BOOK ONE

USA TODAY BESTSELLING AUTHOR

MJ FIELDS

This is a work of fiction. All characters, organizations, and events portrayed in this novel are either products of the author's imagination or are used fictitiously. Any resemblance to actual events, locales, or persons, living or dead, is entirely coincidental.

1st Edition Published: 2015
Published by MJ Fields 2015
Cover Design by: K23 Design
Cover Model: Michael Fagone
Photographer: Shauna Kruse
First Edit by: C&D
Final Edit by: Kellie Montgomery
Formatting by: M.L. Pahl of IndieVention Designs

ISBN-13: 978-1517198756
ISBN-10: 1517198755

10 9 8 7 6 5 4 3 2 1

Disclaimer

This book contains mature content not suitable for those under the age of 18. It involves strong language and sexual situations. All parties portrayed in sexual situations are consenting adults over the age of 18.

Table of Contents

I look in the mirror one last time, noticing my hair is longer on top than it is on the sides. The gel I use to style it makes it look messy and black instead of dark brown. With my black boots, I stand at six-foot-three, and having spent an hour at the gym every night after school, I finally have great definition. I'm stage ready.

I walk out on stage with my guitar strung around my neck, pick in hand, waiting for the nerves to consume me. But they don't.

Why? Because I'm a damn *legend;* that's why. The stadium is sold out, and the crowd is going wild.

"Hello, New Jersey!" I hold the mic out for the crowd's roar, and they give me exactly what I want.

"I am Memphis Black, lead singer and guitarist extraordinairc for—" Fuck, I hate this part. What the hell is the band's name?

"Black Hawks," my sister Madison whispers.

"The Black Hawks!" I yell to the crowd.

"That name is so lame." I hear my sister's friend Tally giggle.

"You two, out."

"No, you said, if we videotaped this, you would—"

"Out!"

"Come on, it's our first dance. We need to learn how!" Madison stomps her foot.

"Well, you didn't hold up your end of the deal, now did you?" I lift the guitar strap over my head.

"Come on, please," Madison says with huge eyes.

"Yeah, please," Tally joins her.

I consider telling them to fuck off, but they would tell Mom. I consider a simple no, but they'd tell her that, too. Therefore, I choose the safest answer.

"Fine. But you both have to shut the hell up."

Tally covers her mouth, looking horrified. The girl is a train wreck in epic, adolescent proportion. She has kinky brown curls and a ribbon always wrapped around her head. Freckles bridge her nose and dot her face, and she always wears cartoon character T-shirts. Today, it's Care Bears.

"What now, Tales?" I huff.

"You said—"

"*Hell*?" I laugh.

She giggles again. "Yeah, you did."

"You know what? I think the both of you should just stay home. All freshman girls do at a dance is stand in a corner, giggle, and look like dweebs." I look at my sister. "Mads, if a boy asks you to dance, you'll start laughing and snorting." Next, I point at her friend. "Tall, you'll get some big-ass grin." I roll my eyes when she covers her mouth again. The little girl can't handle a curse word to save her life. "Just keep smiling and laughing, and they'll think there's something wrong up in those crazy heads of yours. Besides, you're both in that—I don't know—the awkward stage: braces, boobs just budding …"

Tally covers her mouth again, while Madison starts to get really pissed off.

"I mean, look at that hair. Mads, you're so used to wearing a ball cap you have permanent hat head. And you—" I can't resist taking one more shot at Tally—"how the hell are you gonna get a comb through that kinky mess before Saturday?"

That's when Madison finally screams for Mom. Tally just looks at me like that cat from the cartoon, the one with the big, green guy. *Shrek*? Yeah, Shrek. Puss, Puss in Boots. That's what her face looks like.

Looking back at her, I almost feel kind of bad for giving them a hard time.

Mom comes in then and gives me the third degree. She tells me, "Girls are sensitive when they're going through changes," and that I should '*be more thoughtful.*'

Finally, I can't take it anymore.

"Okay, Mom, fine. I will buy into their little girl fantasies about that girl with the blue dress, the one with the mice that turn into horses—"

"Cinderella." In spite of herself, my mom laughs.

"Yeah, her."

Her face goes from amused to suspicious. "What exactly are they doing in your room, anyway?"

"They were supposed to be taping my performance."

I try not to smile as she gives me that look. I know exactly what she's about to say: that my rock star fantasies are just as lame as some dumb fairytale with talking mice.

"It's not the same thing, Mom. This is my *dream*, something I can actually make into a *career* one day."

"I know, Memphis." She pats my back, smiling. "But maybe *their* dream is to dance."

"What do you mean, 'we need a new name'?" I ask Nick DeAngelo.

Nick, or Nickie D as we call him, our manager, crosses his arms, the black ink on his dark skin peeking out from under his shirtsleeve. "Steel is used in *everything* now: the popularity of the tattoo shop, the business, the—"

"Not our fault no one else has an ounce of creativity." Finn stands up, pulls his knit cap down to his eyebrows, pushes his dark hair to the side away from his eyes, and starts pacing. "I mean, really, what the fuck is wrong with people? Get your own shit."

I back him up. "Steel is where it all began. It means something to us, Nick. And to Xavier, to—"

"His wife, Taelyn." River wiggles his eyebrows.

River, our drummer, adores our boss's wife. He should. She saved his ass from being kicked out at least ten times due to his inability to stay sober for more than ten damn minutes.

"Keep Steel, then." Nick throws his hands up. "Just make it different."

"Better," Finn snarls. "Fuckers."

Nick looks at his watch. "I have a meeting to get to. You guys put your creative minds together and come up with something. But don't take too long. This tour is gonna happen. Hell, it *is* happening. We just need a strong name. Something Steel, but—"

River grabs his junk through his torn up jeans. "Deeper."

"*Much* deeper." Finn reaches over to give River a fist bump.

"Balls deep," I join in, making it a three-way fist bump explosion.

Nick shakes his head, rolling his eyes. "Yeah, but 'Balls Deep' isn't gonna fly, boys. Keep brainstorming and shoot me a text. Then I need to get T-shirts and merch' rolling."

"Do we get a cut of that?" River asks.

"River, the money is used to help cover the band's expenses." With that, Nick walks out the door without a backward glance.

Once he's out of earshot, we all look at each other.

"We're sticking with Steel," I declare.

"Hell yes, we are," Finn and River chime in together.

"Steel Rocks?" Finn suggests.

"Lame." Even as I say it, I know River agrees.

"Steel Destruction," I try, and we all look at each other, speculating. "Bad ass, right?"

"Yeah, but it needs to be *totally* bad ass, without question, man. Has to be totally fucking us, totally fucking hard, and hot. Just like our music."

I laugh. "Steel Total Destruction?"

No one says a word; we all just stare at each other.

After a while, River nods. “That’s right. We’ll go so hard, we’ll make anything else look like shit.”

“Ruin it for all the other fucks out there,” Finn adds. “Tear shit up.”

I like where this is headed.

“So, we’re set. We are now ‘Steel Total Destruction’?” I wait for the vote to carry.

“Fuck yes, we are.”

“I’m sending Nick a text.”

I chuckle evilly to myself as I type: WE WILL BE ‘STEEL TOTAL DESTRUCTION,’ THE BADDEST ASSES OUT THERE, GIVING RESPECT TO THE MAN WHO FOUND US.

Not even five seconds later, Nick messages back that he loves it.

“He’s in.” I laugh out loud.

“What’s so funny, man?” River asks.

“Not a damn thing.” I shake my head, laughing inside. Killer fucking name.

***

I wake up to my phone squawking with last night’s audition grumbling, lying bare-assed next to me. Still half asleep, I grab my phone, read the message, and push her off me.

First things first. I stumble out of my room in search of some ibuprofen and a gallon of water to get rid of the hellish hangover I’m sporting. Finn is still awake, writing, and River is asleep in his room with the Bobbsey Twins. Not really twins, but Finn felt inspired. Apparently, the treat he brought home wasn't as important as the lyrics running inside his head, so River got two for the price of one.

"You get a text, too?" I ask Finn after popping the pills.

"Yes." He doesn't even bother to look up. "I just need ten more minutes. This is coming together perfectly." He reaches for the bottle of Firewater sitting next to him and takes a swig.

"Finn, your liver's gonna be pissed at you, man," I say over my shoulder as I head toward the bathroom.

There's no damn way I could do that shit: drink all night, get no sleep, eat no food, score no pussy, and still be awake in the morning, writing. He's crazy.

***

Saturday morning, we walk into *Forever Four*, our label's headquarters, for an impromptu meeting. None of us are feeling it. The whole way over, Finn and River were trying to figure out what the hell is going on.

As soon as the door opens and I hear Xavier Steel's voice booming from the conference lounge, and I know what is up. But fuck if I'm gonna let them know that I know.

"He sounds pissed, man." River's eyebrows are sky high. "His wife is probably not giving it up since I'm sure she is just waiting to tell him she's in love with me. She's going to leave his ass for mine. Of course, I'd try to talk her out of it. Out of respect and shit."

I chuckle. "You'd cream yourself if she ever gave you the time of day." Taelyn Steel is hot, red-haired, tall, thin, and totally in love with her husband, exactly like he is with her. We just allow River this little, indulgent fantasy. It's not hurting a damn thing... and it pisses X-man off, which is always funny.

"I would have brought her on board, let her feel my beat." River cringes. "But she has a kid now."

Whatever. Fucker loves that woman. I know damn well he would hit it and try to keep it.

"They're *kids*," Nick is saying. It sounds like he's trying to calm the X-man down.

"That's just stupid shit, Nick!" X sounds pissed, more pissed than I have ever heard him and I've heard him pissed. "Between you and Rico, neither of you thought I should know? How many thousands were spent on these fucking shirts and hats and—"

"Slow the fuck down, X. One damn question at a time." Nick's laugh is awkwardly placed. "First, you are the one who said the name needed more."

"More, yes. But *this* shit?"

"Rico's design is sick, man." Nick's tone is calm now. "And you got my text and said 'sounds good,' so *your* stamp of approval is on this shit, too. No time to change it. This starts tomorrow if they agree."

"They'd *better* fucking agree. They'd better also realize that the way this company works is shit gets paid back *before* the royalties start getting doled out. Assuming they get a huge cut, they just completely fucked us all with this stunt."

"I disagree." I walk in, wearing my business face.

"What the hell is he talking about?" River follows me in and grabs one of the T-shirts off the table. "This is sick."

He holds it up against himself as Finn and I sit, turning our attention to River like he's working the center pole at a strip club. He takes the black tee with the grey, crackled circle enclosing the different shades of reds and oranges spelling out our band's name as he dry humps the air and rubs it down his front.

"Sick is right!" Xavier doesn't look or sound impressed. "You tell me, River, how well do you think *you're* gonna do at the after parties with the ladies sporting one of those T-shirts?"

"I *always* do well with the ladies." River drops the shirt and plops down next to Finn.

"Are you high?" Xavier scowls at him.

"Just a few hits this morning." He shrugs. "Just pot, though. Not the other stuff."

This is good considering River was shooting up when Xavier found him and then he had a coke habit for a while after that.

Exasperated, Xavier throws his hands up. "Nick, we aren't ready for this shit in three days." He points at the three of us. "You guys want this about as much as anyone wants"—he holds up the shirt—"a fucking STD."

"People love rock, X." River picks up the shirt again and looks at it, paying attention to the details for the first time, and his smile disappears. "That shit's not funny, Memphis."

"So, there we have it." X scowls. "The fucking 'normal' one is behind the name?"

Finn pushes his sleeves up, exposing the ink that covers his arms before he folds his arms over his chest. "All three of us decided on it. It's actually quite genius."

"Nothing funny about a goddamned STD," River growls, adjusting himself under the table.

"River obviously had no idea." Xavier looks between Finn and me, like he's trying to decide which one of us is gonna be sent to stand in the corner.

"River knew," Finn says. "He was just too fucked up to—"

"Bullshit," River sputters. "I haven't smoked in three days… until this morning."

Xavier is now pacing and sputtering under his breath.

"We promote safe sex," I speak up, trying to put a spin on it.

"Yeah, that'll go over like River at an NA meeting," Xavier huffs.

"I should take offense to that," River says, clearly not offended. "And I would if the last one I attended didn't go so, so horribly wrong."

"You know those T-shirt cannons they use at sporting events?" Xavier looks at me like I'm crazy, so I clarify. "I sent a message to a friend last night, and he's building us a condom cannon—"

"Fucking genius." Finn reaches out his fist for me to bump.

"We just need to get some condoms with this

logo on it, and we're golden. Every bitch in the world is gonna want Steel Total Destruction, the only STD that makes their panties as wet as the Jersey Shore." I smirk, feeling proud.

"The one that makes them scream out in pleasure," River adds while typing a note in his phone.

"The burn that doesn't need medicated ointment." Finn reaches out his fist again. This time he gets no bump.

"Nah, man." Nick cringes. "That's just sick."

Knowing Nick's officially in, I smile to myself. Fucking perfect. *Come on, X-man*, I silently plead.

"If you fail, this is on you." Xavier's eyes narrow as they meet mine.

I shrug. "Ain't gonna happen. You knew what we were when you handpicked us, so don't start doubting us now."

We all look up at the door when X's wife Taelyn walks in, holding their baby. She looks up and pushes her long, auburn locks over her shoulder.

"Good morning!" She greets as she sways gently with the baby in her arms. Did I mention she's hot? Yeah she is, and fucking smart, and I knew she would be on our side.

"Good morning, Taelyn." River makes a beeline for her and the kid. "Hello, baby Patrick."

Taelyn smiles. "He's sleeping."

"Perfect," River says with a shit-eating smile. "Then may I hold him?"

"Taelyn," Xavier growls, clearly annoyed.

"Xavier," she mocks back at him, echoing his tone.

We all laugh except Xavier, of course.

"You sober?" she asks River. We all know that's her deal with him. He's sober, or its hands off the kid. As much as River adores older women, he adores kids even more.

I can't help noticing the way River looks at her, like she's the damn Mona Lisa. I expect him to bullshit her, but he doesn't. He has mad respect for her.

He shakes his head, looking guilty, and shrugs. "Maybe next time."

Taelyn gives him a sad look. "Okay."

She goes over to Xavier and hands their son over. She kisses the baby's cheek, then his.

"So, STD, huh?" After seeing the T-shirt, her eyes immediately go to me.

Xavier laughs at my shocked expression. "Seriously, Memphis, you're like one of our kids."

"Except for the fact that you would have been, like, two when you had him," River interjects. "Hot, toddler loving."

"You'd better watch it, drummer boy," Xavier hisses while Taelyn nudges him with her elbow.

"I guess it could work." She holds the shirt up to her chest, smirking. "If anyone can make a venereal disease sound cool, it's the three of you."

"Four," I remind her. "Billy boy could rock an STD shirt like nobody's business."

"He could, right?" She laughs. "He'll be back in a week, very excited."

"Wait, about what?" I ask.

"You're opening up for the Brody Hines band's Burning Souls reunion show, you stupid shit." Xavier speaks in a stern, yet soft I-don't-want-to-wake-the-baby, voice.

River looks like someone just slapped him. "You're fucking joking, right?"

"Nope." Xavier smiles. "So, let me ask you a question."

"Shoot, man." I try to look calm, but shit. *Fuck, fuckity, fucking shit!*

"You ready to spread 'your kind of rock' around like an infectious disease?" The look on his face tells me everything I need to know—X is finally on board.

My laugh is evil and deep. "Hell yes, we are. Hell. Fucking. Yes."

I feel tingly all over. What a fucking rush this business is. *What a motherfucking rush.*

I sit at the kitchen table with my head hung low, waiting for the shiz storm to commence. I know I have crossed some lines—well, not just crossed, more like pirouetted across, moonwalked across while flipping the double bird. Then, when no one was looking, I ran back like the dog I was, tail between my legs, in the middle of the night.

I used the proverbial line like a jump rope, hopping back and forth between who I am and who I never dreamed I could become. Never in a million years did I think I would be called to audition. Never in a billion years did I think I would have the guts to spend an entire day, while my parents thought I was on a trip to the city with Madison's family, actually *auditioning* in front of the most talented and highest esteemed judges at The Julliard School of Performing Arts.

But I did. I crossed that line. I crossed it good. And now I have to pay the price.

After another fifteen minutes, my parents—also known as Pastor Theodore and Andrea Priest—finally come out of my father's office, and I don't dare look up.

"Thou shalt *not covet*. Thou shalt *honor* your father and mother and remember the Sabbath and *keep it holy*." My father's fist strikes the table in front of me, and I jump. "You said dance was a *hobby*! You *lied* to your mother and me. And on a *Sunday*, Tally!"

"Theodore," my mother scolds him weakly.

"Andrea, if you cannot stand beside me in this, then see your way into the next room."

My mom and I both gasp at his retort. My father never speaks to her that way, ever.

As he looks at her, his face softens, but only for a moment. "Love is not always sweet, Andrea. This occasion calls for tough love."

"We should at least hear her out." My mom's voice gets a little stronger as she dares to argue. His outburst must have made her mad. "She is nearly eighteen."

I'm so ashamed, I want to hide underneath the table. I can't believe I made them fight. I can practically hear the shredding of my acceptance letter already. My father has always believed the man rules the house while the wife keeps it pretty, and children are better seen than heard and always obedient. He's a good man, of course, but he can be seriously judgmental.

"I never thought I would get in," I whisper, looking down at my hands. "I just wanted to—I don't know—*try*."

"Try?" My father shakes his head, raising his voice again. "You've already applied to Stanford and NYU. You have already spent more than enough time and money *trying*—"

"But I haven't been accepted yet." I look up at him, wiping my tears away in frustration.

His eyes widen, like that fact doesn't matter in the slightest. I can see his face getting redder, probably because his circulatory system is working overtime. He's never had to deal with a daughter who talks back before. It can't be good for his blood pressure.

After a few seconds of heavy breathing, he points to the stairway. "Go. Go now before I say something I cannot take back!"

I leave the little church parish kitchen as quickly as I can without running. Once I'm alone in my room, I grab the door to slam it, but then I don't. I merely shut it gently and then dramatically throw myself on my bed where I cry, also dramatically.

When a sudden vibration in my pocket makes me jump, I pull out my phone, staring dejectedly at the screen. It's Madison.

"Hey," I whisper into the receiver.

"Hey," she says just as quietly. "Why are we whispering?"

"Madison." I sigh, sniffling. "I have a joy and a concern to share with you."

"Wow. Okay, both in the same conversation? I don't know if I can handle it."

The sound of her laughter makes me want to cry all over again.

"It's not funny, Mad. It's not something to—"

"Ugh, just spill it!"

"Well"—I lick my lips—"my dad got the mail today."

"Wait, which news is this? The joyous or the

concerning?"

"Both," I say. "I told you they were both—"

"Right, right. Go ahead."

"My dad got the mail today," I continue, "and there was a letter from Julliard."

"No fucking way!"

I cover my mouth out of habit. Curse words always tickle my ears, no matter the content or occasion. "Yes, *fluffing* way."

"Oooo, is he, like, really pissed?"

"Of course." I stifle a giggle, not because of how mad he is, but because of the 'P-word.' "There's no way he'd ever let me go."

"I don't think he has the right to tell you what to do, Tally." Madison sounds angry on my behalf. "You're gonna be eighteen in three days."

Of course she doesn't understand. Her parents are nothing like mine. "I don't want to disappoint them, though. I don't—"

"Well, I don't want you to disappoint *you*, Tally." As usual, she bowls right over me. "This is a dream come true. An opportunity of a lifetime, a fucking…"

Suddenly, I hear a soft knock on my door.

"Gotta go."

I hang up the phone and try to act natural just as Mom walks in.

"You okay?"

I sit up, trying to remember Madison's words of encouragement. Maybe I just need to try harder.

"I feel awful, Mom, but I don't want to lie to you. That letter, that acceptance … it makes me happy. So, so happy."

She sits down on the bed and pulls me into her shoulder. "Give him a couple of days, sweetheart. Just let him think, stew, and vent to me for a while. Then, I think he'll get over the betrayal."

Only my mom could make the word 'betrayal' sound so biblical.

"Mom, that's not what I was trying to do. I never dreamed I would get a letter telling me my audition tape was accepted, that they wanted me to come to the auditions, or that I would be chosen to move from ballet to modern dance to …" I trail off when she starts to cry. "I'm sorry."

"Don't be sorry. I'm being selfish. My baby girl is growing up. I always knew you had talent. You shine up there on stage. Year after year, I have watched you at recitals—"

"That Dad hates." I look down, already dreading where this is going.

"No, Tally, he loved watching you dance. He just didn't like the team uniform," she says, pushing my hair away from my face. "Every recital, he sat and watched you, and he was in awe of you. He said you looked like he imagined an angel would."

"I never thought this would happen, but now that it has … I'm so afraid he'll say no."

She smiles faintly. "I know you are nervous, but it's going to be all right." She kisses my forehead. "Get some rest, baby girl. Things always look brighter in the morning light."

I nod, feeling better for the first time, hopeful even. "Okay, but first I'm gonna shower. I haven't had a chance since I got home from the studio."

"Of course."

After my shower, I towel off my hair and throw on my favorite pink pajamas. It's been unusually warm lately, so I open the window and lean out to breathe in the fresh spring air. Then I hear a noise on the street and lean out farther to see what it is.

"Oh, my word!" I freeze when I see him standing under the streetlight.

My breath catches in my throat, but I'm not afraid. I would know him anywhere. Not just because he stands a perfect six-foot-three, but also because of the way he walks—with his head held high, broad shoulders squared—and because of his messy black hair, so effortless and cool. If I could see his eyes in the dark, I would see they are a brilliant blue, like the ocean on a hot day. His jeans hang almost obscenely low. Of course, he's also wearing his signature white tank top, black boots, and that worn, leather jacket.

I must have leaned a little too far, though, because my phone slips out of my hand to clatter loudly across the porch roof and then over the edge to thud dully on the ground below.

Oh, no! I cringe. *Please let that indestructible black case truly be indestructible.*

After a few seconds of standing frozen, waiting for all chaos to break loose, I open the window wider, quietly lowering myself onto the roof. I'm not afraid of getting hurt, because I have done it before. We have practiced fire safety drills twice a year in my house for as long as I can remember.

Keeping my center of gravity low, I slide down on my bottom and roll onto my stomach, scooting down until my body is hanging over the edge, my feet blindly searching for the railing. It takes a few tries, but I figure it out. A few seconds later, I'm bent over, rummaging through the bushes, praying I don't get sprayed by a skunk or bitten by some other inhabitant of the underbrush world. I reach in blindly, poking around until my hand makes contact with something hard and plastic. Then I get out of there as soon as the phone is in my hand.

Once up off the ground, I frisk myself, hoping to remove any dirt or bugs that may have hitched a ride on my pajamas. Confident that I'm not a carrier, I turn around … and scream as a huge hand comes up to cover my mouth.

"If I let go, do you promise not to scream?" The voice is deep and slurred, though undoubtedly Memphis Black's.

I relax a little, nodding against his hand.

"That's a good girl."

He lets go and steps back, eyeballing me suspiciously.

"You don't have a gun, do you?"

"No," I whisper, smiling stupidly.

He crosses his muscled arms and leans back against the corner of the porch. After a few seconds, he starts to slide.

"Memphis." I grab for his arm, trying to keep him upright.

"Shh." He holds his finger to my lips. "If we wake my parents up, I won't have any time to spend with you. Not that engaging in a midnight surprise meet and greet with a fan is normal or deserving of my time, but I will say I am intrigued by your choice of attire. Were you going for the 'little virgin' look? Because 'naughty school girl' is more up my alley."

I frown up at him. "What are you talking about?"

He smirks and his dimple deepens. "Oh, I see." He takes a step closer to me.

"You do?" I honestly have no idea what he's talking about.

"Are you lost, little girl?" His tone is campy and a little creepy as he moves into my personal space.

I take a step back.

"Oh, and she is *shy*." He groans in a sexy way, and I immediately feel my face burst into flames.

"Memphis, I don't understand. Why are you here?"

"Oh, I'm sure you just stumbled across my address on the Internet." He doesn't seem to understand what I'm asking.

"Memphis," I try again. "You know me. I'm—"

"Shhh. No names tonight." His arm snakes around my waist, then pulls me hard against his body. "No names, you sexy, lost, little thing. I'm going to make this little game worth your effort, though. I promise you that."

His right hand slides up the back of my pajama top, and then he gently takes the back of my head in his other hand, leaning in close.

I should step away; I know that. I should, but I don't. And when I try to speak up, my voice just isn't there.

As his lips finally make contact, he slides them

across mine without pressing too hard; instead, it's soft and gentle, the way I always imagined my first kiss, and I feel my body begin to tingle. My eyes close on their own as he kisses my cheek, running his nose along my jaw and down my neck, taking a deep breath as he goes.

"Damn, lost, little one, you smell so sweet."

I find myself moving my head to the side, giving him more room to take in my fragrance.

I have never felt *anything* so amazing. I have never felt more special, never thought in my wildest, most secret dreams that Memphis Black would be my first kiss. I can't believe my childhood dream actually came true.

"Fuck," he says right before turning his head to throw up not once, but three times. The third time, he manages to get vomit all over my bare feet. When he's finally done, he straightens up shakily. "I need to go in and lie down."

I can't think of anything else to do but help him. Somehow, I manage to get him across the road and prop him against his house. Then I dig around the flowerpot for the Black family's hidden key before I unlock the door and push it open.

"Memphis." I shake him awake because he's sliding again. "Memphis, you're home."

He slurs something at me then, some inaudible gibberish. I grab his arm and throw it over my shoulder as I half walk, half drag him inside. We make our way to the couch, and I try to help him sit on it.

His eyes roll back in his head when he tries to look up at me. "You'll sleep here?"

"I really have to go."

"I like the way you smell," he mumbles. "I want you to sleep …" His eyes close, and he starts falling to one side.

I help him lie down, then pull his boots off, lifting his feet and placing them on the couch. I watch him for longer than I should, but he is just so beautiful I can't help myself.

Finally, regretfully, I turn and walk out the door, making sure it locks behind me. Then I put the key back and run across the street, hoping my parents never noticed I was gone.

I look in the mirror one last time. I have on a black hat, white tank, black jeans, and boots. With no time for a fucking haircut as the crazy-ass opening act for the Burning Souls tour, the hat is a must.

It's been like this for a year. Roll out of bed and over whatever piece of ass I snatched to bring back to the bus or hotel room the night before. Roll my ass to the gym because—let's face it—I need to look good naked. Even though there is a no cell phone or camera rule after one of the bitches posted my morning wood on social media, shit could still happen. Thank the stars my dick is impressive, and that mighty oak held that sheet up like a boss. Next, we roll to wherever we're rehearsing, roll to sound checks, roll to an interview or two, roll back to the stage and rock and roll for an hour. There's not nearly enough time to play everything we have.

"Hello, New Jersey!" I hold the mic out for the crowd's roar, and hell yes, they give me exactly what I want. "I am Memphis Black, lead singer and guitarist extraordinaire for Steel Total Destruction!"

Still can't explain the buzz I catch off the roar

from the crowd. It's like a spiritual erection, a transcendent orgy to my soul, a divine intervention within every cell of my body.

"You ready for some STD? You ready to get rocked so hard you can't walk straight for a week?"

There's that noise again: the screams, the shouts, the lust for our music … and for us.

"I like the way you sound." I look off stage to see Xavier pointing and scowling. *Aw, for fuck's sake*, I growl inside. "Get ready, ladies—"

"Prepare yourselves," Finn interrupts, and then the fucking condom cannons jizz all over the crowd.

As they scramble around, screaming and grabbing the fucking condoms like little crack whores, River spanks the drums. The crack and pop of the snare proceeds Finn's finger banging the G and L Tribute, and I begin singing our first hit song, "Going Down."

The crowd screams, and the girls in the front row dance, trying to gain my attention. I see a blonde with a nice rack, and I wink. She freaks and points to herself, so I wink again as I continue singing. Then I turn my attention elsewhere; she needs to work for it, and by work for it, I mean show me some damn titties or I'm gonna look elsewhere.

An hour later, I am sweating balls, quarter chubbed, and we are heading off stage.

"No shit." I hear a smile in Finn's voice, must be Christmas. I look up as he says, "Maddox fucking Hines."

"No shit," I say, just as shocked.

"Which one? Big tits at two o'clock or tiny titties, big ass at four, or the others? " our road manager asks, nodding to the group of girls lined up like a dessert buffet.

"Thanks, Sleazy D, but I think I'm gonna hang out and watch the show. Maddox never plays with his Dad's band anymore. I wanna see if he's as good as his old man."

"Are you serious?" he gasps.

Finn pats him on the back and points. "A fucking legend has returned to stage; do you think he's kidding?"

"Great set, gentleman," T, the drummer for Burning Souls, says as he pats my back while walking by. "Let's hit this shit, Hines," he yells back.

"That his wife?" River asks as we all stand, watching Maddox pull a blonde chick hard against him.

"Yeah, fucking hot, too." I shake my head. "But why the hell get bogged down at the beginning of your career, then walk away?"

"Everyone has a story, man," Finn says. "Google it. Unreal."

River snickers. "I'd bang her like a fucking bass."

Maddox Hines's head snaps right, and he steps back, but his wife catches his hand and shakes her head.

"Sweetness," he growls.

"Get out there and show me you haven't lost it." She blushes.

He smirks. "You know I haven't."

Then she whispers something in his ear, and his eyebrows shoot up.

"It's on." He pulls back and then walks at us. "Say one thing about her, and I'll hear it, even on that stage. I will—"

"Maddox." His wife is next to him instantly.

"Mine," he growls at us before kissing her, then walking on stage.

"Hello, New Jersey!" Maddox yells to the screaming crowd. "This is one hell of a crowd to end the Burning Souls US tour. Thanks for coming out tonight! Feels like déjà vu. It was only three years ago I stood here on this very stage at Bader Field, doing the same damn thing: ending one hell of a tour!"

The crowd screams. They love it.

"Did you miss me? Of course you did. I missed you, too!"

"Sorry about that." His wife smiles at us, then quickly walks to a stool that is obviously purposely set just off stage and sits.

A dark-haired chick almost skips past us to her side, and they hug then begin singing.

I notice Maddox look at her, and apparently, he likes that her friend is present. I kind of like it, too. She has a nice, round ass.

"Squats." I nod.

"Definitely." Finn, River, Billy, and Sleazy laugh.

Being backstage, watching the Burning Souls, is different than being on stage myself. There is electricity, a current surging invisibly in the air, connecting everyone together, including us. I felt that same electricity when I went to my first concert as a kid. Hell, I was only, like, ten. Pearl Jam.

The crowd didn't come to see us; they came to see them. They got us as a little added bonus.

As Burning Souls play their asses off, I'm having fun, even singing along. I know their sets just like I know my own. Don't get me wrong, Steel Total Destruction is better. Well, okay, maybe different is a better choice of words.

"I wanna end tonight with a song that changed my life, a song I hope will change yours, too. When you find that one person who can make you want to spend the rest of your life with them, hold on to them. When you feel that pull, that force that is greater than you, embrace it, follow it. Life changing events can happen when you finally let someone in."

"Fucking pussy whipped," I mumble.

"Did you see his wife? I'd let that pussy whip me." River grabs his dick. "Any fucking day. Her and that little piece next to her."

"To each their own man," Finn says as Maddox Hines begins to sing "Stained."

Waves crash like thunder.
I run.
Inside my mind,
I run.
The sea's grand reflection opens the warmth,
Undone, undone,
Reflecting the love, my soul.
Burning inside my soul,
The sea whispers softly, no longer hide.
Don't hide, don't hide, don't hide, don't hide.

Washed away by the sea's calm,
Nurtured by the wind, the sound of her song.
The breeze gently holds me high.
The weight's lifted up to the sky
Elevated, raised, floating up high.
What remains is a stain, just a stain, a stain.
Lips touching softly on mine, hidden desperations,
An island of questions, my pride.
My pride, my pride, my pride.

The phone vibrates in my pocket, and I take it out to see it's my sister Madison, so I push ignore. Hell, I wish I had that ability growing up.

Twenty seconds later, it goes off again.

911, call me now

I walk away to call her back, expecting the worst.

"Memphis," she whispers.

"Mads, what's going on? Mom and Dad—"

"They're fine. It's Tally."

"Did they get the flowers I sent to the service?"

"Her dad died, like, two months ago."

"So what's the problem, Mads?"

"I want to bring her with me to—"

"Oh, hell no." I laugh. "Can you even imagine her hanging out with the band?"

"She needs to get away. If she can't come, then I'm not coming, either," she huffs the threat.

"All right then. See you next—"

"Memphis!" she screams in the phone.

"Oh, for fuck's sake, Mads, fine. Whatever. Just don't expect me to hang out with her." She starts to argue, but I don't give her the chance. "I'm at my last show, Mads. Chat in a couple days."

I shove my phone back in my pocket just in time to hear the last chorus.

***

Last night, we actually crashed at our place for the first time in as long as I can remember. It was actually nice to dive into my bed—alone—and sleep.

Sleep? Hell, is it possible? A one year tour has ended, a year of traveling across country, spreading STD everywhere. It was a fucking dream come true. Record sales were good, and we were getting airtime on local radio shows and satellite radio.

We rode coattails. It's never been my style, but the opportunity to do so was sick. So, last night, as I lay in my king size bed, butt-ass naked with the fan blowing across my freshly showered body, I couldn't stop the shit-ass grin from spreading across my face.

I cannot believe it. I'm a fucking rock star, bitches!

Now, we sit back at headquarters, *Forever Four*, and wait for Xavier and Nickie D. For once, we're on time, and they are late.

"I can't wait to get away. Need some inspiration," Finn says as he links his hands behind his head.

"And a razor." River smirks.

"Fuck that," Finn grumbles, running his hands over his beard.

"Lumber-sexual," Billy says, and we all look at him like he's lost it. "Read it somewhere."

The door opens, and X-man walks in with

Nickie D behind him.

"You're late," I say smugly.

"We were on an important call," Xavier says as he sits down with a shit-eating grin on his face. "You ready to do this without Burning Souls?"

"Fuck yes—"

"After a vacation, I hope," Billy interrupts. Again, we look at him like he has three fucking heads. "Never wanted in to start."

"You like it, and you know it, Billy-boy. Stop acting like this isn't the greatest fucking thing you've ever done in your life." I laugh, and he looks at me. "Come on, man, tickling the ivory then whatever piece of ass you want after."

"I am a pianist," he states blankly, "not a rock star."

We all look up as Taelyn Steel slides in and shuts the door behind her. "You love it, and you know it, Billy."

"Okay, bottom line"—Xavier stands up—"opening for Burning Souls was an amazing opportunity for Steel Total Destruction." He tries to look annoyed whenever he says the band's name, but I know better—hell, we all do. X-man is amused as hell by the band's name. "But headlining your own tour is insane. It's the difference between twenty-five K a show, which you get eighty percent of, split between four of you after expenses: gas, bus rental, crew, hotels, meals, and whatever incidentals you have. You each probably made seventy K for the year—"

"That's a shit load of money." River rubs his hands together, and all I can think is, *how much of that shit will you spend on candy?*

"It's really good." Xavier nods. "But do you want more?"

"Who doesn't want more? Hell, show me the dough, bro." I laugh.

Instantly, everyone is in hell-yes-we-do mode.

"Irish,"-Xavier's nickname for Taelyn-. "Nickie, and I have lined up a fifteen city tour. The lowest paying gig is two hundred K; highest is two hundred fifty K. That means three million dollars. A million will—"

"What the hell did you just say?" River gasps.

"Fifteen city tour," Xavier says, looking at him.

Finn looks at him suspiciously. "No, man, after that. The money."

"Three mil." Nickie D smirks. "That's saying no one backs out. Contracts are on their way as we speak."

"Fifteen percent stays here," Xavier interjects. "Expect twenty percent to be used for expenses. Merchandise will be split fifty-fifty after expenses. My guess is you'll each make about five hundred K after all is said and done."

"Holy fuck! Holy motherfucking fuck!" River says what we are all thinking.

"If that gets you excited, man, understand that isn't shit compared to what record sales can be if you get your asses writing." Xavier looks at River. "And stay fucking sober."

"Like you did for Burning Souls tour," Taelyn interjects, making a point to her husband about River's ability to keep his shit together for the tour.

"I know you're all heading down to vacay in Miami for a while, but you need to be writing music, too, not just getting laid. You catch me?" Nicki D says sternly. "The more we have out, the better sales are, and the better sales—"

"More money, baby." I high-five Nickie.

"More money." He grins.

My father passed away from a heart attack four month ago. In that time, I have watched Mom, the grieving minister's wife, go from singing his praises in front of the congregation he led for more than fifteen years before the Lord Jesus Christ took him home, to a sobbing mess who is trying to figure out what to do next when she thinks I am asleep.

After his death, I spent spring break helping her pack up the parsonage, where we had lived my entire youth. His church family adored him and whenever there was talk about moving us to another church, they fought to keep him here.

"No, honey, that belongs to the church," she would say as she took pots and pans out of the boxes I was packing them in. Then the same was said for the knives, the plates, the forks, even the furniture.

"This is all you have?" I asked, as I looked at the seven boxes that contained fifteen years of personal property collected between her and my father.

She smiles. "That's more than I'll need."

Once in the tiny, furnished apartment, we put

away those seven boxes, and she was right. In a five hundred square-foot apartment, she would not be able to fit much more.

Today, I look around my side of the empty, shared dorm room. One year under my belt at Julliard was much more than I had ever dreamed or prayed for. *One year of instruction in classical ballet*, I think as I open the dresser drawers one more time to make sure I haven't left anything more behind.

I won't be coming back.

I feel tears prick my eyes, and I push them back. I don't want my mother to see that this is bothersome to me. She has already offered to pay next year's tuition with the money from my father's very small life insurance policy he had from working at the church. However, I refused because that is all she has. That and a social security check that would just barely pay for the rented one bedroom apartment she just moved into and her health insurance premium.

I sit on the bed, looking out the window of Meredith Willson Residence Hall and onto the rooftop of the connecting building that is the school I love so much. Then I stand up and walk to the door when I hear a knock. It's my mother; I know it is. I hold my head against the cool, metal frame and take in a deep breath as I try to brace myself for what may come.

I open the door to find she is spreading fake sunshine through a smile. Her graying hair is piled in a perfect bun on top of her head, and she is dressed in an ankle length skirt and long sleeve, button up in May, perfectly proper.

"Hi, Mom," I say, giving her a hug that I know she needs.

"Hi, sweetheart." Her voice hitches, and I hug her tighter.

"I'm so sorry about this, Tally. All of it. I—"

"Mom." I give her back the sunshine as I throw my backpack over my shoulders and grab my large, wheeled suitcases. "I had a fantastic year. It just wasn't in the plans."

"God has big things in store for you," she says, as she grabs the duffle that has all my dance gear in it.

"I know, Mom," I tell her as I hold the door open.

We get to the KIA, and she gets in the driver's seat.

"You sure, Mom? I can drive."

"No, sweetheart, I have to do these things now." She pauses and swallows down her emotions.

"I really don't mind," I say as I load my bags in the tiny back seat.

"I'm okay," she says, and then the dam breaks.

When I walk over and open the driver's door, she gets out, and I slide in.

"I'm sorry, Tally." She grabs the small purse size packet of Kleenex and then blows her nose.

"Don't be, Mom. I understand."

The entire time we drive through the city, she has a white-knuckle grip on the *oh-shiz* handles: one on the dash and the other over the door. I am careful not to scare her too much, though. I know how she hates city driving. Heck, she hates driving period.

Once we make it through the tunnel and head toward Jersey, she begins to relax a little.

"I should really skip the walk. I should really stay home."

Mom is going on a weeklong Christian women's retreat with some of the ladies at church. It's supposed to bring her closer to God. I hope, when she gets close enough, she can ask Him why He took Dad and left her penniless.

"The walk will do you good, Mom."

Sunshine, always spreading sunshine.

"You can stay, you know. You don't have to go with Madison and her family to Florida, sweetheart. It's so hot there this time of year."

I swallow back the guilt I feel for the little white lie I told her. I am going to stay with Madison, but her parents will not be there. Madison and I still talk all the time, and I certainly can't wait for a two-week vacation with her on the beach in south Florida. I need some healing time myself.

I will definitely be entertained.

After unpacking my bags from the car, Mom makes me a peanut butter and homemade strawberry rhubarb jelly sandwich—my favorite from childhood.

She grabs the step stool and reaches above the cabinet for a coffee can and sets it in front of me. "There is four hundred dollars for you to—"

"No, Mom, I have—"

"There is four hundred dollars, Tally. I won't take no for an answer. I want you to have fun, to be able to buy lunch or a pop when you're on the beach, sunscreen, or whatever you need."

"You need this, Mom." I try to push the can back toward her.

"No. I need to do this for you, Tally. Let me."

***

I land at Miami International Airport at eleven p.m. with my bag over my shoulder and a carry-on in my hand. Madison's flight lands just fifteen minutes after mine.

Not needing to collect my bags from the carousel, I walk over and sit to wait. After half an hour, I look at the screen to see that her flight from South Bend Airport is delayed three hours.

I look at my phone, seeing I still have it set to airplane mode. Once I switch it, I see that I have several missed calls and texts from Madison.

I redial her number and she answers. "What a bunch of fucking shit!"

I laugh at her.

"I just want to get out of this hell hole. I can't wait to see you."

"It's no problem, Madison. I'm fine."

"Like hell you are. I'm gonna text Memphis and ”

"Wait, what?"

"Oh, shit, I forgot to tell you. We're staying with the band." She says it so nonchalantly it's as if I wouldn't be bothered by it. "You still there?"

"Yes."

"Are you mad?"

"Not mad, just wish I had known."

"Well, I wasn't sure what their schedule was, honestly."

"Honestly," I say dryly, hoping she knows I am not buying it.

"I was hoping we'd see them. Hell, last time I saw my brother was on stage. Come on, chin up, Tally. When's the last time you saw Memphis?"

I feel my face flush and am thankful no one sees my embarrassment. "A long time ago."

"Well, I am waiting for him to message me back. I asked him to go pick you up."

"NO! I can wait for you."

"Nonsense, Tally. Who the hell knows when the plane will take off? Neither of us wants you sleeping in the airport."

"Where are we staying?" I can't believe I didn't ask that before.

"85 Palm Avenue, Miami Beach. Google it, Tally. We are living it up for two fucking weeks. Me, you, and let's hope some hot, hot men in super tiny speedos that leave nothing to the imagination."

I laugh. "Gross."

"No, girlfriend. So very far from gross."

We spent the day on the beach, drinks in hand, nearly molested by hot-ass babes sporting dental floss. There was little left to the imagination, very little. I got head in the ocean, which was a first, and now I am pretty confident the two chicks who have been eager for my attention are on board with going back to the beach pad with me, just me.

"You guys ready to head back?" I ask River, Finn, and Billy.

"Yeah," Finn says as he links hands with the tiny, dark-haired chick he is hooking up with.

***

After four and a half hours of no-holds-barred fucking, all three of our bodies are sweat drenched. This little *ménage* was sating, entertaining, and no doubt tiring. *No holds-barred*, I laugh to myself as I smack the little blonde's ass and think, *no holes were barred, either*.

"Just give me a few more minutes," she pants, expecting me to dive in again.

"Sorry, babe." I slam the nightstand drawer shut. "I'm out of papa stopper." I grab the towel off the floor, run it over my hair, grab my wallet, and then throw a hundred on the bed. "Thanks for a very memorable night. There's some cab money. See you around."

"Is he serious?" I hear the brunette whisper to the blonde.

"Yeah, he is." She giggles. "He's a fucking rock star; did you think we were going to stay over?"

"Guess not," she huffs. "But honestly, the band's name is STD, so I didn't think he'd be worried about condoms."

They giggle, talk about me and my impressive cock size, and how they can't believe they did what they did, and did it together. I feel a grin spread across my face as I continue listening to them through the bathroom door. It's almost as good as the applause I get from the sold out crowds we have been opening up for … almost.

When I hear the chick banter end, bedroom door shut, and I know they aren't gonna have to get the eviction notice in order to leave, I turn on the water and hop in the shower. Exhausted or not, I'm going to bed smelling good, feeling clean, and changing the damn sheets. Hell, if I was back in Jersey, I would be flipping the mattress, too.

After my shower, I dry off, throw on a pair of basketball shorts, and strip the sheets. Then I grab the clean set from the linen closet and half-ass make the bed. No flat sheet is necessary until tomorrow when I'm not feeling a hellacious hangover looming.

I decide to head out to grab a drink and a

couple Motrin before falling into a ten hour rest and recoup session.

I hear Finn and River talking and wonder if my chicks are bed hopping. Honestly, I don't give a fuck if they are.

"She's fucking hot," I hear River whisper. "Wonder who the hell left her out here alone." I walk past them, sure as hell not interested. "She one of yours?" he asks me.

"If she was, she's not now," I reply, grabbing a bottle of water out of the bar's mini fridge. "Motrin?"

"Look left. I just took some," Finn answers.

As I open the bottle, I hear a female's startled gasp. I glance over to where the noise came from and pause.

"We scare you?" River asks in his smooth, I'm-putting-the-moves-on voice.

"No. Oh, wow, I'm sorry. I just … Madison gave me the gate code, and the door was unlocked, and …" She stands up and fixes her shirt.

Holy hell, she's a fucking knock out: long, wavy hair, green ass eyes, rocking body… damn, damn, damn.

The pajamas, fucking cartoon characters … Those little blue ones? The girl one, blonde hair … Fuck it. Who cares? That's her.

"No shit," I say in shock, which actually makes her laugh.

Now she is covering her mouth, blushing. I watch as she tugs at her shirt, then runs her hand through her hair.

"Sorry. She said she called."

"Tally?" I know it's her—same voice and nervous laughter—but hot damn. Hot motherfucking damn, she has all sorts of grown up.

"Hi, Memphis."

"You know this sexy, little—"

"Watch it, River," I growl. Shit. Maybe I didn't … Dammit, I know I fucking did.

I look over and see Finn smirk.

"Friend of the family," I say in a much more cool, calm, and collected voice. "Mads didn't call me." I grab another bottle of water and walk it over to her.

"She said it went to voicemail. Her flight was delayed." She can't even look at me, too busy twisting the bottom of that little tee in knots. My balls are doing the same thing.

Her phone chimes, and she looks down. "Cancelled? Oh, dear."

"It's fine. You'll stay with me. She and you can catch up when she gets in."

Before I know it, I have her hand and am dragging her behind me while I snarl at Finn, who is just about ready to bust out laughing. I stop when she tugs her hand away and looks back. She's looking to escape, and those two fuckers are looking like that wolf, the one that wants to eat the little girl, and they aren't going to eat her. Fuck that. I will kill them first.

Red Riding Hood. Yeah, that's it. Little Red Riding Hood.

"If you think for one second I'm gonna leave you out for them to try and snack on, Tales, you have lost your fucking mind." I hold out my hand.

"Let's go."

She hesitates for a moment then grabs her purse and looks up at me. "Where are you taking me?"

"You'll sleep in my room, just until Mads gets here. Then I will lock you both up somewhere." I say it in a way I know makes her nervous, and hell, that's kind of hot, too.

I grab her hand again and pull her behind me. She doesn't fight me; she comes willingly.

I open the door and turn the light on, and all she can say is wow, her eyes wide and full of wonder.

My blood is pooling in a place it shouldn't be right now, and I think of that green ogre chick, the one who's a princess. Then all hell breaks loose, and she is a nasty green ogre. Fuck, Tales, you need to show me your inner, what's her name? Fiona. Yeah, that's her name. Shrek and Fiona.

"Nice, right? Hop in bed," I say, pulling back the covers.

She looks at me all wide-eyed, and damn, damn, damn.

"Where will you sleep?" she asks.

"With you."

Her mouth drops open, and I feel a little off. Not a lot, just a little.

"Is there a problem, Tales? Would you rather be out there where they—"

She shakes her head. "Okay. It's just—"

"I will be a perfect gentleman."

"You promise?" she asks, looking back and forth between the bed and me.

I point to the bed. "Like a slumber party."

"Those two girls?" she asks and a slight frown traces her lips. "They came out of here."

There isn't a question in her voice, and I sure as hell can't lie to her after she saw them. "They left. Clean sheets." I point to the dirty sheets pooled on the floor. "It's been dealt with."

She climbs in, and I am right behind her.

Once we're settled in, I ask, "You comfortable?"

She pulls one of the pillows from the top and puts it in the middle. "I'm fine, and just remember, I'm not like them."

"I know who you are, Tales."

"Right." She rolls to her side, facing away from me.

"What's that supposed to mean?" I ask as I settle in next to … the pillow.

"Nothing. Thank you for a place to sleep, Memphis."

"Of course. Sorry I didn't get Madison's message. Phone wasn't charged."

"But you knew she was coming?"

"Yep." When I think about the statement, I know she is judging me for being, well, me. "It's charging now."

"She'll text me when she gets in," she says, tightening the blanket around her.

I let the quiet hang in the air like a fucking black cloud for as long as I can stand it then finally say, "Tales?"

"Hmm?"

"I'm really sorry about your father."

"Thank you for the flowers."

That statement seems like a big fuck you to me.

"Sorry I couldn't make it."

"He doesn't know you didn't come, Memphis." She yawns. "Goodnight."

I lie there, my body exhausted as it should be, but I can't sleep, not with the way her scent is mixing with the smell of sex still in the air.

I slide out of bed, grab the dirty sheets and blanket, and toss them in the hallway, all with a fucking hard-on that I am sure is caused more by the sweet scent of lilac invading my senses than the already fading memories of my first threesome.

I lie next to her again, inches from her. I know the exhaustion and alcohol that is still mixed in my cells aren't helping me right now, but fuck.

Her hair is almost waist length, and those waves are more inviting than any one of them I rode today. Her neck is long and slender, and I want so badly to run my tongue from right behind her ear, down her neck to her spine, and all the way down. I want to taste her so fucking much right now, and I don't taste.

Her tight, little tee is hugging her body, and I am thankful she has her back to me because I would be testing the little restraint I have if her tits were staring me in the face. Her ass is like POW! She obviously works out. Hell, she's a dancer, I think. Her ass was never POW! before, was it?

I run my hand over my face. *What the fuck are you doing?* I ask myself. *She hadn't even hit puberty the last time you saw her.*

Well, fuck, that shit changed.

I glance back over at POW! My mouth waters, my dick gets a little harder, and then I see those legs: strong, lean, and long. They have two purposes: one, to wrap around my waist while I bang her against every wall in this room and the other to hold up POW!

I want to save her from every one of those fuckers out there who want a taste, and I want to eat her up. I want to make sure no one hurts her, and I want to wreck her, too. I want to do all that to the chick who had little nubs last time I saw her, the girl who still can't handle a curse word, the girl I am sure was wearing a chastity belt that's key went to the grave with her old man, but I can't.

God help me survive the two weeks Mads is going to be here if Tales is going to be here, too.

I lie in his bed, acting as if I'm asleep. I wish I was asleep because then I wouldn't be thinking of that night, the night he kissed me. He was so intoxicated I know he doesn't remember. I mean, why would he? Besides, it made him vomit.

He smells good, looks amazing, and dear God, he's in his underwear next to me, in a bed. What am I doing? I should get up right now and walk out of here. I should, but I am temporarily paralyzed in his bed, his wicked, rock star bed.

I must smell awful since I was on an airplane and in an airport most of the day.

I wonder if he's watching me. I wish I knew. I wish I hadn't lain on my side. Could I move to my back now?

No. Absolutely not.

Worry and sleep deprivation exhaust me, and I must fall asleep because, when I wake, I hear his soft snores, and oh, my, goodness. OH, MY, GOODNESS, he is holding my pinky, and his ankle is linked over mine.

My body tenses immediately, and I can barely breathe.

I hear his sigh, and then he rolls over, moving

his leg across mine, his arm crossing over my body, the opposite hand's pinky still locked with mine.

His nose nuzzles into my hair, and he inhales a deep breath. Then he gives a slow, deep moan.

I feel him. He's hard … And, oh, dear, I think he's waking up.

"Relax, babe. If you're still here, you did real well last night." His nose rubs back and forth against my hair slightly. "Smell good, too."

I push him off me and jump up off the bed. "I did nothing last night, Memphis Black."

The tone in my voice surprises even me, but he deserves it, him and his … hard penis.

"Shit, Tales, I—." He rolls away, taking his erection with him and smirks at me as he starts to open his mouth.

I hold my hand up, and his mouth snaps shut. Then he sucks his lips in, and his chest vibrates.

"You're laughing at me?"

"Wow, what the hell happened to you?" He shakes his head.

My eyes move south, and then I quickly look away.

"Tales, it's morning wood. Don't take offense."

"You're just … you're—"

"Well, you're, just, you're," he teases me as he adjusts himself, "kind of hot now, Tales. I mean, you even have boobs. Nice ones, too." He laughs as he gets out off bed and brushes past me, then stops and leans in. "I'm gonna shower. Wanna save some water?"

"You're disgusting."

"Now, Tales, you and I both know you don't feel that way, and if you were a little more experienced …" He chuckles. "If you were even a little bit experienced, I know damn well you'd be taking me up on that offer. For the good of the environment, of course."

I turn and retreat to the bathroom, slamming the door behind me and quickly locking it.

"Did you just lock me out of my bathroom?" I hear a bang on the door then a deep, dark laugh. "I need to piss, Tales, and I can have that door open in three, two …" I hear the door handle jiggle.

"I'm using the bathroom!" I yell as I jump off the toilet and pull up my pants.

The door opens, and then I am standing there, looking at him with my mouth gaping open as he smirks, walking past me.

He is standing at the toilet when I hear him start to pee while I am right there, like, right in the same room.

"Oh my goodness! You are—"

"Pissing excellence, and you are—"

"Disgusted." I can't help the giggle that escapes as I walk out of the door as quickly as I can.

"Most chicks would pay money to see this, Tales," he says with a loud laugh. "Front row, first class, VIP, and you walk away?"

I hear him flush the toilet before he comes out when I am walking out the door.

"Where you going?" he asks as I hear his footsteps behind me.

"To find my bag, my phone." I pause. "Away from you."

"Wow, you're a little spirited nowadays." He laughs, and I feel his breath hit the back of my neck.

"Good morning."

I look up to see River, and if I wasn't embarrassed, I would be totally fan-girling right now.

"How was it?"

"She's my sister's best friend," Memphis snarls a bit, shocking me at the one-eighty he just did.

"Good morning," I say as I grab my phone and bag off the floor next to the couch where I left it. I look at the phone screen and see it's dead. Grabbing my bag, I open it to find a charger. "Is there a place I can plug this thing in?"

"That's what he said." Finn appears, pointing at Memphis with a sinful grin and winks. "Nothing, man?" He points to me, and my gaping mouth snaps shut.

"You're all—"

"Not all of us." Billy B walks up and extends his hand. "I'm Billy. Welcome."

I shake his hand quickly, then pull away.

"Outlets over there." He points to the kitchen counter. "Set it on airplane mode once you get a screen; charges faster."

"Thank you." I nod, then walk away, trying to act calm and cool, which I'm not, not at all.

Once it's plugged in, I look behind me to ask Memphis if Madison has contacted him to find all four are staring at me.

"You have a nice body," River says as if it's no big deal, but it embarrasses me completely.

Memphis slugs him in the arm.

"What, man? She does. Long, lean, and tight as—"

Memphis punches him in the arm harder this time.

"'Da fuck, man?"

"Memphis," I call his attention back to me. "Did Madison call or message you?"

He shrugs and scowls, not looking away from River. "No idea."

"Could you check?" I ask, and he finally looks back at me. "My phone is—"

"It's in my room. Come on, let's go see."

"She can't stay out here?" Finn asks in a harassing tone.

Memphis doesn't say anything, only looks at them before walking over and grabbing my hand, but I pull mine away quickly.

"Wow." River laughs loudly.

"Back the fuck off," Memphis snarls. "Let's go, Tally." He points to his room.

"You think we're all gonna try to jump her if you leave the room for two seconds? Shit, Black, you are—"

"She's a fucking preacher's kid, probably just sprouted tits two days ago, and she certainly—"

I quickly walk past him and toward the room to see if I can find his phone and get away from the most embarrassing conversation I have ever sort of been involved in.

I hear the door shut behind me as I am searching around the side of the bed and look up.

"You're pissed at me?" He seems shocked.

"I want to know what's going on with Madison. If she's okay, alive, in the air"—I turn and scowl at him—"if she needs a ride from the airport."

"Didn't get the message, Tales. No need to be pissed off at me." He's standing inches in front of me, looking down at me, and my heart speeds up, like it did that night, like it did last night. "You're not pissed at me, are you, Tales?"

I take a step back, retreating because I don't know what he is all hot and cold about. Why one minute I'm a kid he seems annoyed by and the next he comes at me like he is on stage, all "Look at me, I'm Memphis Black, rock star," and it's making me angry.

"Could you please check to see if she—" His laugh interrupts me. "I don't think it's funny."

"You're funny." He smirks, reaching down and grabbing a pair of white shorts that he pulls his phone out of.

I glance down at it, seeing the notifications light up, message after message.

He clicks on one and slowly turns his head, studying the screen, and his brows shoot up. "Dayum."

"What?" I reach for his phone, but he holds it up so I can't get it.

"Oh no, Tales, you don't need to see that," he jokes.

"See what? Is she okay?"

"The naked picture that the chick sent me is more than okay."

"Pig."

“Why am I a pig, and why the hell are you getting so angry at me, Tales?”

“I don’t know what you’re talking about.” I blush.

“You want me.” He plops down on the bed. “Admit it and we can get past the *dis* and head right into the possibilities of the *comfort*—”

“I *want* to know if Madison—”

“Storm’s causing delays,” he reads from his phone. “She hopes to be in tomorrow morning and asks that I take good care of you.” He tosses his phone on the bed and lies on his back, linking his hands behind his head. “I’d take really good care of you if you weren’t a virgin or my—”

“Am not,” I snap, then cover my mouth in surprise.

“Really now?” He sits up slowly and looks me up and down.

“It’s none of your business, Memphis Black.” I turn to walk out, and he grabs the hem of my shirt and pulls me back.

“Where do you think you’re going?”

“To get my things.”

“Not without me, you aren’t.” He stands, his hand still on my shirt.

“Because of your friends? You’re afraid they—” I stop, unable to finish saying what I was going to.

“Hell, yes, because of my friends,” he says, taking my elbow and turning me to face him.

“They aren’t acting any differently than you are. Heck, you’re acting worse, so how ’bout you let go of my shirt and let me take my chances out there?"

"You can't handle them."

"I lived in New York City for a year; I can handle pretty much anything."

"Tough girl, yet you still giggle when the word"—he leans in toward me—"fuck is said."

I thrust my hand up, and it hits his chest, stopping him from coming any closer. He looks shocked. I am shocked, too. There is something else going on, something I have never experienced. I go to pull my hand away, but he holds it still against his hot, bare chest.

"Did you feel that?" he whispers. "That is nothing compared to what—"

"Stop, okay? Please, just stop." I pull my hand away, and he lets me this time.

"Stop what, Tales?" His gaze drifts to my lips, then back to my eyes.

"Whatever it is you are doing."

"We. We are both clearly attracted to one another."

"Apparently, you're attracted to anything with"—I swallow down the fear that comes with being so … racy—"boobs and a vagina."

He tries to suppress a grin, then laughs out loud.

"You're a jerk."

"Wait!" He grabs my elbow again.

"Nope. I am leaving. I'm going to find a hotel—"

"Come on, Tales. Your face …" He laughs again. "You looked like it hurt to say that."

"Well, geesh, Memphis, this is completely

uncomfortable for me," I admit.

"You are staying here. Madison will flip her shit if—" He moves, stopping me from side stepping him.

I try to reason with him. "She doesn't have to know that you were being—"

"Honest?"

"Okay. Uncomfortable again."

He throws his hands up as if to surrender. "Sorry, Tales. You look good. Hot—"

I scowl. "Very, very uncomfortable."

He smirks and runs his hand through his sexy black hair. "You think that's uncomfortable? Hell, you haven't even said you think I look good."

"I don't think you need an ego boost from me. You have a gaggle of groupies to do that for you." I am feeling a little less uncomfortable now.

He smiles and shakes his head. "I suppose you're right, but …"

"Of course there's a but."

"An ego maniac like me still needs daily affirmation, so look at me, Tally, and tell me what you see." I shake my head. "Come on. I won't ask you again."

I shrug. "Fine. I see what everyone else in the country sees: a tall, dark, fit guy with tattoos up and down his arms who is confident and very talented."

"I hear a but." He cocks his eyebrow.

"But"—I shake my head and look away—"if you were so confident, would you need all that *affirmation*?"

"I love the applause. I put my heart and soul into what I do."

I smile and nod. "I think your music is brilliant."

He grins. "Brilliant, huh?"

"I've always thought so." I shrug, feeling my face burning because he is looking at me in that way that makes me uncomfortable. "That's all the applause you should need, Memphis Black. Not all the other nonsense."

"Oh." He smirks. "You mean ass?"

"Well …" I can't help giggling, and he smiles with his whole face. It's beautiful. "Yeah, I suppose."

"Sex is almost better than the applause. Hell, you should know, Miss I'm-not-a-virgin?" He laughs again. "How the hell did you get through it?"

"I have no idea what you're talking about."

"Getting all sweaty and naked in—"

"I am not having this discussion with you." I scrunch my eyes shut.

"Sex is sex, Tales. It's an activity that ends in a rush."

"Memphis," I sigh.

He stands up and swats my backside when he walks past me. "You should really try it with me, Tales. It's not just an activity; it's a fucking adventure."

"Oh, my goodness. Do you ever stop?" I giggle nervously.

"My missile is heat seeking and locked on search and destroy mode, Tales. Don't fucking kid yourself with the emotional bullshit. If you feel up for the challenge, I'll rock you my way."

"Do you have no boundaries? I mean, you

seem to give them to your band mates."

"I have no boundaries, Tales, none." He smirks.

"I do."

He flashes me a wicked grin, and I feel it; everywhere.

"I need a shower."

"I'm all—"

"I'll do it at a hotel," I threaten.

"I'll do it anywhere you want."

"Ugh." I walk out of the room before he has a chance to stop me this time.

I round the corner and run into Billy.

"You okay?" The sincerity in his voice makes me immediately feel at ease.

"She's fine." And the one behind me makes me feel the opposite.

"I am, thank you." I walk past him and into the kitchen to grab my phone and charger. Ten percent battery. I pull it out of the wall, then walk over to my bag and scoop it up.

"Tales." I look up at Memphis. "Go shower. Then you can head to the beach with us."

"I think I am gonna—"

"Go shower and stop being a punk," he says as if he's joking, but I see a glint of annoyance in his eyes.

"You can use the guest bathroom if you'll feel more comfortable, Tally," Billy says, pointing to a hall across the room. "Third door on the right. There are two beds in that room, too. Madison and you will like it, I'm sure."

"Thank you." I glance at Memphis, whose jaw

is squared and the muscles are popping in it, before walking down the hall.

"You better watch it, Billy," I hear Memphis growl.

"You were making her—"

"No, man, I wasn't making her anything. I've known her all my life, and I'm telling you to watch it."

I shut the door behind me and lean against it as I take in a deep breath.

Memphis Black wants to rock me. Thousands would kill to be in this position, but I am not thousands. I am just me.

I look around to find the guys are all looking at me like I have three heads.

"That goes for all of you."

"What, are we supposed to stand around and let you make an ass out of yourself and make our guest feel uncomfortable?" Billy asks.

"*My* guest," I snap, "and you're supposed to mind your damn business."

"Reel it in, man. Shit, didn't you get enough last night?" River pats my shoulder before he shoves his hand in his pocket, feeling around for something. He pulls out a pipe. "One toke and you'll chill."

"Not in the fucking house, River." Finn shakes his head.

"Fine. Out by the pool, then. Come on, Memphis, you need to hit chillz at least once. She's got you wound up tighter than," he pauses, "a preacher's daughter." He laughs as he walks to the French doors leading outside. "Suit yourself."

I couldn't agree more with River. I am wound so fucking tightly I'm going to snap.

I walk out and see River around the corner, toking on his one hitter. His lips curl up as he taps out the ash and shoves the pipe into the snuff box, then taps it a few times, packing it tight. He hands it to me with the lighter.

"Easy. It's pretty bad ass," River warns.

I nod but don't listen. Pot never affected me in high school. That's why I rarely touched the shit.

"You like that chick?"

I suck in a deep breath and hold it, even though my lungs are on fire immediately. Exhaling slowly, I say, "Sister's"—I pause so I won't choke—"best friend."

"And your reason for having a mad-on."

I exhale and look at him like he's nuts because, let's face it, he kind of is. "What?"

"Mad-on, bro." He takes the one hitter and taps the ash out before packing it up again. "You can't tap that ass, so instead of a hard-on resulting in a set of blue balls, you get a fucking mad-on."

"Mad-on." I lean against the white stucco wall and shake my head. "Not mad at all."

"You wanna tap that, though," he says, before sparking up the tiny pipe and inhaling.

"Her ass is nice."

"Yeah, it is," he says as he inhales deeper.

"You steer clear."

He coughs out the smoke and laughs as the door opens. He shoves the one hitter deep in his pocket and smirks as Finn and Billy walk out.

"You ready?" Finn hisses.

"Let me change," River says, then looks at me and laughs, and hell if I don't laugh, too. "Black, you're in your underwear still."

I look down and laugh harder. "Looks good,

though, right?"

"Looks really good." He winks.

"Fuck you."

"Good enough that I'm thinking I wouldn't mind tapping in the front, and you in the back of—"

"You may not want to finish that sentence. I don't do double rainbow," I say as I walk inside to change.

"Daisy chain." He chuckles, following me inside.

"Shut the hell up, man."

"The four of us, DVDA," he says, still laughing.

"DVDA'ing your mother." I push him.

"She likes that shit, man."

As soon as we walk in, I see Tally standing at the end of the counter with her back turned.

"Three blocks, thank you." She continues, "How much a night?"

I haul ass in front of her, take her phone, and hang it up.

"What are you doing?"

I grab a quarter off the counter. "Heads, you go. Tales, you stay."

"Memphis, it's—"

"Heads, you go. Tails, you stay," I repeat.

She shakes her head then says, "Fine."

I flip the coin, and it lands on tails. "Go get changed."

"Memphis—" She looks around and stops as she spots River out of her peripheral.

"I'll back off. Shit, Tales, I thought you were

all badass now, being a New Yorker and all." Fuck, I hope she bought that.

She looks skeptical, and I know damn well I fucked up. And, well, I'm buzzing pretty hard now, but I feel much less wound up, kind of chillz.

"Promise me."

"Damn, girl, I was fucking with you. Not like I really need to work at gaining panty access, Tales. Women throw that shit at me."

"Okay."

"Okay?" What the hell does okay mean?

"Yes, but I'm not going to the beach with you guys."

"Like hell." I laugh, but she's not having it.

Her shoulders square up a bit, and she stands taller. If I push any harder, she will be at a hotel, and that will land me on the shit list with Mads. I am being fucking ridiculous. There are hundreds—hell, thousands—of women I can have in my bed without issue.

"Fine. Help yourself to anything in the fridge, and if you need anything, I'll send the boat back to give you a lift to the beach." I grab a pen and the pad of paper, then write down my number and hand it to her.

"Thank you."

"Yeah." I stare too long; I know I do because she gets squirmy, so I take off to my room to dress.

When I come out, she is on the phone again.

"You're staying, right?"

She pushes mute and whispers, "My mom."

There is sadness in her eyes, and I feel even more like a turd. I can't imagine losing my old man, but if I hang out, she will think I'm trying to fuck her because, well, I would really like to be between her legs, but it's Tally. Tally all grown up, and Tally hot as hell, and Tally—fuck! Note to self: chillz is evil with a capital E.

"You need something?" she asks.

"No, but we'll be right—"

She nods. "I know."

I give her a nod then pull my shades down, covering my eyes before forcing my sorry ass out the door. I must seem like that one guy with the gun and red shirt, the one who hates books and hunts and is all hot over that chick in the blue dress and white apron. I laugh because I'm fucked up, wondering why they didn't make the douche sport wood in the cartoon while chasing after that beast—*Beauty and the Beast*. Yeah, that's the movie.

"You ready yet?"

I snap back to reality when I look up at Finn.

"Fuck, yes, I'm ready. When am I ever not ready? Hell, I'm always ready."

"You shouldn't touch that shit, man. Makes you act like him." He thumbs behind him at River.

"Fuck you, Finn," River snaps.

River hands me a beer. "Chaser?"

"Don't remind him that he already almost drove that poor girl out of here," Billy says, only half joking.

"Back off, Billy. She's a good girl."

"I'm a good boy, the best behaved one—"

"I swear to God above, man, if you touch that—" I step to him, and River slaps my chest, stopping me.

"You calling lead on her?" River smirks.

"I'm calling, if you touch her—any one of you—I'll kill you." I look them all in the eyes. They are a little taken aback—okay, a lot taken aback. "She's my sister's best friend."

"That you went all caveman on and—"

"I was fucked up," I defend.

"Not this morning you weren't," Finn points out as we walk down the beach.

I ignore the comment. So I'm an ass, but I will not be concentrating on her ass. As fucking perfect as it may be, I will focus fully on the ones sprawled out, soaking up the Florida sun.

The boat is by the dock, waiting for us. Talk about service; we get to ride in style.

We take off and pass the other yachts and boats anchored in the bay.

"Look around, men. There is a lot to take in right here and right now. Fuck this morning." Don't need the drama, anyway. It's not like she'd want it any different than I give to the rest of them. I'm a fucking experience… My leather is *not* made of the boyfriend material, girls like Tallia want.

Ten minutes later, we're docked, and River dives in.

When he pops up out of the water, he laughs. "Let's go."

None of us follow his lead; we all take the short walk down the dock right to the white sand and hot as hell chicks. River is walking out of the water, and all eyes are glued to his crazy ass. Leave it to him to take the path much less taken.

"Damn, check out that little peach," River says

when he meets up with us, running his hands back and forth through his hair, ridding it of some of the Atlantic. He points to a chick laid out on a beach towel, all oiled up, top already undone, and she is turning around to lie on her back.

"Oh, fuck no." I almost laugh as we get past her, heading for the volleyball net.

"Sascrotch," Finn mumbles under his breath.

We all bust up laughing.

"She's hot and all, but who the fuck doesn't look in the mirror and see they need a fucking trim before—"

"That's more than a trim, man; that would require a bush hog." I laugh.

"She's a moped," River chimes in. "I'd ride the hell out of her for fun, but I sure as fuck wouldn't want any one of you to see me on her."

"Hair grows there for a reason," Billy says.

"So does facial hair, man, but you trim that shit so you don't look like a mountain man or a—"

"Bah, bah." River laughs. "Billy goat."

As soon as he leaves the house, I uncover the phone, hoping Mom didn't hear him.

"Tally, was that Memphis Black I heard?"

Well, I guess that cat was out of the bag.

"Yep, he is here, Mom."

"How is he? Has he changed? Has the—?"

"He's the same, just older," I lie, hoping she doesn't notice.

"Can you ask him why on Earth a nice boy like him would agree to a band name like," she whispers, "STD?"

"I'll ask," I say to appease her, but there is no way I will ask him that question. "Okay, Mom, I'm going to the beach now. I love you and will call in a couple days."

"Love you, too, Tally," she says before hanging up.

I grab an apple off the counter and a bottle of water, yawning. Exhausted, that's what I am. Totally exhausted. I decide to go back in the guest room and message Madison to see when she'll be in, and then I need to search online to see what tomorrow holds for me.

I eat the apple as I sit down on the bed and grab my phone, and it's … dead. Of course it's dead. I shove the charger plug into the wall, throw the now eaten apple in the wastebasket, and give it ten minutes. My phone is shot. The battery life is horrible, but I don't have the money to spend to get a new one, not now.

I lie down so I can use it while it's plugged in then send Madison a message.

When will you be here?

She replies immediately.

Tomorrow at ten a.m. Make sure you and my brother pick me up at ten on the nose. I am so fucking excited to see you!

It's followed up by a bunch of emojis.

Can't wait to see you, either!

I follow that up with the smiley face and tears emoji.

I click on the Internet browser on my phone and search jobs for dancers in New York City. I enjoyed living in New York. It was busy; there was always something to do; and you were never alone, even if you were alone.

There are plenty of auditions available and a lot of instructor jobs. I screenshot the ones I think look the most promising. Heck, they all look promising when you need a job.

I then spend an hour or more reading, taking more screenshots, and then I Google the nearest public library because I don't have access to a computer, and I want this task completed. I want to know that, when I tell Madison the secret I have been keeping from her, she doesn't go all Mads on me and try to help.

I am an adult now, and I need to take care of myself.

***

When I return from the library, I am hot and ready for a shower, then maybe a nap. I am exhausted from the walk, the heat, the emotions, and the lack of sleep I got last night while I lay next to Memphis.

As I walk down the brick drive, my breath is taken away by the place. It's like a dream. Heck, it's nothing I ever even dreamed of. The three buildings connected by lanais are beyond luxurious.

I round the corner, hoping the back door is unlocked because my phone has died again, of course, and I forgot the code. I walk past the marble infinity pool that seemingly spills into the bay to the door, and of course, it is locked.

I knock, hoping someone will answer, but when no one does, I look toward the dock to see if the boat Memphis said would be back is there. My fingers cross, hoping the man driving the boat knows the code.

He isn't here. The boat isn't even back. I kick off my shorts and pull my tank top over my head, deciding to dive into the pool and hoping I won't feel as disgusting as I do right now when I come out.

Once in, I carefully watch for the boat. I don't want to be in the pool when they come back. I don't want to be in this stupid, teeny bikini that Madison sent me, either, but it's the only one I have.

The water feels like silk, and it's warm, almost to the point that it's not refreshing, but it's not quite as warm as I'm sure it will be by evening.

Once I swim a bit and feel better, I walk out and wring out my hair, grab a towel, dry off as best I can, and then pull my shorts and tank back on.

I lie down under one of the lanais and decide to let the sun dry me off. The chaise lounge is so incredibly comfortable I drift off, knowing the loud motor from the boat, or the even louder band members from STD, will wake me as soon as they return.

"You're right; she has a really nice ass," I hear River and quickly roll to my side, keeping my eyes closed.

"Careful. Don't let Memphis hear you talk like that." It's Finn. I can tell by the deep baritone in his voice.

"Memphis is busy." River chuckles.

"Uh-huh," Finn says. Then I hear them walk away.

I hear girls giggling, and then I hear *him* laugh.

"Nuh-uh. I invited you here for a party, not to get grabby there, girls."

Girls, as in plural. So the stories I have read online are true. Memphis is a man-whore.

"Why?" one whines. "Come on, we really want an STD."

I can't sit here and listen anymore, so I open my eyes, taking in my surroundings, and then find the quickest escape to the house.

There are tons of people around. It's sick that my ears are tuned in on his conversation when there are dozens of others surrounding me.

I stand quickly after my route is planned and start walking toward the glass doors.

"Where do you think you're going, gorgeous?" I hear a stranger's voice before someone grabs my elbow.

I don't look back. I look straight ahead and see Billy walking quickly toward me.

"Dude, I'd let go of that one if I were you," he says, reaching out to me.

"It's Wolf, and I don't think that's any of your concern."

"No, man, he's serious," River says, grabbing my hand. "Come on, little one."

I look up at the man, Wolf. He is tall with copper hair and blue eyes, and he is smiling at me. It's a smile that would send you running for the woods if his name wasn't Wolf, and you hadn't been raised having the bejeepers scared out of you by those fairytales. Nope, no woods for me. I'll take my chances with River.

"What's going on here?" Memphis asks, standing in front of me, his arms crossed over his shirtless chest.

I feel immediately at ease.

"The little one and I are going inside," River says in a tone meant to egg him on.

Memphis grabs my free hand and holds it up. "Fingers straight up." His whisper in my ear makes the hair on the back of my neck stand up as I do what he asks. He looks at River as he turns my wrist from side to side. “If you like it, you better put a ring on it. She’s a good kid and deserves better than anyone of us, so back off.”

“Oh, my God, man.” River laughs. “You’re serious.”

“Serious as a bona fide STD. If you touch her, you better plan on wife-ing it, and you better be fucking sober when you do it.”

I cover my mouth when he says fucking and try not to giggle.

He shakes his head and rolls his eyes that are sparkling. “On second thought, if you touch her, I’ll kill you.”

“You staking claim to that?” Finn asks as he walks out of the house, trying not to smirk.

“She’s off limits, you feel me?” He finally lets go of my hand, turns his head, and looks into my eyes. “Anyone of these bastar—” I cover my mouth, and his angry glare threatens to turn into a smile. “Tales, you have no business being here.”

It stings a little. I don’t want it to, but it does.

“I tried to leave earlier.”

His eyes narrow a bit. Then he takes in a deep breath and runs his hand through his hair. “I don’t need Mads pissed off.”

“But with me”—I swallow—“pissed off is fine?”

He looks around, and I do, too. Everyone is staring at us.

Apparently, when he speaks, they listen, too.

“You pissed off at me for trying to save your virtue?” He looks at me like I’m crazy.

Maybe I am because I say, “I already told you

there is nothing there to save."

"Ooooooh," echoes around us.

He throws his hands up in the air. "Fine. Have at it. But, when one of these fucks puts their hands on you and I bust it, don't say I didn't warn you." He looks around. "All of you." Then he looks back at me and points. "And, when I fuck them up, Tales, it's on your conscious."

With that, I storm into the house, but before I can shut the door behind me, Billy walks in.

"You okay?"

"I'm fine!" I yell at him, then realize it's not him I am angry at. "Sorry."

"Need a drink?" River asks.

"Yes, please," I say, surprising myself.

"You eat today?" Billy asks.

"Yes." It's not a lie. I had an apple.

"I can't drink unless I eat. You wanna with me so I don't look like even more of a pussy before we drink?"

"Ruins the buzz, man." River, who came into the house behind us, shakes his head disapprovingly.

I look up at Billy. He is smiling sincerely, so I smile back. "Sure."

"Chicken breast and salad. Crackers between drinks and water. Don't forget to drink water," he warns with his finger pointed at me.

I nod. He knows I am full of it, though.

I don't drink. I have had two glasses of wine, and I wound up in Franco's bed the first and only time I have ever had sex. I was gonna do it, wine or not. I was sick of believing that the one person I had ever allowed myself to fantasize about was a big man-whore.

After eating, River hands me a drink, then hands one to Billy. “Bottoms up, bitches.”

“Cheers,” Billy says with a look of caution in his eyes.

I take a drink and nearly choke. It tastes awful, followed by a burn in my belly, and then … Well, then the taste of cinnamon fills my mouth.

I like it, a lot.

Evidently, River notices and fills it up again.

“River, she’s had enough,” Billy says.

“No, I like it. A lot.” I grab the glass and slam it down.

Burn in the throat.

Burn in the belly.

Burst of cinnamon in my mouth.

Yum.

“Another.” I push the glass back to him.

“Damn, girl.” River smirks as he fills it up again.

I take it and drink it down.

Burn in the throat.

Burn in the belly.

Burst of cinnamon in my mouth.

Yum.

“What the hell is going on in here?” I look up to see Memphis with two girls, one on each arm.

“Tally loves the Fireball.”

"Fireball, please." Tally pushes the fucking glass back to River. When I say glass, I mean, glass. Not a fucking shot glass, either.

"River, Billy, what the fuck are you doing?" I yell at them.

River smirks at me. "She likes it."

I look at Billy, who shrugs and shakes his head. "She asked for it."

I glance at her as she downs the damn whiskey. "How many is that?"

"Four, man, chill."

She is looking at the glass and slowly blows out a breath. Her face is turning a little green, and she is holding onto the table with one hand and her stomach with the other.

"Fucking idiots," I tell them as I pick her up.

I look over at what would have been tonight's auditions and shake my head, "Goodnight, ladies."

I hear them whine a bit. Can't fucking blame them.

"I don't feel very well," she slurs before wrapping her arms around my neck.

"I leave you alone for twenty fucking minutes—"

"Spreading your ST-whatevers," she says, and her stomach heaves.

"You puke on me, and I swear to fuck, Tally," I warn, as I try my best to stay upright myself while hauling ass to my room.

"I owe you one." She giggles then hiccups. "Uh-oh."

I kick open my door right as she chucks all over my chest.

"Aw, fuck, Tales."

She giggles, then hurls again.

"Sorry?" she says as I set her in the Jacuzzi tub fully dressed.

"You think?" I ask as I start the water. "You made me stink. I don't do stink."

"You can't serious—" she pauses. "Serious—"

"Seriously, Tales," I tell her, as I climb in the tub.

"What are you—?"

"You stink." I sit down and the water is rising over my board shorts.

"*You* stink," she says, narrowing her eyes.

"Not for long." I grab the faucet hose and spray myself down, then soap up my chest. "Good thing you didn't blow chunks, Tales."

I look up to see she is looking at me, her eyes glassy and her mouth gaping. She swallows hard.

I shake my head, erasing the thought that her look is the same every other chick gives me. Tally is fucked up with a capital F, and that look is—

"Shit," I scramble back, avoiding her next hurl.

She doesn't stop, either. She throws up again

and again.

"Sweet Jesus, Tally."

I jump out and grab a fist full of her hair, trying to keep it out of the way as her eyes roll back.

"Don't fucking pass out on me," I warn.

She is wobbling from side to side as she dry heaves.

"Hold the side of the tub, girl." I grab the back of her little, green frog tee shirt, the one that's married to the pig. What's his name? Fuck it, who cares? I pull it over the back of her head. "All right, arms out."

"Naughty," she slurs.

"Stinky, Tales," I tell her. "Nothing naughty going on in my head." I see a bright pink swimsuit top covering her. "Besides, you have on a swimsuit."

She pulls her arms out, then flops back, panting as her stomach muscles visibly contract with each dry heave that occurs after each hiccup.

"Hurts," she mumbles as she places her hand over her tight as hell, little stomach.

"I know, babe." And I fucking do know throwing up sucks.

Her teeth start to chatter, and I know damn well she's gonna be pissed when I hose her down, but I can't leave her in here, and I won't put her in bed smelling like that.

"I'm gonna wash you up." She shakes her head very slightly no. "Sure am," I confirm, releasing the drain so all that puke washes away. "And I'm thinking you have bottoms on that match this top?" She nods. "Don't be pissed."

I pull off her shorts, then start hosing her down from head to toe. Her body is instantly covered in goose bumps, and her teeth start chattering louder. I squeeze out some shampoo into her hair and lather it up as best I can. She tries to help, but she's like a little shivering rag doll.

"I can do it faster alone."

"Conditioner," she whimpers.

"I don't think we should be worried about—"

"Afro," she groans.

"You're really not gonna give a shit, Tally," I try again.

"Conditioner," she insists.

Her stomach lurches again, followed by a hiccup as I squirt conditioner in her hair. After I rinse it out, I hose down her body again, and only when she leans forward, hugging her knees and shivering, do I see her back is fried.

Once she is rinsed clean, I have her lie back. She covers her face while I grab the white terrycloth bathrobe off the back of the bathroom door.

"Can you stand up?" She nods, but makes no attempt. "Okay, arms around me." When she wraps her arms around my neck, I notice the tears running down her face. "Come on, Tales," I coo gently. "Rookie mistake; don't be upset. Just listen to me and not those assholes, got it?"

I lift her up, then walk out to the bedroom and push the covers down as she holds on, crying and hiccupping.

"Okay, listen, no tears in my bed."

"I am not stay—"

"Like hell you aren't. If you pass out and throw up, you're fucked. Not on my watch."

She doesn't say shit, which amuses me.

"No argument?'

"No, you owe me," she mumbles.

"So you said."

I drop my swim trunks, then grab some boxers out of the dresser drawer before grabbing a towel and mopping up the little drops of puke on the floor.

"Care to tell me how I owe you?"

"Senior year." Her teeth chatter as she curls into a fluffy, white ball. "You came for a visit …" She pauses as she shakes violently. "Came to my house, kissed me, and threw up on my feet. We're even."

"Did River give you something to smoke, too, Tales?" She is definitely fucked up. *Kissed her?* Yeah, right.

She is still shaking when I grab her clothes out of the bathroom and my shorts, wrap them in a towel, and throw them out the door, knowing the cleaning chicks will grab them in the morning.

Still curious about this little fantasy of hers, I flop down on the bed and pull her against me, hoping to give off some body heat and warm her up.

"Tell me about this little fantasy of yours."

"I'm so cold." She shivers, so I pull her in more tightly, wrapping the comforter around both of us.

"Spill it."

"I helped you in the right house." She yawns. "Took your black boots off."

I would have pushed for more if this scenario

didn't seem a little too familiar to me.

"I kissed you?"

"Uh-huh." She shivers again. "Best kiss ever."

Fuck! "Was it now?"

"First kiss ever."

"Really?"

"Uh-huh. Don't tell Memphis."

"Wouldn't dream of it," I say as I now feel really fucking stupid that I kissed this chick when she was way too young. "I puked on you?"

She doesn't answer. She is out cold, and still her teeth chatter as her body shakes.

I hop out of bed and walk to the dresser to grab a sweatshirt. The black STD one will work. I laugh, thinking about how pissed off the X-man was when he saw the shocker symbol.

I uncover her, then pull her long, wavy, wet hair to the side, and she flops to her back. I pull her up and take her arm out of the robe and then the other.

Rag doll. Complete and total rag doll.

Her eyes flutter open. "What are you doing?" She looks confused, but not scared like she should fucking be to have some man taking her damn clothes off.

Before I can answer, she jumps off the bed and darts to the bathroom. I follow her to make sure she doesn't pass out and fall.

I see her looking in the mirror and then around the vanity. She grabs my toothbrush—my fucking toothbrush—and toothpaste, and then she starts brushing her teeth. She spits into the sink and brushes again. When she is finished, she holds her head in her hands and walks past me in that pink bikini.

I follow her out, and she grabs the sweatshirt I had on the bed for her and puts it on. Then she climbs into bed, still shaking, and pulls the comforter up around her tightly and closes her eyes.

"Well, damn." I laugh out loud.

I put the bathrobe back in the bathroom and then come back to the bed, lying back down again.

"I locked the door," she whispers.

What in the fuck did she just say? I can't hold back the laughter. Tales is talking crazy shit and walking around like she owns the joint. She has no clue.

She groans, and her eyes blink a few times. She opens her eyes and looks at me, then holds her head.

"Where's Madison?"

"She'll be here in the morning."

"I don't feel good," she mumbles.

"I know. Sleep."

"I'm cold," she says as her teeth clank together.

I pull her closer. Her long, lean, tight body fits perfectly against mine, and she smells so good. Her body starts to relax, and I know she is asleep—well, passed out … again.

I lie next to her, knowing I shouldn't enjoy it so much. I shouldn't feel the way I feel about her. The protectiveness I understand because, hell, she is the most innocent chick I have ever been around. Even if she has been with someone in the 'biblical' sense, she's still Tally. Regardless, with a body like mmm, and an ass like POW!, I can't shake the desire to be all up inside of her.

***

I wake up to the sound of my alarm, lying on my back with a sweet smelling, tight, little body draped over me. As fucked up as I got last night, I know who it is.

"Oh, my dear." She tries to pull away, but my arm is underneath her side and wrapped around her with POW! in my hand.

"Morning, buzz kill. How are you feeling?"

"How did I end up"—she huffs as she gives up the fight, yet unravels her leg from between mine—"here."

Reluctantly, I release POW! and let her go. "You were doing shots, got all fucked up in five minutes, threw up on me—"

"I'm so sorry," she begins.

"Evidently, I had it coming," I tell her as I roll to my side, facing her as she sits up, looking mortified when she sees the sweatshirt she's wearing.

"Where are my clothes?"

"Hopefully in the washing machine. Smelled awful." I can't help enjoying watching her eyes widen, so I keep it going. "I gave you a bath and—"

"You didn't," she gasps.

"Would I lie to you?" I sit up and bow my head so I am eye to eye with her. Except, her eyes aren't connecting; she is avoiding looking at me. "Tales?"

"Did we …?"

"Take a bath together? Yes. Did I strip you? Yes. Did I wash you? Yes."

She shakes her head. "Why? Why did you do all that?"

I take in a deep breath and let it out slowly as I get up and turn off the damn alarm. "I needed to clean up after the little vomit shower you gave me. Couldn't get the stink off you without getting rid of the shorts and T-shirt. Wouldn't have been cool if I plopped you in the tub and left you. You could have drowned." I grab a pair of shorts and throw them on over my boxers. Then I grab my black Pearl Jam T-shirt and throw it on before looking back at her.

Finally, she looks up at me. "Did—"

"Tales, does your pussy feel like it went ten rounds with the heavyweight champion of—"

"Memphis!" she yells at me, then grabs her head.

"Well, fuck, Tales, I kind of prefer a warm, active participant in the sheets, not a dry heaving, goose bump covered, shaking, little drunk," I tease.

She tries not to laugh when I swear, and I try not to laugh at the hellacious mess of curls going every which way on her head.

"We have thirty minutes to get to the airport, and if we're late, I will have even more hell to pay from Madison than I already do."

"Is she angry at you?" she asks, running her fingers through her hair.

"I don't know. Is she?"

She swings her long, lean legs over the side of the bed. "What do you mean?"

"When you told her I kissed you, was she

pissed?"

Her jaw drops, and her head jerks back so she's looking at me like a deer caught in the headlights.

"Well?"

Chapter Ten
Hung Over

"I need clothes," I say after far too much uncomfortable silence.

"That's all you're gonna say?" he asks.

"What do you want me to say?" I look down. I feel like garbage. My head is pounding, my stomach hurts, and now there are butterflies dancing inside of it.

"Does she know?"

I shake my head.

"Why not?" he asks.

"You were drunk. It wasn't a big deal."

"Right." He laughs. "Is your bag in the guest room?"

"Yes," I whisper.

"I'll grab it. Feel free to brush your teeth. You already used my toothbrush last night."

I hear him walk out the door, and I quickly walk to the bathroom and then shut and lock the door, as if that matters. I take off the sweatshirt and jump in the shower, washing as fast as I can while still in my bathing suit in case he comes in. I condition my crazy hair and then quickly rinse.

After I get out, I throw my hair up in a towel

and see the bathrobe hanging on the back of the door; it reads, *HIS*. But right now, it's mine.

My head is still pounding, but my stomach—whenever he's not around—doesn't feel so off.

I walk out as he walks in.

He smirks. "Ten minutes," he warns. "I'll leave you to it. Hurry up, okay?" With that, he starts to walk out.

"Memphis?"

He looks back at me.

"Thank you."

He gives me a sly, little grin. "Now *you* owe *me*."

The past two days have been insane, totally insane. I have spent two nights sleeping in the bed of a boy I had a crush on growing up, who happens to also be my first kiss and a rock star, for goodness sakes. If I didn't know better, I would certainly allow my mind to entertain the little fairytale buzzing around inside it, maybe even serve it tea.

I am dressed, and my hair is wet, yet tamed with product. I brush my teeth with my own toothbrush, and as I am flossing, he walks in.

"Tales, come on; you can do that shit later." He snaps his fingers. "Queenie is arriving soon, and I sure as hell don't want to be late. I'll catch hell."

I throw the floss away and reach in my bag. "Memphis?"

"Tales?"

"Do you know where my phone is?"

He shakes his head. "Where did you have it last?"

"Probably my pocket? I don't know."

His eyes widen, and he cringes. “Clothes are gone to the laundry.”

“Someone is washing my clothes?”

“And mine. Can you imagine what they must be doing in that washing machine?”

I completely ignore his sexual innuendo. “Did you check the pockets before you put them in?”

“I don’t do laundry.” He looks at his phone. “Time, Tales. Let’s roll, or we’ll be late.” He hurries out the door, and I follow behind. “I’ll send a text; we’ll find it.”

Once outside, he hits the key fob and unlocks the doors to a black Escalade. Then he opens the passenger door.

“Chop, chop, sweet cheeks.”

I feel a blush rising on my face as I climb in, and I’m pretty sure he groans behind me before shutting the door.

He hops in the driver’s seat, then moves the seat back. “Haven’t driven in a while”—he laughs—“so buckle up.”

“How long?” I ask, and he merely chuckles.

“Been on the road for a year, so I’d say a year. Might get a little hairy out there.” He reaches out and messes up my hair.

He has always poked fun at my hair. Apparently, he still does. How stupid am I for thinking he was attracted to me? His sexual innuendoes were nothing except a joke, or maybe he just wanted to have sex, which he obviously gets a lot of.

“You’re quiet. Felling shitty?”

I smirk and shake my head.

"Tales, you really need to get over the giggles when someone curses." He pulls out and starts down the brick driveway. "Tell me about school, about your father. How is your mom?"

"Why?"

"'Cause I want to know what I've missed."

"Tell me about being on the road for a year."

He stops in front of the gate and looks at me as we wait for it to open. "I really am sorry about your dad, Tales."

"Thanks."

"He's in a better place, right?" he asks sincerely.

I nod. "Yes, he's where he'd want to be."

"Your mom? Church family taking care of her?"

"She's okay. She misses Dad, but she has a new place, and—"

"A new place? She isn't in the house?" he asks in shock.

"It belongs to the church."

"Probably easier being away from the house, though, right?" he asks, pulling out onto the road, where he guns it. "Memories and shit?" I grab the handle above the passenger window, and he snickers. "You know what that's called, Tales?"

"What?"

"The handle. It's the *oh-shit* handle."

"You drive like a maniac." I grab the one on the dash while he weaves into traffic at a speed I am sure is higher than it should be.

"I drive how I bang, Tales. I get you from start to screaming orgasm in record time."

"That must be why they don't stick around." I am terrified of the way he drives. "Memphis Black, slow down!"

He laughs. "They don't want to leave, Tales; trust me. Never had a complaint, just requests for an encore."

He hits the gas, and I see the airport sign.

"Left lane, Memphis"

"Shit." He guns it again. "You keep fucking me up with all the sex talk, Tales, and we'll either be in the back of an ambulance or in the backseat."

"I'd like to get to the airport without either detour, thank you."

"Damn, sweet cheeks is cracking funnies," he says.

Once settled into the proper lane, he reaches up and turns on the radio.

"Love this song."

I look at the radio, seeing "I Followed Fires" by Matthew and the Atlas scrolling across the display.

He begins strumming on the steering wheel, and his head starts bobbing slightly. He gets that look of intensity on his face, exactly like when we were younger, and starts to sing along.

"*There's a devil at your door, and he grows, he grows. So I've been told he had a heart of gold …*"

He continues singing as I lean back in the seat and take in the smooth sound of his voice, watching his incredibly handsome face as he sings a story, his facial expression—heck, he puts everything into it. He feels every word, and watching him, you do the same. He is truly an artist, always has been.

The song ends and the next begins.

He laughs. "Want some chocolate, Tales?"

"What?" I ask, confused.

In the blink of an eye, he starts singing this crazy song about chocolate. He sings it to me, smiling and bobbing his head. He grabs my hand and holds it up like a microphone and starts singing into it. I can't help laughing, which he does, too, but doesn't miss a beat.

The dash reads "Chocolate" by The 1975.

The way he is looking at me is best described as sinful because it makes me think of his mouth and his perfectly shaped lips. His hair is a mess, his T-shirt fits him like a glove, and his shorts are white. I have no idea why I am checking him out in such detail, but I am. When I realize it, I look up, our eyes meet, and his lip curls up at the corner.

"I'd give my left nut to know what the hell you were just thinking." His voice is thick and raspy.

"I was thinking you're going to miss the turn," I say, pulling my hand away and grabbing those handles.

He crosses over two lanes to the sound of horns from angry drivers, and he is laughing.

"You're going to kill us!" I screech.

"Fuck that. They have breaks, and I had plenty of time, sweet cheeks."

"Have you always been such an awful driver?" I ask in anger as I hold my hand over my chest, thinking any moment my heart is going to beat out of it.

"I drive just fine. And would you look at the time. Damn near perfect."

He pulls up in front of Virgin Air and smiles as he grabs his phone. "Mads is at baggage claim now." He taps a reply on his screen, then tosses it on the dash before reaching in the back and grabbing something. He turns around and shows me the sign.

"*The Mad Queen's Ride*. You think she'll like it?"

"You know she will." I laugh.

"Yeah, I do. As much of a pain in the ass as she is, I've kind of missed her, Tales." He hits his hazard lights and opens his door. He quickly walks around the vehicle and opens my door.

"Come on. I think she'll be happier to see you than me."

I get out and start for the door, but he grabs my elbow.

"No way, Tales. You're gonna stand here with me and look like an idiot holding the other half of this sign."

"Shouldn't we go in?"

"Nah. I can't be that easy. She'll think I actually like her." He winks. "Gotta play hard to get, you know."

The way he looks at me makes me think he's talking about me. The way he's still staring at me makes me realize I'm right.

His thumb is running slowly back and forth on the side of my elbow.

"Memphis?"

"Tales?"

"You're holding my arm."

"Shit." He lets go. "Sorry, sweet cheeks."

I turn around when I hear his name behind me and see three girls whispering.

He grabs me with one arm around my waist and pulls me against his side.

"What are you—?"

"Are you Memphis Black from STD?" a blonde with a very short shirt and huge breasts asks.

"What gave it away?" he asks in a very flirtatious manner.

"The hair," a brunette swoons.

"The ink," the blonde purrs.

"The total package," the other girl with ambrosia hair says, blatantly staring at his crotch.

"Can we give you our number?" one asks.

"I am dying for an STD," the brunette who ends everything in a purr says.

"Gave her one two months ago," he says, pulling me tighter. "In about seven more months, she'll be giving birth to it, so I will have to pass this time, ladies."

I look up at him, ready to let him have it, but he pushes my head so my face is buried in his chest.

"Well," one huffs as the others … congratulate us.

I try to pull away, but he holds the back of my head tighter.

"She's shy," he excuses.

I dig my nails into his chest, and he lets go, but only after a few more seconds.

"What the heck did you just do?"

"What the hell did you just do?" He lifts his shirt to see red marks where I dug into him. "Damn." He smirks. "You need to kiss it better."

"Memphis, you just told them I was—"

"So?" He shrugs.

"Well, not only is it a lie, but it's possible it will start a rumor, and my mother …" I cover my face. "Dear God, Memphis, my mother will stroke out. And you, you idiot, you just messed up the whole"—I wave my hand in the air, and somehow it ends up pointing at his, lower half—"rock star, man-whore thing."

"First, you can call your mother and tell her I did it to push three chicks away who wanted in my pants, and they were not my type, Tales."

"I thought everyone was your type," I huff.

"No, Tales, not everyone." He looks at me.

"Right. I get it. Fine. But you just screwed that up. Every kinky-haired, thrift store queen is gonna think they have a shot with Memphis Black and—"

"She's coming. Do you think you could chill the fuck out for a minute?" He laughs.

"No. No, I don't," I say honestly.

"Tally, Memphis! Eek, hugs!" Madison runs up and hugs us both. "Tales, you're too damn skinny. What the hell happened to the freshman fifteen?"

I feel tears filling my eyes. I have missed her so much. She is and always has been what balances me.

I sniff back the tears, and she pulls back and looks at me.

"Don't you do that, okay? We cried too damn much last time I saw you."

I feel my lips tremble and I hug her more

tightly.

"Aw, Tales."

"Just missed you," I whisper.

"I missed you, too."

I pull back and plaster a smile on my face, and she wipes the tears off my cheeks as two women approach Memphis.

"Aren't you the lead singer from—?"

"Not right now," he says in a gruff voice, and I look up at him. His eyes are locked on me. "Come on, Mads. Let's get sweet cheeks something to eat. I think she's probably hungry."

"But you're Memphis Black, right?" the girls ask as he opens the door to the Escalade.

"Right now, he's a brother and a friend," Madison says as she hops in the back seat and pulls me in behind her.

"And apparently, Queenie's driver." He shuts the door and grabs her bag.

"Talk to me," Madison says as she buckles up, then grabs my hand.

"Just, just …" I don't even want to have this conversation.

"Just what, Tally? You can tell me anything, you know that." Her eyes are like his; brilliant blue and inviting.

The door opens and Memphis gets in, turns around, and holds up the sign. "Did you even notice this?"

"Nice." Madison flashes him a smile, then turns back to me. "Spill it."

I expect Memphis to start up the vehicle, but he doesn't. When I look up, his eyes are slightly crinkled, and he looks to be trying to figure something out.

"Tales got shit-faced last night."

"You did not!" Madison gasps.

"Fireball. By the fucking glass. One after another." Memphis winks at me.

"You're shitting me," Madison says, and I smirk.

"I wouldn't shit you, Mads. You're my favorite turd."

"Shut up and tell me everything." Madison grins and looks at me.

I shake my head. "Wasn't really my best day."

"Fucking whiskey? You chose to get drunk the first time on whiskey, Tales?" She laughs. "How do you feel?"

"Surprisingly, not as bad as I should," I answer.

"That's because she fucking ralphed all over me." Memphis smirks at me through the rearview mirror.

"No way," she gasps.

"Yes way. And more than once."

"How did that happen?"

"She turned green, and I snatched her up before she tossed it all over in front of the band and some friends. She'd have never lived that shit down."

"Did you feel better after? I always do," Madison says.

"She got hosed down in the bath tub and passed out." Memphis snickers as he pulls out onto the road.

"No way. Who …?" She pauses. "Did you

hose her down?"

"Hell yes, I did, right after I hosed myself down. She smelled awful."

"Aw, my brother can be a gentleman."

"A perfect gentleman."

I sit back and listen to the two of them talk back and forth. I have always loved watching how they interact. They may have driven each other crazy growing up, but they love each other immensely.

Then I realize how differently he is driving.

I shake my head and look up. He is staring at me in the rearview. He looks forward and grabs his sunglasses off the dash and puts them on as he cautiously drives us back to the house.

Once Mads and Tally are in the house and settled in their room, I call and order brunch. I'm starving. Everyone is still asleep, but I know, once they smell steak and eggs, they'll come running like the dogs they are.

While I wait for the food, I decide to take a shower since I didn't get to it this morning; my bed was too damn comfortable. Mmm-mmm.

What the hell am I going to do about this little obsession with POW!? I need to tap that ass, but she's—well, she's fucking Tales.

I kick off my slides, pull my tee shirt over my head, and shed my shorts.

I look down and shake my head, looking at my cock. "You need to take a fucking break right now, anyway. Tour time, you'll be well fed and exercised. You won't be frowning forever."

Freshly showered and feeling like a million bucks, I hop out and towel off before dressing.

When I walk into the kitchen, the food is spread out on the island, and no one is eating. I grab a piece of bacon and shove it in my mouth before grabbing a croissant and heading down the hall to tell Ta … Mads that it's time to eat.

The door is cracked, and I hear Mads chewing off Tally's ear.

"No fucking way," she gasps, and I can picture Tally's face turning pink. "The senior? Tall, dark, and smoking hot?"

"Handsome, talented, and kind," Tales corrects her.

"Throw a ball cap and some ink on his arms, and he'd be hot as hell, just sayin'," Mads says.

"He isn't that kind of—"

"Fine. I get it. So tell me; how was it?" Mads interrupts.

I'm leaning in closer to hear because I want to know, too.

"It was sex, Madison," she whispers.

"Like hot, sweaty, all night long, ass smacking—"

"Dear God, Madison! No, of course not. Gross."

"No, not gross at all."

I'm ready to bust in and demand a name, an address, and all that shit from Madison.

"I don't want to hear about you and what's-his-name."

"Well, sometimes it's what's-his-name and sometimes it's what's-*his*-name." Madison laughs.

I grip the door jamb and hold myself back from kicking the door open and demanding to know all that information when I feel a tap on my shoulder and jump back.

Finn is standing there with his arms crossed over his chest and a shit-ass grin on his face, shaking his head.

"What?" I whisper in a hiss.

"Don't do it, man."

"Do what?"

"Go in there, ready to be the white knight for little sis when you wanna go dark knight all over her friend."

I glare at him, and he shakes his head, steps around me, and raps on the door.

"Chow time."

I storm down the hall, and he follows. Annoyed, I look over my shoulder at Finn chuckling.

"Laugh it up, asshole," I snap, which makes him laugh louder. "Why don't you…?"

"Don't I, what?" He laughs.

"Go shave your fucking beard or something," I snap as I grab a plate.

"Fuck that. Ladies love it." He smirks as he strokes it.

"Especially those whose beaver curtains are bare," River comes in and says with a wink.

"How the fuck do you know?" I snap at him.

He sticks his tongue out slowly, then pulls it back in. "Most rode tongue in the state."

"If you read the Internet gossip pages, that would be my brother. Lead singer with the tongue made for her pl—"

"You clearly mean the drummer," River says with a perma-grin on his face.

River's high. I know it, Finn knows it, and Billy … Yeah, he doesn't know it. I laugh to myself.

I've dabbled in some heavier stuff. When we

first started playing together, River and I got fucked up a couple times, but a couple times of doing a line or two wasn't enough for him. No, fucker would go on a binge, and then he'd crash. As a result, I only take a couple hits of chillz once in a while when I am feeling froggy, like yesterday. I didn't want to put that temptation in his face again.

Finn doesn't touch shit. He smokes cigs, drinks like a fish when he's in a mood, but he hates drugs. I knew there was a story behind it the day I had to pull him off River. He spilled it about someone OD'ing and told River he was a selfish fuck. When I asked him later if he wanted to talk, he simply said no.

Billy walks in. "Good morning."

We all say it back, and as we load our plates, I see him and Tally exchange a look that pisses me the fuck off. Mads notices the exchange, too, and she elbows Tally and giggles. Tally looks at her with a clueless confusion, and I can't help smirking. Tally sees me, shrugs, and continues placing bird-sized portions on her plate. She is clearly uncomfortable, and it pisses me off.

"Tales, you have got to eat more than that, girl."

Billy smiles at her. "She ate well last night."

She ate well last night, I mock him in my head.

"Then she threw up. Eat, Tales."

"Memphis." Madison looks at me like I'm crazy. "She's a grown woman. I think she can handle herself."

"Yeah, you're both all sorts of grown up now, aren't you?" I sneer, then walk to the door with a full plate. I decide to eat outside because I already want to kick Billy's ass, lock up Mads, and tie up Tally and show her a thing or twenty about sex.

I sit at the outdoor high top where the sun is already blazing. There is a breeze that feels really good, but even as beautiful as this place is, nothing is distracting enough to un-hear your kid sister talking about banging his or *his*.

"What's your problem?"

I look up to see Mads walking out and shutting the door behind her.

"How's school?" I can't help the irritation in my voice.

"Great."

"Learning a lot?"

"Why the inquisition?"

"Why avoiding the question, Mads?"

"Okay, I love it. I get up and finish my classes by one in the afternoon. Most of the time, I am done with my homework by four or five, and then I hang out with friends."

"What kind of friends?"

Tally walks out now, sets her plate on the table, and pulls her shades down.

Mads and I stare at each other. She's clearly pissed, and so am I. Neither of us says a word.

"Should I go?" Tally thumbs behind her toward the door.

Mads says no, I say yes, and Tales sits, looking down.

"Don't be a dick, Memphis," Madison snaps at me.

"Or what? You'll tell Mom?" I snap back

In true Madison form, she dramatically shoves her chair back and storms back into the house.

"Why are you fighting with her?" Tally asks in an even tone that kind of infuriates me.

"I heard you two. She's banging all sorts of boys at school and …" I stop when Tally starts to smirk. "I said bang, not fuck, Tales. Jesus, keep it together."

"It wasn't the word, Memphis." She scowls. "I'm kind of used to them by now. It was the fact that you're judging her, yet live the life you do."

"Me, judging?" I gasp. "This coming from the preacher's daughter."

Her mouth forms a straight line.

"I didn't mean it to hurt you, Tales."

"Well, just so you know, I don't judge. There is a huge difference between being religious and being a Christian." She's pissed, but so am I.

"So what would Jesus say about you fornicating in the dorms, Tales?"

She pushes back and stands. "That's none of your business. Who are you to judge me or her?"

"Wait just a damn minute. I'm not judging—"

"It's okay for you to sleep with everything with two legs and boobs?" She blushes immediately.

"You just wait a minute, Tales. I'm a little bit pickier than two legs and tits—"

"I find that questionable when you've been trying to get me in bed."

"Tales, I don't try. I do. Don't kid yourself. If I wanted to fuck you, I would. Then your little dorm indiscretion that, I assume, left a bad taste in your mouth would be like fucking crack, and you'd be all but dry humping my—"

Without warning, she slaps me across the face, and hard, too. Then she runs into the house.

Angry is not a strong enough word to describe what the hell I'm feeling right now. I storm toward the house and see the guys looking out the window. They saw everything.

Embarrassed? I probably should be, but I'm not.

"What the fuck are you doing?" Finn asks, and he's not laughing, either.

I don't answer. I go to my room and grab a duffel bag.

"I asked you a fucking question, man. Don't disrespect." Finn's voice is low and angry.

"Tell them motherfuckers, if they touch Mads or Tally, I will quit this fucking band." I throw a change of clothes in my bag and walk past him.

His voice booms behind me. "Where are you going?"

"To the fucking woodshed," is all I say.

He steps back and gives me a nod. "Any idea when you'll be back?"

"Two days, tops," I answer.

"Work it out, bro. I've got this covered."

***

I crawl out of the bed and look down at the chick from the hotel bar. She's hot, blonde, tall, has big titties, and a nice ass. I worked it out, all right, for three hours, and she took it like a champ. I will definitely be giving her a VIP pass if we tour down here.

I look at my phone lying on the floor next to my shorts. It has fifteen missed calls and ten text messages, all from Madison.

I shoot her one back.

Mads, I will see you in a day or two. Stay put and enjoy.

Her reply is immediate.

Where is the woodshed?

I laugh to myself and shake my head as I type.

Ask Finn. See you soon. Airplane mode commencing.

I sit, and I write.

I look down at the paper, pretty content with myself. I haven't worked something like this out in a year. Finn is the man behind the lyrics lately when it used to be my thing. Today, it all comes back.

I feel hands resting on my shoulders.

"How did you do?" she asks in the raspy tone I have admired for a few years now.

"Inspiration at its finest."

"I see that."

I look up and see she is looking at my notepad.

"No way, babe. This is mine." I flip it over.

"And every time I hear it on the radio, I'll think about what happened next."

"Oh, yeah, not before?" I ask, pushing back in the wheeled chair and turning it so I am eye level to her jugs.

"I've seen you live in concert, Memphis. I know how well you perform, but your encore … Nothing beats that."

"You ready to be rocked my way?"

"Rock me any way you want."

And I did.

She didn't stay over. I didn't ask.

***

I spend the entire next day writing in the hotel room.

Two songs in two days.

X-man asked for five. I knew Finn had two, so that meant only one more.

When I walk into the house, Madison glares at me.

"That's a nice welcome back," I say with an eye roll.

"Tally is leaving," she yells.

"When?" I ask, trying to ignore the anger boiling inside of me.

"In a couple hours, and she told me everything."

"Madison, don't."

I look up to see Tally walking toward us.

"Memphis, did you ever find my phone?"

"Shit, Tales." I run my hand through my hair. "Give me a second. I'll—"

I stop when she nods and then head to my room, seeing the laundry basket of clean clothes sitting on my bed. I only brought one change of clothes when I left, and I need a change, so I pull my shirt off, then grab a white tank out of the basket of folded clothes and throw it on.

I dig through the clothes and find her phone. "Fuck."

"You found it?" I hear her behind me and spin around.

"Yeah." I feel anxious. "Look, Tales, we'll get you a new one if this one is shit now. And please don't leave. Mads will be … well, mad, and I feel like shit about—" I stop when I see her eyes widen, and her mouth make a little O. "Who is your phone provider? I'll call right after I call and have your flight changed back. You can't leave, Tales. Come on."

"I can't stay," she says in a more hostile tone than I expected.

"Please, Tales. I'm sorry, okay?"

"You don't get to say sorry, Memphis. I slapped you. I got drunk. I let you"—the way she says you is like a kick to the nuts, the disdain nearly taking my breath away—"make me sleep in that bed." She points at said bed and then stops.

I see tears pool in her eyes, and the pain in my chest is worse than the one that felt like a kick.

"I need to leave."

"No. No, you don't. I won't say a word. I won't do a damn thing. I want you two to have fun." I go to reach out to grab her hands, and she jumps back. "Tales, come on; it's me. I promise. My word is good, okay?"

She turns to walk away.

"Tales, tell me you'll stay."

"Tell me you'll leave me the hell alone," she retorts as she walks out.

"Thank you," I call behind her.

When the door shuts, I about bust up laughing. She said hell.

I walk in the bathroom and grab my toothbrush, the one Tales used. I squirt some paste on it and look in the mirror.

"Da fuck!" I say as I see the fucking hickies and scratch marks all over my neck. "Son. Of. A. Bitch."

There is a knock on the door when Madison is in the shower. I hesitate, not wanting to see him. Fearing I will stare at the … *love marks* all over him.

I hate that I allowed myself to believe for only a short time that he was interested in me. I hate that I wasted a year daydreaming about that stupid night.

There is another knock, and then the door opens. “Tales?”

“Oh, sorry.” I stand up and straighten my shirt. He notices, and his lips curl up, but there is no smile in his eyes.

“What’s that guy’s name? The one with the crazy orange hair on your shirt, the one—”

“Beaker,” I answer.

“Right, meep meep?” He smirks, handing me a box.

“What is it?” I ask as I look down. “Oh, no. No way.”

“Yours was ruined,” he says, pushing the box with the Apple logo on it back toward me.

“This is way too much.”

"Renter's insurance," he answers quickly.

"Oh, come on, Memphis. An hour after my phone shows up damaged, the insurance company—"

He nods his head, and I shake mine.

"Fine, but the claim's been filed, so I'll get the cash back. Just take the phone, Tales. You need it."

"Renter's insurance?"

"Yeah." His eyes shift, and I am almost certain he's full of bologna. "Same number, but they couldn't retrieve the contacts." He sighs. "Tales, just take the phone."

"I—"

"Please?"

"Fine, but how did you do it without my permission? I mean—"

"I can be pretty persuasive."

"Yeah." I nod, looking down at the box in my hand. "My old plan was grandfathered in, so I should call them and—"

"No need to call; it's the same plan." I give him a questioning look. "Okay, it's not, but you just give me, like, ten bucks a month and—" I try to hand it back to him. "Nope. It's yours."

Madison walks out of the bathroom, toweling her hair off. "Is he pissing you off?"

I shake my head. "He needs to take back the phone."

"Oh, wow," she says, looking at the box then at him. "Feeling like a douche? Don't forget you pretty much ruined my first couple days of this vacation, too. Making my best friend cry and—"

"Madison," I say quietly, closing my eyes and

wishing I was invisible.

"I'll take it in diamonds and—"

"Mads, I told her I was sorry. Now I'll say it to you, and then we move the fuck on, got it?"

"Fine," she huffs.

"I can't take this phone. It's too expensive, and I am sure ten dollars a month is not truly what it costs, anyway."

"It is. Mine's on his plan, so are our parents. He gets a discount because he is affiliated with Steel Inc., and it's an added line." She looks at Memphis. "But I don't think she owes dick a month."

"I don't care about the money," he huffs.

"Oh, that's right, Mr. Bigtime," Madison says in an exaggerated tone as she grabs her clothes and walks in the bathroom. "You're taking us out to dinner tonight."

She shuts the door, and I am left looking at the box in my hand and trying not to look at him.

"Where do you wanna go, Tales?"

"I really don't want to go out." I shake my head and look up at him.

"I'm really sorry. I crossed a few lines."

I nod, then shrug. "I have never hit anyone in my life." I swallow down the guilt and clear my throat.

"I deserved it," he says, searching my face.

I'm not sure if he's waiting for a smile, for tears, or for me to tell him he didn't deserve it. Therefore, I give him a true version of the latter.

"No one deserves to be hit."

His eyes scrunch together.

"What?" I ask, knowing he wants to say something.

He shakes his head. "Nothing, Tales. Thanks for the apology. Please accept mine."

With that, he looks at me for a few more excruciatingly silent moments and then walks to the door.

"Phone's charged. Mads can show you how to use it if you don't know how." And then he walks out the door.

I am left with an iPhone Six in my hands, the big one, too. It's huge, probably too big, definitely too expensive, and he won't take it back.

When Madison and I walk out, we can hear the guys on the patio. I go to the sink to grab a glass of water and see River in the pool, floating around with sticks in his hand. Finn is sitting on the edge of the chaise, strumming a bass guitar. Billy is seemingly playing the invisible keyboard on his lap, and Memphis is sitting opposite Finn, strumming an acoustic. I can hear him singing. His voice isn't the booming onstage rocker voice; it's softer.

"Might as well shit-can the idea of going out." Madison looks over my shoulder.

"Why?"

"He's been in a funk for a while now, and it looks to me like he's out of it." She smiles adoringly in his direction.

"A funk?"

"Finn's written almost all of the lyrics."

"Since when?"

"Since we went away that spring break, right

before going on tour with Burning Souls. He doesn't say anything to me, of course, but he told our father he thinks the road took something from him, and he's been looking for it ever since." She looks at me and rolls her eyes. "Mostly between chicks' legs, but …" She shrugs, as if to say whatever.

I grab a glass of water and drink it down.

"You wanna go listen?"

"Should we interrupt?" I ask, thinking it's a bad idea.

"Give him a few minutes." She starts opening drawers until she finds what she's looking for and then pulls out a pile of take-out menus. "Let's order dinner."

We order Mexican—it's always been Madison's favorite—quietly as we listen to Steel Total Destruction play in the background.

I have never seen them live. Even though I was invited plenty of times, I just couldn't. I didn't have the time or money. Now I have the time. I have lots and lots of time.

I know I will have to tell Madison soon. I have avoided it so far, just wanting to enjoy my time with her. So far, it's been a total disaster.

Madison is smiling. "Do you hear him, Tales?" I nod. "He's amazing."

"Not sure if it should be called "Bang, Bang" or "Loners Syndrome"," we hear Memphis say as he strums his guitar. "The chorus, you all join in at bang, bang. One, two, three. Two, two, three," he says then starts doing what Memphis does best.

Her dress is devil red and skin tight.

She's made up her mind; she has plans for the night.
Smoke filled room, the music plays.
Her eyes cut through the sweet smelling haze.
I sit. I wait. I drink a few.
I watch her dance, wait for her cue.
No lines, no promise, no future plan,
Just desire and a need of a woman for a man.
Room key in hand, I follow her.
One touch of hands, and she purrs.
That smell, that taste, that wild plum.
Look in her eyes.
Come on, give me some.

Bang, bang. My heart beats like a drum.
Bang, bang. No choice but to succumb.
Bang, bang. Not sent from above.
Bang, bang. Fits like a glove
Bang, bang. I'm driving it home.
Bang, bang. A loner's syndrome
Bang, bang. I'm a loaded gun.
Bang, bang. Two seconds to run.
Bang, bang. No room for love.
Bang, bang. Not sent from above.

"Yeah, he sure is." I force a smile then excuse myself to go to the bathroom.

Once the door is shut behind me, I close my eyes and wrap my arms around myself, feeling sick to my stomach. The marks he wore, the words he sung, it all makes me sick. What made me even more ill is the fact that I know deep down I still want him. I would be lying to myself if I said otherwise.

I walk out as Madison is juggling bags in her arms.

"Let me help." I go over and grab two as she kicks the door shut behind her.

"Nice save. You know you are always there when I need you."

We set up the food on the table as they change chords and timing then sing the song again. It will no doubt be a hit, but I think that will be one song by STD that I will not be buying.

"What did you think?" I hear Memphis ask as he sets his guitar down and looks in our direction. His eyes train on me, and then he looks to Madison.

"Effing love it, of course," she says, beaming.

"Thanks," he says and doesn't look at me. "Wrote two others, too."

"And you're holding out?" Madison pushes him in jest.

"One, I'll let you hear after dinner. The other—well, I'm still working on it."

I look at him out of the corner of my eye and see he is looking at me out of the corner of his eye with his head down.

"What did you think?" he asks.

I give him a forced smile and nod. I say nothing, because if I do, I will say the wrong thing.

After dinner, I help clean up. Mads hands me a glass of wine, and I drink it down. I see the guys all heading back outside, but I don't think I can take another "tell all" by Memphis Black right now.

I need a break from the intensity that comes with him. The feelings he evokes are like a storm, a disease, an STD, I think, shaking my head and trying to rid the picture I have in it.

"Spill it," Mads says as she pours me another drink.

"No, it's nothing." I laugh uncomfortably, and without thinking, I drink down the glass of wine she just poured.

It's bitter and doesn't really feel all that great on my belly, but it makes me kind of numb. I like it.

"Shit." Madison laughs. "Thirsty much?"

"Yeah. Another please."

She pours the glass of dry white.

Note to self: if I ever decide to become a lush, dry white is not something I will ever purchase.

Purchase. I laugh at the thought. An indulgence. I can't afford just getting by; how the hell would I even consider something I might indulge upon?

I look up to find Madison laughing.

"Damn, girl." She fills the glass again, and I suddenly feel hot. I also feel like I just don't care anymore. I like that feeling.

"Come on, I have the bottle," she teases as she holds it in front of me like I'm a dog being lured by a treat. "Let's go listen to the boys."

Everyone is sitting around the outdoor fireplace. River is tapping his sticks on the tiled table, Memphis and Finn have their guitars, and Billy is doing something with his laptop.

I sit next to Billy, who smiles, and I lean in to see what he's doing, feeling the weight of someone's very blue eyes, but I ignore it.

Madison is on the other side of Billy, doing the

same.

Three glasses of wine later, I'm hot and tired. They have played two songs, both ones Finn has been working on, and I am glad not to hear "Bang, Bang" again.

They end the song, and I expect them to discuss it like they did the last, but Memphis speaks.

"You do remember you're still underage, right, Madison?"

"Are you serious right now?" she snorts.

"Just don't want you getting all fucked up and throwing up all over the place."

I look up and see him blatantly staring at me.

"I think he just doesn't want to see the two of you going inside with Billy boy and banging the fuck out of him," River begins, and Memphis draws back his fist.

"I will knock your goddamned teeth—"

"Oh, please." Finn rolls his eyes. "If it wasn't your sister or the girl who—"

"Watch it, man," he warns.

"—grew up next door, you'd be the first inside with the both of them."

"Respect, man. Show some." Memphis stands up, sets his guitar down, and then storms into the house.

I look around to see everyone is laughing. It's funny if you know it isn't you who caused his grim mood.

I finish my drink and stand. "I'm gonna go to bed."

"I'm not ready yet," Madison says as she fills her glass and takes a sip. "But I'll come with if you want me to."

"To do what? Watch me sleep?" I smile. "Stay, have fun."

"You feeling okay?" Billy asks as I take a step and nearly trip. "Apparently not. I'll walk you in."

"Not necessary," I say, but he is immediately next to me, holding my elbow.

"It's not a problem. I need to use the bathroom, anyway."

We walk in, and I quickly scan the area. No Memphis.

"Thanks, Billy, but I'm okay."

"Have a glass of water and a Motrin," he says as he grabs the bottle off the counter, then a glass from the cupboard. "You'll feel better in the morning."

"Thanks."

He walks out of the room as I swallow down the Motrin with the water. I clean the glass and then head to bed.

When I round the corner, Memphis is standing against the wall with his arms crossed over his chest. His eyes are angry as he stares directly at me.

"You scared me," I whisper.

"Not my intention," he says, looking up at the ceiling. "Look, Tales, I don't know if I'm losing my fucking mind or if this shit I feel when I'm around you is—"

"Memphis, I am clearly making this vacation miserable for you. I—"

"I have been a fucking wreck for a year. Over a year. I finally figured out why."

I shake my head and swallow hard, waiting for

him to tell me how I jinxed him, how I messed up his music mojo.

"I'm sorry," is all that comes out.

"Don't be sorry. Help me fix it."

"By letting you do all those things you say you want to do, Memphis? The things that I'm not sure if you're joking about or if it's just you and your … testosterone levels amped up like a damn electric guitar?"

He sucks in his lips and tries not to laugh.

"It's not funny, Memphis."

He is suddenly serious. "I wanna do all sorts of shit to you."

"Well, you wrote two songs, or was it three? So, I think you are all straight now, you and your"—I point to his upper body—"torn up torso."

"Wasn't the ass I had, Tales. It was the ass I've wanted since that night."

"You're—"

"Honest? Would you like me not to be? I could lie; would that be better?" His voice raises, and I am suddenly fearful that Madison will hear us.

"Shh," I tell him, and his eyes narrow.

"No, sweet cheeks. You and I are gonna work this out. I couldn't give a fuck less who hears me."

"She doesn't know about that night. It wasn't even a big deal, Memphis."

"That's not what you said while your ass was pressed up against me in my bed the other night."

"I was drunk."

"Then get drunk again. Press in harder this time."

"You are something else."

My heart is racing. His lips never looked so good, and I am sure the air conditioner is on way too low because my nipples are straining against my padded, push-up bra.

"I am something you want, and you are something I want."

"Well, it'll never happen." I attempt to step around him, but my wobbly knees betray me, and I stumble.

He grabs me and pushes me against the wall. "Tell me what your doubts are."

"Why?"

"So I can blow them out of the water." His hands are on my waist, and his face is inches from mine as his chiseled chest rises and falls quickly underneath his shirt. "Boyfriend?" I shake my head. "So he humped you and dumped you? Fucking idiot. Does he know he's an idiot?"

I don't respond. I don't want him to know he's right. Then he'll figure out that I am not worth even one night.

"Madison," I say.

"She doesn't find out until we both figure out if this is physical or more."

Dear God, he said or more.

I close my eyes and try to slow my breathing, but it's not happening. I feel his thumb on my chin as he pushes my head to the side. He inhales a slow, deep breath, running his nose from my collarbone up to the spot right behind my ear, and I moan. I flippin' moan, and he does, too, at the same time.

"You're promiscuous."

"Ask me not to be." He moves my head back

and pushes my chin up with his thumb. His tongue lightly slides down my throat and stops at the base. Again, I moan, and again, he does, too.

"Your tour."

"Your school."

"I'm not ready for a relationship," I pant out as his lips run across my jawline.

"Give me this week."

"To be your groupie?" I shake my head.

"To be mine." He sucks on my earlobe. "All mine."

"Madison," I remind him.

"After hours."

"Fine," I concede.

"You are not going to regret it." He steps back and cups my jaw.

"I already do."

"Why?"

"I'm not a whore."

"I promise, Tales, whatever the swimsuit or underoos cover is off limits."

I can't help smiling as I open my eyes. He looks happy, and I feel giddy.

He pushes his forehead against mine and runs his nose back and forth across mine. "You tell me if it gets to be too much."

"This is a bad idca."

"I won't hurt you. I've never made a girl cry yet." He smirks that sinful grin. "Okay, maybe a few, but they survived."

"Why?"

"Contrary to what you believe, I think it was you who gave me my inspiration back."

"Your floozies did."

He shakes his head. "Nah."

"I won't sleep with someone who sleeps with everyone under the spotlight."

"I'm really not like that, Tales." I can't help huffing. "No, you started this. I've been like that little, blonde girl, the one with the bears, eating all that porridge, sleeping in all those beds until I found the one I was looking for."

I look away from his mesmerizing eyes. "Goldilocks."

"Low and behold, she was right under my nose. I can't wait to kiss those lips and see if they're the ones I have been trying to find. You know, like the glass shoe that the prince makes everyone try on 'cause the girl he—"

I spare him the rambling, albeit adorable. "Cinderella."

"Yeah, Cinderella."

His lips are centimeters from mine, and I am ready for him to kiss me. I want to know if it's true. At the very least, I want him to kiss me just once without throwing up on my shoes.

He moves closer, and I close my eyes and lift my chin, giving myself to him. He kisses … my cheek.

Stunned, I open my eyes.

"Sober. Come to me sober so I know I'm not pushing you into something."

"But you said—"

"Tales, I wanna kiss you so fucking badly right now." He leans against me with his whole body. "My tongue isn't the only thing that wants in." He nudges me with his erection, and I gasp. "But sober, sweet cheeks. I won't do you like that."

Then he walks away, leaving me buzzed, turned on, and wanting more than ever to give everything I have to Memphis Black.

I don't go back outside, although it's not like I can when I am as hard as nails and feeling guilty as fuck. Tallia Annabel Priest, the sweetest girl on the entire planet, and my dick can't keep my mind occupied enough to leave her alone.

I flop down in bed and stare at the ceiling, willing this hard-on away. I know what will do the trick—think about her father and the day he caught me staring at his little girl when I was in church.

"Do you know what happens to sinners, young man?" he asked me.

"Not really, sir," I answered honestly.

"They burn in hell." He scowled at me, and what did I do? I fucking chuckled. Hell, he was my minister. The one who preached God's love was now pegging me at ten years old as a sinner. He didn't think that shit was funny, but here's the shit kicker: I wasn't thinking of banging his daughter until he went on with, "If you have sexual desires for her, you best get down on your knees and pray, young man."

Sexual fucking desires at ten? Hell, I was too busy trying to figure out what the hell that thing was there for and hating it because the shit hurt when it got all hard. I figured out really quickly after that man's warning what a sexual desire was, and from that moment on, I spent a lot of time in the damn shower. I mean, why the fuck would he even say that shit?

I spent the next eight years tormenting her because I wasn't hot for her. She was the opposite of hot—well, maybe not the opposite, but she was … angelic? Sweet, kind, innocent—all the things you want to protect from the little asshole tormentors who picked on her, and she just smiled in their faces.

Well, that day I flipped a switch, and I sure as hell didn't want to be a sinner, much less want everyone to think I had sexual desires for Tallia Annabelle Priest, the awkward preacher's kid, so then I became a pain in hers and Madison's asses.

Forgive me, papa Priest. Now I have some hellacious sexual desires, and there isn't a damn thing you can do about it. Hell, I can't do shit about it now.

I look down, erection gone. Minister Priest is the opposite of Viagra, and I will use that shit to my advantage.

* * *

I wake up and open my eyes. Tally is standing at the foot of my bed, staring at me. She isn't saying shit, only staring.

I look over at my phone, and it says three in the morning.

"Tales?" I sit up, and she mumbles some

incoherent shit then sighs, yawns, and sits down.

"You still fucked up?"

She shakes her head.

"You wanna play around?" I ask, grabbing her hips and pulling her closer to me as I sit up.

"Sleep."

"Couldn't sleep?" I have no clue what she is doing, but when she is dead weight, I know she's asleep. "Tales?"

Nothing.

Da fuck? I think.

I lay her down, go take a piss, wash my hands, brush my teeth—just in case she wants a little something-something—and then lie down and pull her closer.

She mumbles something more, then falls into what must be a comfortable place, and I hear soft, little purrs.

I push my nose against her hair, trying my damnedest to figure out what it is that makes her smell so damn good while she sleeps peacefully in my arms.

I wake when her body jolts as if lightning struck her.

"What? What is going on?"

She's like a deer in the headlights, and she scared the shit out of me. Hell if I know what's going on, I just want her back in bed. "It's five in the morning, girl. Climb back in here and—"

"Oh, wow." She looks around.

"Wow, what?" I pat the bed, beckoning her back.

She shakes her head and sighs.

"Care to tell me what you're thinking?"

"Sometimes I take walks at night." She crosses her arms. "Sorry."

"You mean sleep walk?" I smirk because of the way she says it.

"No walks." She yawns.

"Right, well, 'toh-may-toh,' 'toh-mah-toh.' Come on. I was comfortable."

"I can't."

"Tell me you weren't too fucked up to remember our talk last night."

She looks down and slowly shakes her head.

"Good. Now that you're sober, climb back in here." She hesitates. "Tales ..."

She looks up at me. "It's a bad idea."

"It's a damn good idea."

"I don't know." She sighs.

"Then come back when you straighten it all out in your head." When she hesitates again, I pull the covers back and pat the bed one more time. "Just let me spoon you."

She sighs again, then takes the first step back. She sits on the edge of the bed, and I am quick to pull her down and into my arms.

"I'll spork you later."

She gives a silent chuckle. "This is a bad idea."

"Does it feel bad right now, Tales?" I ask, rubbing her back over her shirt and not her fine, fine ass like I want to.

"No."

"Why do you sound so sad, then?" I question, as I inhale the scent that calms and ignites me at the same time.

"I don't want to hurt Madison."

"Me, either."

"She will be up at, like, nine."

"Just stay another hour, maybe two?"

"Will you make sure I'm awake?"

"Sure will."

She yawns, and even her breath smells sweet.

What the fuck am I doing?

Minister Priest, I repeat over and over in my head until I fall asleep.

***

"What the hell?" I hear Madison's voice, and both Tally and I are instantly all sorts of tangled and trying to jump up. It's a mess, a complete fucking mess, and there is nothing I can do except laugh.

"Morning, Mads."

"I … I …"

"Did you?" Madison shrieks, charging at me.

"No," Tally gasps in a disgusted tone that quite frankly pisses me off, but it stops my crazy-ass sister.

"Madison, get out!" I snap at her and immediately regret it. However, I'm a little pissed.

"Don't talk to her like that," Tally scolds, and here I am, the innocent in this.

"She walked in here and decided to take a fucking nap," I defend. "I didn't drag her by her hair, so you can—"

"Oh, my God, are you sleep walking again?" Madison gasps.

Tally shrugs. "I guess so."

"Why?"

I think it's an odd question, but I know damn well I want the equally as odd answer.

"I don't know."

"You're having bad dreams again?"

Tally shakes her head, glances at me, and then quickly looks away.

"You only do this when you do."

"Everything's fine."

"Not really." I stand up and look at both of them. "What the hell would have happened if you had walked out in the street or, worse yet, into River's room?"

"River's room is worse than the street?" Madison laughs sarcastically.

"Depends on how fucked up he was, yeah."

"Well, she's managed to stay alive all these years and—"

"What if it happens at school? What if she ends up in some guy's room, and he—" I stop when I see the look exchanged between the two of them. Fuck it has already happened! "Spill it."

"It's really none of your concern, brother dear."

"Da fuck it's not." I am livid. "Did you get—?"

"No, Memphis, no. Okay, geesh, sorry I wandered in," Tally says like it's no big deal.

"Why didn't you wake her up?" Madison asks, her brows shooting up and her hands on her hips.

"'Cause I like the way—"

"Madison," Tally interrupts, "I'm not easy to wake up. Think about it."

"Fine." Madison seems to give up. "But next time, you come get me."

"Why? Do you think you—?"

Madison narrows her eyes. "I'll cut you."

"You'll fucking what?" I gasp.

"She's joking."

"Maybe I'm not."

"I'm your fucking brother. Shit, Mads, what would be the big deal if I was into Tally?"

She covers her ears and starts "la-la-la-ing" like she did when she was a kid.

Tally gives me a look as if to say, *please don't,* and I want to kick my sister right in the ass, just once. The little queen deserves it.

"Conference call. X-man is on," Finn yells into my room.

"What?" I ask

"Billy sent him the songs."

"What? When? I'm not even done."

"Come on, man. He looks happy as hell."

I walk past Madison and Tally, scooping up my shorts. They stop whispering, and Mads rolls her eyes and walks out. Her being pissed at me is nothing new.

"Probably got dome this morning," River says, rubbing his hands over his messy ass hair as he walks out of his suite.

I want to laugh, but Tally is looking at me all nervously and shit.

I stop and step into my shorts, waiting for everyone to get out of earshot. I look up to see she is staring at my chest, so I pop my pecs, but she doesn't look impressed when her eyes meet mine.

"I can't do this," she whispers.

"She won't find out," I whisper back.

"It's not her; it's—" She stops, and her eyes are on my chest again. I recognize the look immediately.

"They'll be gone in a couple days."

"Just like the many you've shared a bed with."

"Tales, stop coming up with excuses. You want me or you don't." I'm getting really sick of this conversation. "You want me." I walk past her, unwilling to hear whatever comes out next. Her excuses are bullshit, and my patience is wearing thin, but there is fuck-not that I can do about it now.

I stop and turn back. Apparently, walking away is a problem for me, too.

"Sleep walking. What's got you worried?"

She huffs and rolls her eyes. "Everything."

"Okay, let me help you figure out whatever it is that's not about me. Talk to me, Tales."

She looks confused, maybe even sad, and then the emotions are gone. "You have a call. I'm fine. Go."

"Tales—"

"Really, Memphis, go."

I reluctantly walk out into the living room where X-man is on the smart TV. Technology, I have a love/hate relationship with it.

"Good, you're all here." X-man starts. "Finn, Memphis, I am proud as hell of you two. The lyrics are edgy but commercial enough—"

"Commercial?" I scowl as I sit on the arm of the couch.

"But edgy," he responds. "It's good. That

being said, we need to lay down the tracks and get production rolling because …" He looks behind him.

Taelyn looks over his shoulder. "We have dates, lots of dates. Twenty cities in—"

"Twenty cities?" River grins at her.

"Starting right here, where you left off." X beams.

"The coolest part, man. Get to it," Nickie D urges in the background.

"Irish," X says, looking at his wife. "Your idea, so you tell the band."

She sits down on his lap and looks into the screen. "The opening acts."

"No, you've got it wrong, Mrs. X. STD is the coolest part." River winks.

"River, you keep that shit up and you'll be Def Leppard-ing that drum set. I'll rip your motherfucking arm off and beat—"

"Enough, Xavier." Taelyn laughs. "Xavier and I or Nickie will join you all at each city where we'll hold open auditions for local bands to try out to be opening acts."

"What's it pay?" Finn asks.

"Finn." I nudge him.

"What? I'm gonna do this shit for free? Hell no," he says, scowling at me.

"Anyone else have reservations?" Xavier asks, and I know he's trying to keep his cool.

"Will you explain the process a little?" I ask, hoping to chill Finn out a little.

"We're currently scouring the Internet to find talent that is untouched or—"

"To sign," Finn interrupts.

"Well, if we all like them, and they're committed like you four, then yes, of course that's what we would like to do," Xavier answers.

"So we become sink or swim. You just throw us on stage and walk the fuck—"

"What the fuck did you just say?" X-man is pissed. "Sink or swim, Finn? Really? Are we not in this together? Forever fucking Steel isn't just something to lure you in, asshole."

"All right, Xavier." Taelyn situates herself in front of her very pissed off husband. "Finn, think about who we are and not what you know of the industry."

"But?" Finn snaps.

"But nothing, Becket." Xavier shakes his head. "Are you here for us, too, or is this all about what we can do for you? Because look around. We've pushed our asses off because we believe in you four fuck-sticks."

"Hey, X, he's a fuck-stick; I am just—"

"Innocent?" X lets out a forced laugh. "STD?"

I can't help smiling. "Epic name."

"You guys have four days till you return. I was gonna make you come back early, but my wife reminded me I'm not a dictator, or some shit like that, and I agree. You've busted your asses for a year and deserve to have some fun. So think about this, Finn: we aren't trying to fuck you here. You should know that by now. Okay, STD, keep it wrapped and see you soon."

"Have fun," Taelyn says.

"Peace," Nickie D chimes in. "Out."

The screen goes blank, and I look at Finn. “Can’t you just trust them?”

“Trust?” he huffs as he stands up. “Wait until you get dicked over just once, and that shit will harden you, too, and not just your cock. Get fucked twice, and you’re stone.”

“You trust us, don’t you?” Billy asks.

“You don’t even want to be here half the time, so I don’t think you’re gonna fuck us unless you leave. River is, well, River, and I know he’s cool.” He looks at me. “You, you are true blue, but the past few days, you’ve been a little—how do I say this?—in your head.”

“You wanna give me what?” I laugh, standing up.

“In your wildest dreams,” he snaps.

“You wouldn’t?” I joke. “If I really needed it?”

“Not if we were the last people on Earth and armless so I couldn’t jerk off.” Finn gets up and walks back to his room.

“Going to shower,” River yawns. I know he’s not, though; he’s going back to bed.

Billy takes off, too.

I look around and see Tally standing in front of the stainless, walk-in, industrial-sized fridge.

I get up and walk over. “Where is the queen?”

“Shower,” she says, turning to look up at me, not showing a bit of awkwardness. “You need to be nice to her.”

“Ask me nicely.” I can’t help putting my hand on the base of her elegant, long neck and using my thumb to turn her chin to the side. “Your neck is pornographic.”

She sighs, and I see her emerald greens roll.

Mesmerizing.

"Fuck, Tales, you are a very, very sexy young woman."

She moves her head back, looks at me, and clears her throat. "You have a lot coming up, huh?"

"So do you, right, Tales?" I hold eye contact, not backing down. She is gonna give me another excuse; I know she is.

"Well, then I guess we should just get this out of the way so you can move on with your life." She grabs my face in both hands and pulls it toward her, but I pull back. She looks stunned and embarrassed, but she'll get over it.

"When I kiss you, it'll be from head to toe, in a very private setting, Tales. It won't be in the kitchen or hurried. It will be slow, hot, wet kisses that, regardless of where they are placed, will cause you to feel it just about…" I put my hand flat to her stomach and then push my fingers below her waistband. Her body quivers, and her eyes close as her mouth gapes. "Tonight, we're all going out to dinner, but I want you to sit next to me and pretend the same fucking thing I will be—that the dinner is a prelude to a kiss and to what is about to … come."

"Memphis." She stops my hand's slow descent.

I hear a door open, and Memphis slowly moves his hand away and winks at me. “Prepare yourself.” He steps away, leaving me in a state of disarray.

I watch as he lifts his hand to his nose and inhales deeply before licking his fingers, one by one, as he continues walking away.

Prepare myself? Prepare myself for what?

“You guys wanna play?” I hear Memphis from around the corner.

“This early?” River asks.

“I am pumped up, feeling inspired, ready to fuck shit up,” Memphis says in his sexy rasp.

Dear Lord, prepare myself.

I walk in the room to find Madison sitting on the bed, wrapped in a towel.

“Talk to me, Tales,” she says as she looks at me curiously.

“I just have a lot going on.”

She is sitting on a towel, knees open a bit wider than they should be, and I must look shocked because she laughs.

“Bikini area.”

"What?"

"Hair removal lotion. Two more minutes and then I get to rinse, Tales. Then you'll be less uncomfortable."

"I'm not uncomfortable," I say in the most uncomfortable sounding voice on the planet.

"Okay." She laughs. "Sleep walking again?"

"I guess."

"To Memphis's room?"

I nod.

"Thank God he knows I'd de-nut him if he ever touched you."

"I'm pretty sure you wouldn't do that; he's your brother," I say, before I even think about what I'm saying.

She looks at me oddly.

"Madison, I'm not as innocent as I used to be," I say as if it's no big deal.

"I know, but guys like Memphis—"

I should shut my mouth, but I can't. It's Mads, and even though I am not telling her what is … not going on, I can't shut my mouth.

"Memphis isn't all that bad, really. I mean, he has been decent to me. I threw up on him, sleep walked into his room, and well, he was nice."

I am knotting my shirt as she looks at me as if she knows. Dear Lord, she knows.

"Tales, I know my brother, and I know you." I expect more, but she remains silent.

"What's that supposed to mean?"

"You're going through a lot. Even though you won't talk about what is bothering you right now, you need to. I feel like you're projecting. You're going to make rash decisions. You're fixating." She swallows back emotions, and my heart cracks a little. "I am not judging, Tales. I've been there."

Madison never gets like this. She never gets emotional.

"I think you need to talk to me. Tell me where it is you've been."

She smiles and it's a sham; I know it is.

"I need to rinse this stuff off before I get a rash or something." With that, she leaves the room.

Warning from Madison or not, I have had feelings for Memphis Black for a long time. Be it annoyance, a crush, a fascination, or a fixation, I am going to explore them.

I look over at the bottle on the nightstand, then pick it up and read the information.

Prepare yourself? That I will.

When Madison comes out, she smiles. "Let's do something fun today, just you and me."

"Sounds perfect. I'm gonna shower first."

"Then come meet me outside?" she asks.

"Of course."

I walk into the bathroom with the lotion tucked under the bath towel.

***

"We can all go," Memphis says sternly to Madison, "then come back here, and we'll all go out to dinner."

"I'm sure the guys don't really want to go shopping and then to dinner with your sister, Memphis," she replies with an exaggerated eye roll.

He looks back at them, and despite the aviators they are all wearing, I can tell she is right.

"I'll go," Billy offers.

Memphis's head whips around, and in a gruff tone, he says, "Thanks." He looks at me, then at Madison. "See? It'll be fun."

"Pedicures and bikini waxes sound like fun?" she shoots at him.

"Watching might be," River chimes in.

"I'm driving. Let's roll."

We get in the Escalade, and Madison and I are in the back, Billy is sitting shotgun. Memphis is driving like a normal human being.

"Where do you wanna go?"

"Shopping, the pedicures, then—"

"Let's get the shopping out of the way, skip the pedicures, and do some swimming?"

She grins at him. "Miami Design District, and I'll think about it."

"You do know I'm not loaded yet, Mads." He smirks.

An hour later, Memphis comes around the corner, while I am looking at a Louis Vuitton bag.

"Are we having fun yet?" he asks.

"She is." I nod to Madison. "She is looking at the same bag she spotted when we came in. She keeps walking away, but then ends up right there." I look up at him and see he is smiling.

"What caught your eye?"

"What?"

"If you could have anything in here, what would it be?"

"Honestly, nothing," I answer.

He grips the bottom of my T-shirt, his lips curling up on the side. “That’s right; you’re more retro.”

“Right,” I say as his knuckles run across my skin, causing my nipples to harden immediately and my face to feel hot, because retro, I am not.

He looks down. “I love the look on you, Tales. There’s only one thing that would look better.”

“What?” comes out in a whisper.

“Me.”

“Tales, come over here,” Madison calls out.

“The queen has spoken,” he mumbles, and I giggle. “You better go.”

I walk over to where she and Billy are laughing. I’m so glad she’s happy, but I wish I knew what it was that was bringing her down.

The entire time shopping, Memphis would show up at the most random moments, always when Madison was talking with Billy, and he always had something sexy and … naughty—very, very naughty—to say to me.

We didn’t get pedicures or waxed, thank the Lord. I can’t imagine having pink eyebrows for the next couple days.

Back at the house, Madison holds up a beautiful white slip dress against her as she stands in front of the mirror. “We get to dress up.”

“What’s the place called?” I ask as I push Madison’s hanging clothes to the side and spot my black and white, long, floral, wrap skirt and a black tank top.

“LIV, I think. Memphis and Billy both said it was a cool, chic place.”

I look down at my attire, feeling a little uncomfortable.

"It's perfect, Tales." She smiles as she drops her bra and pulls the dress over her head.

After messing with my hair and realizing the Florida humidity is not my friend, I go with a loose twist.

"You done yet?" Mads asks, putting on one more swipe of mascara.

"I just need a couple minutes."

"Need my help?"

"No," comes out rather quickly. Madison likes makeup. I, however, do not.

She laughs.

"Go spend some time with your brother. I'm sure I can manage."

She smacks my butt. "You have the best ass in the world. So jelly."

I smile. "You have the best hair on the planet and a perfect body, so don't hate."

She turns to walk out of the bathroom. "Mascara would make those green eyes pop, just sayin'."

I look in the mirror, seeing the girl next door. I will once again pale in comparison to Madison's stunning beauty. I decide to swipe one coat of mascara on my lashes because she's right; a little pop wouldn't hurt when I am almost certain I am going to be hanging on to every naughty word Memphis Black rock star says in a club full of beautiful, well-dressed women.

When I walk out, Memphis stops mid-sentence and smirks. "Damn, Tales."

"Leave her alone." Madison swats his arm jokingly.

"Leave her alone? I'm going to have to watch out for you both tonight. No motherfucker within a five foot radius or he's going down."

His eyes are locked on me the entire time he says it. My gaze is taking in the black T-shirt that fits his muscular build like a glove. He is wearing dark denim jeans and those black boots. He looks hot. So, so hot.

"Let's roll. The car is waiting," Finn says, walking into sight.

His hair is long on top and cut close on the sides. Tonight, he has it pulled back and has trimmed his beard. He is wearing an unbuttoned, black button-down with a white tank, black jeans, and black boots.

River walks in, smirking. "Be right back." Then he walks toward his room.

"Chillz." Finn shakes his head.

"Hey, at least he remembered to put it away and didn't bring it with him this time," Billy says.

Billy is dressed in a white linen shirt, khaki shorts, and loafers. *No black boots*, I think to myself. He sticks out, but not like a sore thumb. He is beautiful yet much less the stereotypical rock star.

River walks out in a white tee, black pants, and yes, black boots.

After dinner, we stand in line to get into the club, and Memphis is behind me. I feel his breath on my bare neck when he whispers, "Neck porn. Fuck, that's hot."

I glance back at him, eye level to his chest. "I like that shirt."

"Looks better on the bedroom floor."

I can't help laughing.

He leans against the wall. "Do you know how badly I want those long, sexy legs wrapped around my waist, Tales?"

I roll my eyes.

He laughs and pulls a coin out of his pocket. "Heads, I get whatever I want from you tonight. Tails, I make you cry out my name."

I look around to see if anyone heard him. All three of the guys are surrounding Madison and listening to a story about Memphis when he was younger.

"Wing men." He winks.

"OMG, I think that's Zach Efron," I hear a whisper behind us.

"Here we go," he huffs.

"Is he here?" I whisper.

"Could be, but I am pretty sure they're talking about—"

One of them taps him on the shoulder. "Are you—?"

"Yes," he answers before she even asks a question.

"We loved you in *High School Musical*. Aren't you dating Vanessa H—?" Again, he cuts her off.

"Broke up with her because she wouldn't swallow."

They all gasp while I laugh.

"It's important," he says, defending himself or, rather, defending the real Zac Efron.

"Some girls just don't like to do that," the dark-haired one says.

"Understandable. I just won't waste my time with them. I need my girl to swallow. I mean, honestly, I can't imagine going through life—"

"You ready?" I interrupt him, nodding toward the door.

"She must swallow, then."

I whip my head around and look at the girl who just said that.

"She does, and she likes anal. Begs for it even."

"You are a pig." I try to be angry, but my nerves get the best of me, and I laugh.

"Can we get a picture?" one calls out from behind us.

Memphis doesn't respond, only looks up at the bouncer. "They're asking for pictures."

"Thank you, sir." He nods.

We walk in, and I look behind us, expecting them to follow, but they don't. They are denied access.

We walk up to the bar where Memphis orders a round of slippery nipples.

"Are they good?" I ask.

"I'll tell you later. Have I mentioned how hot you look tonight?"

"Come on, Tales; let's dance," Madison shouts over the noise.

It is then that I look around and see just how beautiful the club is. Not only is the club architecturally appealing and extravagantly designed, but it's a mix between an exclusive lounge and an ultra-modern nightclub, and the people are just as beautiful.

I look back as Madison drags me to the dance floor and expect to see Memphis looking at everyone, watching all the women dressed beautifully in couture, practically see-through clothing and expensive jewelry, but he's not. He's staring at me.

"This is DJ Drunken Monkey in the house! Let me hear you say 'Whoa-oh.' " He waits for the crowd to respond and they do. "Say 'Whoa-oh,' " he says again, and it continues until "Pretty Girls" by Iggy and Britney starts to play.

Mads and I start to dance and sing along. Mads sings Iggy's part, and I get Britney's.

The floor is packed as we dance, bodies rubbing up from behind us as the music takes control. It's the only time I feel free, no inhibitions, so I go with it.

"One Hot Mess" by Malea starts, and now it's not just bodies pressed tightly, there are hands on my hips and a little grinding. Mads has a guy behind her, too.

I look back, expecting to see Memphis, but I don't. It's a Ricky Martin look alike with amazing moves. I look at Mads and put my palms up and shrug,

With my hands in the air and Ricky's on my waist, I tip my head up and see the very angry eyes of Memphis Black from the second level, getting a bird's eye view of the dance floor.

"Mads!" I yell over the noise and point up. "Your brother is angry."

She looks up. "Where?"

I laugh. “He was right up there.”

“Fuck him, Tales. It’s me and you, dancing.” She hands me a blue drink she took off the cocktail waitress’ tray. “Bottoms up.”

We slam down the drinks. They don’t taste like alcohol; they taste like Kool-Aid.

I feel a tap on my shoulder and turn to see Memphis standing behind me.

He looks at the Ricky Martin look alike. “That’s mine.” He slams back his drink and shoves the glass into the guy’s hand. “Take that up for me.”

Whoa, what was that? I think to myself.

“You looking for a fight? ’Cause you’ve got one,” Ricky snaps.

Finn steps between them. “Walk, man, while you can.”

Memphis looks at me. “If we’re gonna be playing around for the next couple of days, it’s one on one, you feel me?”

“I was just dancing.” I blush and look to see if Mads is watching this. She’s not; she’s dancing with River and Billy.

“That wasn’t dancing, Tallia. That was fucking foreplay,” he says, stepping into my space as “Teacher” by Nick Jonas starts. He then takes my hands and puts them on his hips. “Your little hands go here, not on his, feel me?”

I nod as he places his hands over mine and drags them up under his shirt as his hips start swaying to the music.

As Nick’s voice booms “Oh my, oh my, oh my God” over the speakers, Memphis’s hips circle while he moves down slowly until he is hip level with my hands on his shoulders. I close my eyes and start swaying as his hands run up the back of my thighs and stop right below my butt. Then he lifts the hem of my tank top with his nose and runs it across my stomach before I feel his tongue against my skin.

My knees weaken, and I clutch his incredibly strong shoulders while he continues to lick, kiss, and graze his teeth across my now exposed flesh. He senses it and places a kiss on my hip as he slowly kisses up my side and then turns me so my back is against his body. He takes my hands in his and runs them up my body as he sings, "So let me teach ya," in my ear, sending chills all over my body.

My hands now rub up my front and over my chest, and he groans in my ear.

"So let me teach ya," he sings again, my hands now behind his neck.

"Hold tight; don't let go," he commands against my neck. "Rock with me."

He sways, and I follow his lead as his hands grip my hips and pull me toward his hard body. And his body is hard *everywhere*.

"Feel what you do to me?" I say in her ear. I am in a club with hundreds of people around and hard as steel. "Fuck, Tales, you can move."

While her body presses more tightly to mine, I see her chest rising quickly up and down.

"So sexy, Tallia. Fucking heartbreaker." I know she is. I feel it deep.

"Me?" She looks up at me like I'm nuts, flashing me those eyes. They look like that place with the witch, the dog, the lion, and the scarecrow. Aw, fuck, what's it called? The Elton John song's one. "Good-bye, Yellow Brick Road"?

I move back to those fucking eyes. Fuck!

"You make me insane. Those emerald eyes, that tight body, those lips, and don't even get me started on POW!" I say, turning her back to me.

"Pow?"

"Your ass, Tales, it's like POW!"

She blushes, giggles, and shakes her head. "You're crazy."

"Crazy in lust over you," I tell her, and I'm not kidding. "Tonight's the night, Tales. I'm going to show you what it's like to be rocked."

Once she swallows hard and gives a slight nod,

I look up and see the boys surrounding Madison. She is laughing, and so are they. When Finn looks at me, I mouth, "*Cover me,*" and he nods, stepping in front of Madison's view.

I run my hand up Tally's back and she squirms. I love it. I grip the back of her neck gently enough but also letting her know who is in control. Then I use my other hand to lift her chin, and her eyes roll slightly and close.

I lick my lips at the same time she licks hers before pressing my lips and swiping my tongue against hers. She opens to me, and I slowly stroke my tongue along hers, unable to hold back the urgent growl rising in my throat.

My hand leaves her face, grabbing her ass and pulling her body to mine. She takes in a quick breath as I roll my hips against hers, showing her exactly what I was talking about, showing her what she does to me. When I lick inside of her mouth again, I am that little blonde chick, and this porridge is just fucking right: clean, sweet, fucking mine.

I open my eyes to find she has hers open. Emerald City, that's what they are.

"Fuck, Tales. You taste like fucking more. I want more." My lips crash against hers, and she meets me with just as much urgency, her tongue coming out to play. How she strokes my tongue is hot and sweet.

I bring my hands to the side of her face, tilting her head so I can get in farther. My tongue needs control—I need control—so I take it.

Breathless, I eventually pull back while she

leans into me, wanting more.

"Damn, Tallia."

She opens up Emerald City, her chest rising and falling, nipples hard as hell. She is trying hard to control her breathing, looking confused.

"Talk to me, Tales," I say, knowing she can't.

"I-I—"

I take her hand and pull her behind me, walking by Madison and the boys.

"Tales needs a break. We'll be upstairs."

"You okay?" Madison yells to her over the crowd.

"Stubbed my toe," Tales responds.

I have to bite my cheek so I don't laugh.

We get upstairs to a private box overlooking the dance floor, and I shut and lock the door behind me.

"Breaking all the rules, are you?" I smile a little as I turn to look at her.

"I lied. I know it's wrong, but—"

"And you suck at it," I say, taking her hand and leading her to the U-shaped couch.

"Do you think she knows?" she asks as she sits down and clasps her hands together on her lap.

"No," I answer, grabbing two bottles of water. I open one and hand it to her. "You drunk?"

"No," she says, looking at me like I'm crazy.

"I don't want any excuses, Tales. When we do this, it's us—you and me, sober."

"Do this?" Her voice squeaks.

I look at her and try to push away the annoyance the question gives me.

"This happens tonight, you feel me?"

"This?"

"You and me, naked and sweaty. I have three more nights after tonight, and I am telling you right now, I need to get this out of my system. I want you so fucking badly, and I know damn well you want me, too."

"Everyone wants you, Memphis," she whispers, looking down at her tangled hands.

I sit down next to her. "I'm sure anyone who got close enough to smell that … that fucking smell you emit feels the same."

"What's that supposed to mean?" She scowls slightly.

"Pheromones? Your perfume? You? Fuck, whatever it is, it's insanely sexy." I want out of this conversation and into her. It's confusing, that smell.

She opens her mouth to respond, but I don't give her a chance.

I grab the back of her head and pull her toward me. My lips smash against hers, and she whimpers. My tongue pushes into her mouth as I pull her on top of me.

"Memphis," she moans as I kiss down that pornographic neck, licking, sucking, tasting, and trying my best not to eat it or mark its perfection. As my lips come to the base, I have no desire to stop there, so I don't.

I pull the back of her tank top up and unclip her bra with one hand. Her back arches, and she whimpers again.

Her shirt is off, and her bra is fucking next. I would tear it, but I need to slow down, or it's going to be over before it begins.

"Tales, no one has ever made me feel so fucking insane before. I am losing my mind," I say between kissing and nipping down her shoulder, pushing her bra strap down as I go.

Her body trembles as I pull her leg up so she is straddling me while taking the strap in my teeth and lifting her arm as I pull it free.

"Memphis," she gasps as I kiss the soft silhouette of her perfect, little globes, heading toward her peaked, little ruby reds. "Stop."

Fuck, I scream in my head and look up.

She looks stunned, covering her mouth.

I pull it away. "Talk to me, Tales. Tell me what you need me to say, to do in order to get deeper inside of you."

"This is wrong," she says quietly, looking down and covering her breasts.

"What feels wrong about it?"

"You, me. It's not like—"

"Like what?" I ask as my hands rest on her thighs.

"We'll see each other again."

"We'll be seeing a whole lot of each other for the next few days, a *lot* more if we can get this hashed out quickly."

"Right and it will be uncomfortable."

"Only for a while." I can't help smirking. "You'll stretch, get accustomed to my—"

She slaps my shoulder lightly and covers her mouth to muffle her laugh, completely letting her tits show again. She notices when I make it obvious, so being the … gentleman I am, I pull her against me so they're covered.

"What are you doing?"

"Trying to make you more comfortable," I tell her, holding her tightly to me with one hand as I lean forward, looking into Emerald City as I pull my shirt over my head and kiss her hot, little mouth again.

When I pull the shirt out from between us, she gasps into my mouth, and I kiss her harder. Her hands grab my shoulders, and I feel her push slightly. Then she shocks me by pulling me closer.

Her tongue strokes mine, and I release her back to cup POW!, pulling her snuggly up against my rock hard erection.

She whimpers, then tangles her hands in my hair. I feel the muscles in her ass clench. She's trying to hold back, so I raise my hips a bit and give her a nudge. She cries out and tries to pull away.

"Tales, did that feel wrong?" I nudge her again.

She cries out, "No."

"No as in stop? Or no as in it feels fucking good, Memphis?" I ask with another nudge.

Her body quivers, and she bites my collarbone as she cries out against my flesh.

I grab her hips, knowing she's on edge, and I know damn well I am going to be the one to push her right the fuck over.

I guide her back and forth against my strained, denim-covered cock.

"Memphis, stop. Oh, please stop," she says, so I ease up, but she is rocking it now.

Back and forth, her hips move as I kiss her neck with POW! firmly in my hands.

"I can't—"

"You're there, babe. Let go. Take what you want, what you need," I groan as I suck on her neck.

"Oh, Lord," she says as her body stiffens, and then she cries out my name.

"Fuck," I whisper, pulling her closer as her body relaxes against mine.

She is panting, and I feel her heart racing, beating like a drum.

I rub slowly up and down her back as she comes down from an orgasm. She doesn't move, even when I know she has come back down from cloud Memphis. Her body grows tight again, less relaxed.

I let her sit there for a moment because, quite frankly, my cock is hard as fuck, and the pressure against it is welcome.

Finally, she sits up and scurries off my lap, her knee nailing my sack.

"What the hell, Tales?" I half-laugh, half-groan as I grab myself. "Da fuck?"

"Sorry. That was … um—"

"You better get over here and kiss it better, Tales," I groan.

"What?" She looks at me in confusion.

"You kneed me in the nuts." I rub myself a little.

She gasps and covers her mouth. "Sorry."

"Kiss it better, and I'll—"

"Will not." She laughs nervously.

"Fine." I give an exaggerated sigh. "At least come back over here."

She shakes her head as she grabs her tank top and puts it on.

"What's the problem?"

"Embarrassed," she mumbles.

"Because you got off on my lap?"

"Memphis, good Lord," she grumbles, making me smile.

"It was fucking hot, Tales," I say, standing up and reaching down my pants to adjust myself. "That's a first for me, sweet cheeks."

"Well, me, too," she says as she reaches behind her and tries to snap her bra back on.

I get up and walk behind her. "I am giving you a hand." I do it slowly, purposefully. "Why is this going back on?"

"Because," she says and steps forward, "they'll wonder where we are."

"They know where we are, fixing your banged-up toe." I pull her back by her bra strap and attack her neck.

She squirms. "Tickles."

"Tastes fucking good." I lick her again.

The door handle jiggles. "Open the door!"

"Oh no, oh no, no, no—"

"Sit. I've got this." I walk toward the door and get hit on the back of the head with my shirt. I look back and give her a what-the-hell look, and she smiles and shakes her head, then looks down. "Foot up on the couch, sweet cheeks."

I throw my shirt on and open the door as Mads is about ready to beat it down again.

"I can handle my *damn self*," she huffs with a smirking River and Finn following her in. Billy looks annoyed.

"What the hell's going on?" I fixate on Billy.

"Those guys came back. I was dancing with them and he"—she points at Billy—"started shit with them."

"No, Madison, they pushed past me and—"

"Man the fuck up, Billy. You want a piece of me, take it," Madison steps up to him.

"Whoa, whoa! What the hell did you just say?" Billy gasps.

"*Pft.*" Madison pushes past me and heads to Tallia. "He's lyin', and denyin', Tales. Who the hell wouldn't want a piece of this?" Tally laughs as Mads puts her head on her shoulder. "How's the piggy?"

"Fine." Tally leans her head against Mads.

"Did my brother try to get down your pants? 'Cause, if he did that, I would cut—"

I smirk. "She tried to get in mine."

"Lyin' and denyin'." Tally giggles.

Her giggle hits me in the junk, too. It makes me smile.

"Tell yourself whatever it is you need to, Tallia Annabelle Priest. You know you want me." I wink.

"Her initials are T.A.P.?" River laughs. "If that's not an omen, man …"

I smirk because I have thought about those initials for years, but I never wanted to embarrass her that badly.

Billy starts to walk out.

"Where are you going?"

"Your sister told those guys to back off; they didn't listen."

"How do you know? You weren't even…" Madison snaps, and he interrupts.

"I just do," Billy snaps back then walks out.

River follows. "It's about to get fun up in here."

"Let's go, ladies." I nod to the door.

"No," Madison whines, sticking out her bottom lip and the whole thing.

"Queenie, get your ass—"

She stands up. "I have to pee first."

"Right there." I point to the private bathroom.

"Right there," she mocks, then stomps and whines all the way there.

"Meet me out front?"

"Yeah, man. You get the chicks. I'll grab the dicks," Finn says as he walks out.

As soon as he's out of earshot, Tally jumps up. "Your shirt is on backwards."

I look down. "So?"

"So, they'll notice."

"I'm pretty sure they're gonna notice what's going on between us. I have no intention of hiding it."

"I don't want Madison to think less of me, Memphis."

"Less of you for wanting me?" I point to myself 'cause I'm pretty sure she just insulted me.

"The way she talks about your groupies … I don't want her thinking I'm like—"

"You're nothing like any of them, Tales. Come on, she would never—"

"She would, because I do," she says quickly then covers her mouth, surprised by what she said. She clears her throat. "Your shirt, please."

"If you want it fixed, come and fix it. I couldn't

give a fuck less what anyone thinks about me."

She groans before walking over and pulling my shirt up. "Happy?"

"No, not fucking really."

I pull my arms out, and she turns the shirt over.

"All better." She steps back, and I grab her hand.

"Let me ask you something, Tales?"

Her eyes dart to the door and back to me. She is panicking a little.

"How do you think I feel about this situation? Do you think I consider you to be like the women I've fucked?"

She pulls her hand back. "You haven't fucked me."

I swear to God my jaw hits the ground when she says fuck. At the same time, my dick is instantly hard.

"Tales." I can't even hide the growl. I am amped up and ready to rock. "You're right, but you've fucked me, so let me ask you something: do you see me the same way they do, like a conquest, like something you can check off your bucket list?"

"Screw you, Memphis!"

"What did he do now?" Madison asks as she walks out of the bathroom.

"Nothing," Tally says as she hurries away.

"I stubbed my fucking toe," I say, opening the door. "Ladies." I pause, hoping that stings her a little, exactly like she just stung me. "Let's go."

We are at the top of the stairs when I see Billy swing and connect with some preppy fuck's nose.

"Get the fuck out of here!" I yell at Madison

and Tally as I skip about twenty stairs to get to the bottom.

It's a fucking brawl. Finn is lifting some fucker up by the collar, and River is ducking, weaving, jabbing, and laughing his ass off. Billy sees me out of the corner of his eye.

"Look out!" I yell as the bastard he hit nails him in the nose.

I dive into the crowd, swinging. Motherfuckers don't fuck with my friends.

I feel someone grab my arm, and I swing and make contact with the face of the same fucker that was giving me hell about Tales. I feel something sharp hit the back of my head, and then liquid heat.

I turn and swing, and before I can stop myself, I see the broken bottle.

"Fuck!" I scream when I connect with the broken bottle. "Motherfucker!"

I swing with my other hand, knocking the fucker out with a right uppercut. I then feel someone pulling me by the back of my shirt.

"Get him the fuck out of here."

I grab my left hand and pull it tightly to my chest where blood is pouring out. I am getting dizzy.

"Where are the girls? Mads, Tales! Where the fuck are they?"

"Memphis!" I hear Madison screaming. "Oh, God!"

Blackness overtakes me.

I grab Madison and pull her to the door, feeling sick to my stomach as I open the door to the awaiting car.

"Get in, Mads."

"But, but—"

"Get in the fucking car!" I scream, not even covering my mouth after the expletive.

"What the hell did I do to you?" I hear Memphis behind me. "Swearing and—"

"Get in." I have to hold back the tears when I see he's awake now.

"Sweet cheeks, only if you don't mind my head on your lap." He sounds drunk.

I smile and nod. "Of course."

In the car, I am seated on the black leather bench that backs against the driver's seat while Memphis lies with his head on my lap, just like he warned. I rap on the partition, calling out "Hospital!" when the driver opens it.

"Tell him fucking fast. Not feeling all that good," Memphis moans out.

"Fast!"

"No, say 'fucking fast'." He smirks, and then

his eyes squint in pain.

"Fucking fast," I yell, knowing it will make him open his eyes.

"You're making me hard, sweet cheeks," he mumbles.

I push his hair out of his eyes and lean down. "Aren't you always?"

He smirks. "Lately, yeah." After a minute, he says, "Your father." He shakes his head.

"What?"

"He made me this way." His eyes get droopy.

"Give me your shirt." I hold my hand out to the guys. "One of you, give me your shirt," I snap. "He's bleeding more."

"You can have mine." Memphis's full lips curl up in one corner. "Oh, hell, take my boxers, too, Tales."

"Very funny."

"If I die, you'll be so pissed you missed that experience."

He's bleeding everywhere. There's blood on him, on me, on the seats and he's still being… Memphis.

"Then don't you dare." I feel tears in my eyes.

Finn leans over and wraps his shirt around Memphis's arm.

"Easy, motherfucker." Memphis cringes. "I really don't wanna cry like a little bitch in front of Tales," he pauses and looks at Madison, who is hysterically crying into Billy's shirt, "or Mads, man."

I smile as he grins up at me, tears falling freely down my face.

"Aw, man. Don't cry, sweet cheeks," he groans while Finn tightens the shirt on his wound.

"How far?" I half yell, half cry to the driver.

"Five minutes," he snaps back and hits the accelerator.

"How's our girl?" Memphis asks me, and I know he's talking about Madison.

"A mess, Memphis." I push his hair back, then lean down and kiss him. "If you don't get better, I'm going to die." He looks at me like I'm nuts, and I don't even care. I smile through my tears and whisper. "I want you that badly."

I am shocked that I said that to him, especially now of all times, but you can't take even a moment for granted and I needed him to know. I needed to give him ...something to look forward to? God, what was I thinking? Well it's too late now.

His eyes open wide, and then his dark brow creeps up. "What do you want from me?"

I lean down, kiss his nose, and then whisper the truth, "I want you to get better fast, and then I want you to rock me your way."

"I'm gonna rock you every way. Move back down here."

I lean back down, and he inhales deeply.

"I'm not the guy you think I am, Tales, and you're nobody's groupie."

I dig deep for courage. "I wanna be *your* groupie."

"Fuck, you better not just be saying that 'cause I'm bleeding out, Tales."

"Memphis, I've been your groupie since I was, like, seven." Even if I become merely one of many,

I will not regret admitting that to him, not ever. Not after the way it makes him smile.

"We're here." I tell him.

I feel the car speed into the emergency room's drop off zone.

"We'll find you a hot nurse, man," River says jokingly, and Memphis smirks.

I already feel stupid. So, so stupid.

"River, you're gonna be my bitch, change my bed pan, give me sponge baths," he groans as he sits up, then slips back. I catch him. "Nice save, sweet cheeks."

"Anytime," I say sadly and hang back.

He looks back. "Where you going?"

"What?"

"You were just right fucking here a second ago. Don't duck out now. I'm gonna hold you to it, Tales."

It gets really noisy and confusing when we go through the emergency entrance. Finn and River carry Memphis, and Billy is bleeding, too.

"Bar fight?" The ER nurse laughs.

"Excuse me, miss, but it's really not funny," Madison cries. "Not fucking funny at all!"

"Get her the hell out of here," Memphis says as his eyes roll slightly.

"Come on, Madison; let's go call your folks."

She wraps her arms around my waist and cries as we walk out the way we came in.

"Want me to call—?"

"No," she cries. "He has to be okay. He just has to be."

"I know, and he will be," I say, hugging her

tightly.

I lead her to the bench to the right of the entrance, and we sit.

"No, he won't be."

"He will, dammit!" She looks up at me, surprised. "Sorry."

"I know. I know! Tally, our parents—"

"I'll call them." I look for the car since my bag is in it.

"No, that's just the thing. They aren't okay. They split up six months ago. Dad came to see me at school during one of his trips. He stayed at a hotel. I … Well, I went to surprise him, and he wasn't alone."

"Your mom was …" I stop when I see her lip quiver, and she shakes her head. "Oh! Oh, Madison. Why haven't you talked to me?"

"I haven't told anyone," she cries. "God, what a mess. What a fucking mess."

Her face is in her hands, and she is trembling from her silent sobs. I place my hands on her leg.

"How did your mom take it?"

She shakes her head. "I couldn't … I couldn't tell her."

My heart breaks for her. "You've gone through this alone?"

"I couldn't tell Memphis. Dad told me I couldn't, or I would fuck things up for him."

"He put that on you?" She nods. "What an asshole."

She smiles and wipes away her tears. "You have a *Black* mouth."

"A what?" I wipe my face.

"Like a potty mouth, but worse." She smiles, and I squeeze her in a hug again.

"How come you didn't talk to me?"

"You lost your father, and I want mine dead half the time, Tales. I just couldn't."

"I understand." I hug her more tightly. "Don't do it again, or I'll cut you." I smile, repeating what she says to Memphis all the time.

"What's up with you and my brother?" she asks, pulling free from my bear hug.

"What do you mean?" I look away for a moment, hoping she won't see the lie on my face.

"Tales, if he hurts you…" She grabs my hand.

"Madison, it's flirting," I tell her, looking back at her.

She gives me the uh-huh look. "Talk to me when you're ready."

"I'm ready for you to call your parents and then go back in and check on Memphis," I say, standing up from the bench we sat on.

"And Billy."

"Talk to me about that when you're ready." I smile, taking her hand. "Let's go get our purses from the car."

When we walk in, Finn looks up and says loudly, "Come on." The nurse gives him a look. "They're his sisters."

"And you're all his brothers," she says, obviously not believing him.

"That's what he told you, isn't it?"

She shakes her head. "Go on in."

When we walk in, I can immediately tell Memphis has been given something for the pain.

His eyes are not vibrant and showy like they always are. His arm is bandaged from the fingertips to all the way up past his elbow.

"You okay?" Madison asks quietly.

"No, I'm not fucking okay, Mads," he slurs. "They think I have nerve damage. I have to have surg—"

"Ery," River finishes for him.

Memphis covers his face, saying nothing.

"He is worried about the tour," River whispers, none too quietly.

"I'm a fucking guitarist," he mumbles. "I play fucking guitar."

The room falls quiet.

"And you sing, Memphis," I say, trying to give him some hope.

"Yeah, now we have to find another guitarist. Fucking bullshit."

"You'll be okay, Memphis. You'll see." Madison's voice cracks.

"And how the hell do you know that? You a doctor, Mads? Or you just going to college to do him or *him*?"

"Memphis," I gasp.

"It's my best diddling hand, Tales, so you may want to rethink the groupie thing, sweet cheeks."

I feel my face burst into flames as he looks out from under his arm.

"Still got my lap, though. You can still get yourself—"

I turn and walk out. I walk out of the room, out of the ER, and outside.

"Wait up." I turn back to see River running

behind me. "Tally, he's all fucked up on morphine. He is a mess. He's going on tour in just a couple months, and there is no way in hell he's gonna recover that quickly."

"He could," I say, rather forcefully for me.

"No." He runs his hands through his hair. "Pretty sure the doctor said, 'There is no fucking way, young man'." He smiles sadly and looks down. "He is going into surgery in about fifteen minutes. He has you and Madison, who by the way, is a train wreck of epic proportions, and that's coming from me, the cause of most train wrecks of epic proportions. Fuck!" he roars suddenly. "Look, you are, like, the most normal person in his life who's here; go tell him the bullshit about him being okay."

"He won't believe me," I argue.

"He'll want to. Fuck, tell him, if he pulls through, you'll give him dome or some shit."

"What?" I honestly have no clue what dome is.

"You have two point two seconds before I claim fucked up on drugs when I get arrested for throwing you over my shoulder and marching POW! back in that hospital."

"What?" The word doesn't even leave my mouth before he has me up and over his shoulder, walking toward the ER entrance. "I'll scream," I threaten.

"Like I said, I'm fucked up and will get off; trust me, Tales. I've been there, done that, gotten the T-shirt."

"River, put her down, for fuck's sake," I hear Finn's voice before I get dropped on my feet.

"He needs you. Pull your shit together, stop acting holier-than-thou, and man the fuck up," River says as Finn takes my hand and leads me back in. No sense in fighting; he's a damn house.

He stops in front of his room and releases my hand. "Madison is making a phone call. You do whatever you gotta do in there, understand?"

"I don't like you very much right now; do you understand me?" I ask, straightening my skirt and trying to push my mess of a hair-do back in place.

"Don't give one fuck, let alone two. Now go," he says in a harsh whisper as he opens the door.

I turn to walk in and feel a sharp smack to my backside, and I turn around to see River.

"POW!" he whispers.

I would rather take my chances with the crude and rude Memphis than that motley crew.

Memphis gives a slight huff. "You came back."

"Yeah, well," I say as I walk toward him, "I just needed a break from tonight, you know? And, well, your band mates don't seem to get that."

"You left because I was a dick. That's what Madison told me, anyway. But I need you to do me a favor."

I sit down next to him and look into his drugged and hopeless eyes.

"Your dream of being with a rock star, that shit's not gonna happen here, girl, so you're off the hook."

"Off the hook for …?"

"Me banging you into oblivion."

"Memphis?"

"Seriously, you can walk. You deserve something better than a twenty-three-year-old coffee jockey."

"What are you talking about?"

"I'll be serving coffee again soon."

"You'll be singing onstage while you heal and melting panties in the process."

"I'm all fucked up on pain meds, and I'm chubbing up, Tales. They should bottle you up and sell you to those poor fucks who can't get it up."

"They could replace that pink pill with your voice, Memphis."

"Ooo, she's good," he says, looking up.

"He's amazing," I say, looking at him.

"If I ever hurt you, cut my dick off."

I laugh. "What?"

"Hmm." He smirks. "I don't deserve a good girl like you."

"Well, I am a hundred percent sure the girls who have had you would disagree."

He is dozing off, so I take his hand.

"Tales?"

"Yes."

"I don't deserve you, but everything inside and outside of me wants to take you and keep you."

"You should rest; you're talking—"

"Truth. I'm talking truth."

"Under the influence, so I won't hold you to it, Memphis."

He slowly drags my hand to his stomach and then down … there. "Take them with you." He uses my hand to grab his … balls. "You should have them."

Wow, just, wow. I am blushing from head to toe and slightly turned on, while he's a mess. What the hell is wrong with me?

"Sweet cheeks?"

"Yeah, Memphis?"

"The least you could do is give them a tug."

"A what?" I laugh.

"Hmm," he sighs.

"You really want me to …"

"Fuck, yeah," he says in a medicated, slow drawl. "When I wake up, I want them slapping POW!"

I'm totally confused, so I stand, hands still under his … on his … balls. I lean over him and kiss him.

"I fucking love your mouth. I can't wait to taste your—"

I kiss him again, then tug.

He groans in my mouth, and … I do it again.

***

Four hours. That's how long it has been since we arrived here at this godforsaken hospital. Between the band, Madison, and me, I think the nurses are growing tired of us.

I look up when I hear Finn say, "X-Man, what the fuck are you doing here?"

This guy… X-man is in jeans and a T-shirt. His arms are covered in tattoos and he's bulky, like he works out. He's very, very good-looking, just like everyone Memphis hangs out with, but none of them are as handsome as Memphis.

"Forever Steel, man. How is he?"

"Still in surgery. He's a fucking mess."

"How's your head, man?" Xavier asks, walking around him.

"Twelve stitches. I'll be fine," Billy answers. "This shit's my fault. If he can't play, it's—"

"Then you'll play," the man covered in tattoos that looks very intimidating walks over to me. "Rough night?"

I nod.

Finn introduces me and Madison, who is asleep on my lap, in his own way. "That's his sister and the girl he wants to—"

"His sister's best friend," Billy interrupts.

"I'm Xavier Steel." He reaches his hand out. "Someone call his parents?"

"I'm Tallia, and yes, Madison called them."

"He has a great team of doctors; he'll be fine." Xavier sits down. When he's not hovering, he looks far less intimidating. "Billy here is gonna learn acoustic—"

"I can't."

"The fuck you can't; you will." Xavier laughs, but I really don't think he's joking.

"Xavier …" Billy begins.

"Forever Steel, Billy," is all he says before he turns back to me and shakes his head. "Where's his head at?"

I look up at Finn and then River who is sleeping on the hard plastic waiting room couch.

Xavier clears his throat. "I saw you in the video monitor during our call the other day, saw him looking at you. So, I'm not asking them, I am asking"—he points at me—"you. Where's his head at?"

I swallow back tears. "Scared, doesn't think he's going to be all right, but he will. I know he will. He has an amazing voice, and his talent is God given and—"

"Where's your head at?" he interrupts.

"I don't understand."

"You gonna keep his head straight and mind focused?"

How? I scream in my head. How am I supposed to do that and what the hell is he talking about?

"I don't understand," I repeat.

He nods. "I see."

I can't find her. Fuck, I don't even know who it is I'm looking for. I just know I need her, like now. Someone has me. Someone is keeping me away from her, and I don't know who they are, either.

I look around. Darkness is everywhere. I see shadows, but nothing recognizable. They still have me, and I fight with all I am, all I have.

"Please, stop. Just leave him alone. God!"

I hear a cry, and then I see a light. And nothing good comes when you see a light. Fuck, what happened? Where am I? Why is she crying?

"Memphis, just open your eyes. Please just open your eyes."

I force myself to do just that. I blink at the brightness a few times then finally …

"Fuck," I groan.

"He's awake," I hear Mads. "He's awake."

"Shit, Mads, did you think I wouldn't wake up?" I growl at her. "Fucking throat hurts."

"You had a tube down your throat. That's normal after surgery," the nurse says.

"You shoved a fucking tube down my throat? You never said you were shoving shit down my throat. So help me God, you better not have fucked that up." I try to sit up, but I can't. "Am I tied the fuck down?"

"You were fighting. We had no choice but to restrain you for your own—"

"Un-fucking-believable," I groan. It hurts. It hurts really fucking badly. "How long am I gonna feel like shit?"

"A few days. And you'll—"

"Then knock me the fuck out. Fuck, I have to piss."

"You have a catheter in—"

"Fucking masochists. I will end your lives if that shit doesn't work again."

"Memphis, shut it down, man. You'll be fine."

I look left. "X-man, if they fuck everything up for me, and I'm back to serving coffee—"

"I'll hire you on to wipe River's ass." He smirks at me.

"Fuck you."

"If it still works, I'll get you a hooker, but you aren't fucking me," he jokes.

"Man, what a fucking mess." I look toward Madison, who starts sobbing.

"I'm sorry. This is all my fault. If I—"

"Mads, you're fine. Just muffle that cry; my fucking head hurts, okay?"

"I have to tell you something," she says, standing beside me.

"Mom and Dad here?"

"No, I didn't call them," she says and that lip pokes out.

I laugh. "You didn't what?"

"They don't deserve to be here. They've only come to two of your shows and—"

"They're busy, Mads. Shit, Dad busts his ass making bank, and Mom busts hers making everything perfect for all of us."

"Dad's been cheating on her. I caught him, and I don't know how to tell—"

I gasp. "What the fuck did you just say?"

"Madison," I hear X as the room spins. "Not a good time for this conversation."

"Someone knock me the fuck out," I beg.

***

I wake up in the dark. I swallow, finding my throat is still sore. I try to move my hand, but it hurts like a bitch, and my head is spinning, and not because of the drugs, but because of what Madison told me.

"I am gonna kill that mother—"

"You're awake?"

I look right to find Tally is sitting there. I give a nod.

"You're in pain?"

I nod again.

"The nurse said you can drink. It might make you feel better."

"I don't see how it could."

She looks at me sadly.

"Don't look at me like that, Tales. I mean, shit happens. Maybe not all at once like today, but shit happens."

"You're going to be okay."

"Yeah." I nod.

"Wasn't asking." She gets up and sits on my right side, taking the cup off the rolling stand then bending the straw as she leans toward me. "Hydrate, rest, heal."

"It's that easy?"

She nods. "Hydrate, rest, heal." Then she leans in and kisses my head.

"Where's Mads?"

"Your band mates took her back to the house to sleep. She's kind of … tired."

"She okay?"

"She will be."

I take a drink, and then she sets it down and turns her body toward me.

"You will be, too."

"My old man fucked around on a woman he told he loved every day on the phone or in person."

"Things happen. I know it sucks, but they do."

"You lost your old man," I whisper because it hurts to talk.

"Madison said she wants to kill yours," she says with a sad smile.

"She's not alone."

"Can I get you anything?"

I smirk, and she laughs, shaking her head.

"Even in pain, I want whatever it is your offering."

"A kiss?"

"No."

She looks hurt.

"Tales, I haven't brushed my teeth in a while. It's definitely me being a gentleman."

"A toothbrush?"

"Now you're talking."

"I'll be right back." She walks towards the door.

"I'm not going anywhere."

"They did untie you." She smiles a sweet smile.

"That was fucked up, right?" It still pisses me off.

"This is all fucked up."

"Tales." I stop her before she leaves. "Tell one of them chicks I am taking this tube out of my dick if they don't get in here and do it. That shit's not natural."

The nurse comes in a few minutes later. "I'm Sandy. I'll be removing the tubing."

"Good. Can I brush my teeth first?"

She hands me a toothbrush with paste on it and a pan to spit in. When I'm done, she pulls the sheet away. I am looking down at my dick with a hose coming out of it. So fucking not cool.

"You may feel a slight tug or pull when it comes out, but it won't hurt."

"Gotcha." I brace myself for it, anyway.

"You'll feel relieved, but you might pass urine when you don't want to."

"You're kidding, right?" I snarl.

She looks at me deadpan, and I realize Nurse Sandy isn't fucking kidding.

"This is an incontinence pad." She shows it to me. "Lift your bum."

"I don't have a bum; I have an ass." I try my best not to be pissy, but fuck this shit.

She gives me that look again. “It’ll get better over time.”

“How much time?” I ask as she pulls the tubing out of my dick.

“Not long.”

“Sandy, when my dick is in your hand, I don’t wanna hear ‘not long,’ because it is.” She turns her back to walk out. “Tell me I’m lying?”

“Goodnight, Mr. Black.”

You have got to be fucking kidding me. I’m gonna lie here and piss myself, and she can’t even laugh at that shit. Fucking healthcare.

The good news is, I’m not pissing myself. The bad news is, Tales hasn’t returned.

I sit and wait and wait some more.

When she finally comes back in, she is all wide-eyed, and her face is red.

“You’re back,” I state happily.

“Yep.” She takes my water cup and holds it up. “Drink.”

“Not sure if that’s a good idea.”

“Your throat.”

I look at her, she looks at me, and neither one of us says a word. I see it in her eyes, though; she is questioning something.

I shake my head.

“Memphis …” she says in a warning, squaring her shoulders. “Hydration is necessary, so if you’re worried about”—she glances down at my dick; I swear to fuck she does—“something, just don’t. You’ve been through—”

“Worried about what?”

She glances down again.

I shake my head. "Spill it."

"I heard the nurses giggling at their station," she whispers.

"About me?"

She shrugs. "Something about an ass and not a bum and then length and—"

"I'm not pissing myself, Tales."

She holds out the cup. "Take a drink, Memphis Black, or you won't be pissing at all, and then you'll get an infection, and you might just end up all sorts of"—she pauses—"fucked up. Your hand, your throat, and your penis, Memphis. Do you want those things most important in your life to remain … injured, or are you more worried about a little leakage?"

"You said fuck, and my dick heard you." I can't help messing with her. "And it's seems to have blood flowing in the right direction, so …"

"You're a pig." She smirks as she sits down next to me.

"Careful, sweet cheeks, don't get too close."

She laughs, and then her eyes fill up with tears. "You're going to be okay."

"Yeah, I'm going to be fine," I tell her so she doesn't worry, but fuck if doubt isn't on stage under the spotlight, center stage in my head. "I brushed my teeth."

"So did I."

"You wanna lean down here and kiss me? Make it easier on me?"

"Of course."

Her lips are gentle on mine, soft and sweet, not like before and maybe not ever again, but right now, nothing has ever felt so good.

***

I wake up to a blood pressure cuff strangling my arm.

"You people are bound and determined to fuck something up on me, aren't you?" I cringe and open my eyes.

Mom.

"You're okay?" she chokes out on a sob.

"I'm good, Mom," I say through gritted teeth. I don't know for how much longer, though. Shit, I don't know how people survive in these places.

"The good news is that you can go home today." She forces a smile. "Also good news, I'll be staying here until they release you to fly, so I am going to spoil my little boy and help him get well."

"Mom …" I whisper.

"Don't, Memphis. I need to do this."

"Yeah, well, when I heal, I have a thing or two I need to do, as well."

She shakes her head. "Heal."

"I will, Mom. So will you."

"I'm worried about the two of you. You and Madison are my life."

"He needs to get the fuck out."

"He has."

"Good."

"He's still your father."

"He ain't shit."

"Memphis, I won't have you talk about him like that. He provided a good life for us and—"

"He funded a life; you provided it."

She sits down on the bed as tears spill out of her eyes, and I pull her head down to my chest. As she cries, my heart breaks for her.

***

I walk into the house, the guys are all standing there, looking at me.

"Is someone gonna say something? This isn't a fucking funeral. I'm walking; my throat is fine." I pull my mom's head to my chest and cover the ear that is not crushed against me. "And my dick isn't leaking and works just fine." I look around, then let go of my mom. "Where are the girls?"

"Grocery shopping," Mom says as she shakes her head. "And I heard you." She starts to walk away while all the guys laugh.

"We have a cook available," I call out to her.

"I came to take care of you," she says, walking into the kitchen, "so the cook gets a break. I'm sure it's well deserved."

I look back as the Escalade pulls in. Tally is in the driver's seat, looking smoking hot in that big thing.

Madison gets out of the passenger side and wipes her eyes. She's been crying. Again.

I look at the guys. "Sorry shit's messed up. I don't like the drama. Really don't like bringing it to you all." The fucking hospital, the wreck my family has become, and now the fuck pad has been invaded by women no one can fuck.

"This ain't fucking drama; this is life. Shit drama." River chuckles as he walks down the hall.

I look at Finn.

"Step the fuck out of your bitch pants, man. Tear off the Depends." He grins.

"Shit's not funny. Could be leaking today because of this shit."

"But you're not, so tug on your balls, get laid, and look around, motherfucker. Life is good. We're in Miami, baby, and because of you getting your ass kicked—"

"I didn't get my fucking ass kicked, you asshole!"

"You may have busted a nose."

I grin. "I broke his nose?"

"Hell yes, you did, and you were bleeding like a stuck pig when you did it. I'd high-five your ass, but I don't wanna make you cry."

I laugh and shake my head. "You think Billy can pull off lead guitar?"

"It's acoustic; a trained monkey could pull it off. Now, if it was bass, we'd be fucked."

Speaking of fucked, I smell her as she walks by, and my fully functional, heat-seeking missile is … fully functioning.

"Good afternoon, ladies."

"Wow, someone's in a good mood." Tally smiles over her shoulder.

"I feel like I just got sprung after being in county for twelve months," I say behind her.

River walks out, chuckling. "Hashtag: white boy problems."

"Hashtag: suck it."

"Hashtag: not my job, man. Oh, and hashtag: you sure it still works?"

I scowl at him and he smirks. I know the

fucker's just sucked on something, and its named chillz.

"Oh, darn it," Tally says, looking through a bag. "We forgot the chicken."

"How do you girls forget chicken when I am making chicken enchiladas?" Mom laughs.

"Hashtag: blonde moment." River grins like a fool.

"You do know they're both brunette, don't you?" I comment, looking at his foolish face.

"Hashtag: don't give a fuck. But hashtag: your mom has a smokin' body."

"I will fuck you up if you ever say shit like that in front of me again," I hiss at him.

"Come on, River; let's go for a walk," Billy says, shaking his head. Then I hear him say, "You really should stop smoking that shit."

"Mom, wanna come with?" Madison asks, grabbing the key fob.

"I can go," Tally offers, grabbing her bag.

"No, I need some Mom time. Memphis has been hogging her." She sticks her tongue out at me, and I smile.

"Be right back. We'll grab your prescription from the pharmacy, too." Mads and Mom walk to the door.

"They can deliver it, Mom," I call to her as she walks out.

"I'm your mom, Memphis."

I look over at Finn, then Tally. "I'm going to—" He doesn't finish as he walks out.

"Tales," I say.

She sighs and looks up. "You need to let her

take care of you."

"Come again?" I can't help thinking about how badly I want to make her do just that.

"Your mom needs you to need her right now."

"How about you?"

She nods, but her eyes aren't sparkling. Emerald City has lost its luster, and I don't like that at all.

"Wanna help me out?"

"With?" She tugs at her shirt. It has those robot-looking people on it. The green, red, blue, and pink— "Memphis?"

Aw, fuck it. "I need a bath. Run some water?"

"Sure." She walks quickly by me, then stops and turns around. "I'm happy you're going to be okay." Then she walks back, grips my shirt, pushes herself up on her toes, and kisses me. Plants one right on me.

She starts to pull away, but I grab her T-shirt and try to kiss her. However, she manages to step back.

"Come on." She all but runs into the bedroom.

When I get in there, the water is already running. She stands there, fussing with that shirt.

"Do you know how sexy you look in all those vintage tees, Tales?" I ask as I shut the door behind me. She shakes her head. "I always preferred the glamour shit, and now, when I look at you, I have no fucking idea why."

"It might have something to do with the pain medication," she says as she nervously tangles her long, wavy locks around her finger.

"The hair, too, Tales. I love it. I used to pick on

you tirelessly about it, and now I've decided, when I get my first interview in Rolling Stone, I'm gonna tell all the little boys out there that the tight, kinky curls tame, and when they do, damn." I pull my shirt up and then over my head, groaning in pain.

"Let me help." She steps over to me and drags my T-shirt slowly down my arm. "Does it hurt?"

"At this moment, I have no clue, and I don't really give a shit." Tales is stripping me.

She folds my shirt and sets it on the counter behind me. Then she takes a deep breath and reaches out, her hands going toward my waistband.

"I'll get these." Her voice is no more than a whisper. She's nervous and I swear if I say some stupid shit and fuck this up, I'm gonna kick my own ass but I have to make sure she knows it's not an expectation.

"You sure you wanna do that?"

She nods, biting down on her lip, and then, as if she has found enough courage, she unbuttons me as she breathes out slowly.

I grab the back of her head and pull it so her forehead is touching my chest as I smell her hair before kissing the back of her head.

She pushes my jeans down until she is kneeling in front of me. Her eyes are wide, eye level with the bulge in my boxers.

"Step out?"

"Yeah, Tales, yeah." I step out, slow and easy, all sorts of turned on.

She leans back on her heels and folds my jeans, before pushing herself up on her knees and setting them on the counter. Then she turns and looks up at me, swallows hard, and her eyes … Her fucking eyes are illuminated with want and desire.

"I'm just gonna …" she says, hooking her little fingers on the waistband at my hips and slowly pulls them down. My dick is hard and centimeters from her face. "Step out," she says, then clears her throat. She leans back and folds them before setting them on my jeans.

Her folding the clothes is like a slow seduction, and if that was the intention, it fucking worked. I hope this is leading where I think it is. I never wanted any woman more.

She pushes herself up on her knees, closes her eyes, and takes in a big breath of courage before she licks her lips then leans forward, placing her hands flat on my abs.

"You've complimented me so many times over the past few days, and I don't know if I have once told you, with every defense I have down, how amazing you look or how much you make me feel."

"Tales," I say, gripping the base of my dick and rubbing her cheek with its head. "Don't tell me; show me." I want her mouth on me so fucking bad, and I know damn well she wants that too. No. Fucking. Doubt.

"I plan on it." She leans forward and licks me from tip to base.

"That's it, Tales. Show me more," I growl.

She opens her mouth and gently places her lips around my cock.

"Fuck yes," Hallelujah.

She moves up and down slowly as her nails dig into my flesh. She then looks up, seeking approval.

"Perfect, Tallia. Absolutely perfect, babe."

She closes her eyes as she moves up and down on me a little faster, her tongue swirling. She sucks and takes me deeper.

"Fuck. Fuck yeah."

Tales places her hand over mine, and together, we pump my dick as she sucks and licks. She finds a rhythm, so I take my hand away as she pumps my cock all on her own. She moans and licks me, her other hand cupping my sac and giving it a tug.

I immediately feel the heat, the burn, the pull. *Not fucking yet*, I tell myself.

She takes me a little too deep and gags a little.

"Easy, babe. Don't hurt yourself."

She pulls her mouth off me and lifts my dick so it points up, and then she licks me from sac to tip over and over.

She has saliva pooling in the corner of her mouth, and I am so fucking turned on by how raw she is with me right now.

Her mouth covers my cock, and she whimpers as her strokes become faster while she sucks harder.

"Babe, I'm gonna come."

She looks up at me, eyes watering, her hand wrapped around the base of my cock, and nearly all of it in her mouth. She sucks, licks, and pumps.

"Fuck!" I roar as I rapid fire my cum in her mouth. "Fuck, Tales, fuck. That was … Fuck!"

I pull her face to my thigh and praise her the only way I can right now, because the words aren't coming. I pet her hair—her soft, wavy, deep brown hair—as I try to catch my breath after the most powerful sexual experience of my life.

How the fuck do you recover from that?

I want to scoot under the vanity and hide.

I'm embarrassed at what I just did … *needed* to do.

I think I did well. I think.

"Can you let go of my leg and stand up now?" His voice is thick, husky, the way it gets when we are near, and good Lord, we have just been intimately near.

"Not yet," I say honestly.

"Tales, up now." There is a command in his voice, and for some reason, I like it.

I stand up, yet I can't look at him.

"My cock was in your mouth, and you were showing me Emerald City, but you can't now, Tales? Come on, shit just got real here, and I won't let you hide from me." He pulls the back of my hair, making me look up. "That was incredible. Amazing. Fuck, Tales, incred-amaze. Is that a word?"

I shake my head as he pulls me to him firmly. "I owed you."

"Is this a competition? Please say yes," he teases.

He releases my head, then spreads his hand across my ass. Then, with one hand, he lifts, and I squeal until he sets me on the vanity.

"Batter up!" He drops to his knees, pushes my skirt up, and spreads my legs.

"What are you …? Oh, God!"

His mouth covers my panties. I feel his tongue moving up and down the fabric, and I am unraveling … reeling. If I am dying, I will take it now.

"Oh, Memphis." I grip the edge of the counter and fall back slightly.

I feel a tug and hear a rip.

"Fucking hate those things."

He pushes his tongue into me, and I try to scoot back, but he captures my knee and lifts my leg over his shoulder. "Stays there," he growls as his tongue pushes in again.

"Don't think I—"

"Don't think, Tales. Feel." I feel him shoving something—his finger—inside me, and he hisses as he looks up, while still licking and sucking around my clit. "Mmm," he moans, and the vibration causes me to buck.

"Oh, don't, don't …" I beg.

Mischief and desire dance in his eyes, and he does it again and again and again until I crumple apart.

He doesn't give me a chance to catch my breath. He is sucking me and using his fingers, and … I look down to see he is watching me fall apart … again.

"Water," I pant. "Memphis …"

"Mmm," his mouth vibrates against me again.

"I don't want to hurt you, but … Oh, God," I cry again, this time less forcefully, because he is sucking the little force I have left out of me … with his mouth.

He sits back and licks his lips, smiling a cocky little smile as I try to get my ultra-relaxed muscles working again.

"Sweet cheeks?"

"Huh?" As I open my eyes, he is looking over at the massive Jacuzzi tub.

"You wanna turn that off?" He smirks, lowering my leg, then standing.

"Oh … hell." I jump up and scurry over, turning the water off.

I feel his hand on my hip and the soft covering of his wrapped arm on the other. "Don't. Move."

"Memphis …" I begin to object.

"Sweet Jesus, Tallia, your ass is so, like, POW!" he grumbles.

"Can I move now?" My voice hitches as his hand cups me between my legs.

"Uh-huh." He pushes my skirt up, and then I feel his lips touch my bare behind. He growls.

Either he's hungry, or he's *hungry.*

"Any chance you're on the pill?" his voice rasps as his finger runs between my legs, causing me to tremble.

"No."

"Any chance you'll consider it?"

"Doesn't work that way," I moan, arching into his touch.

"What way is that?" He kisses me again.

"Not instant—oh, God."

"Not looking for instant, Tales. Looking forward and behind." He nips my butt cheek, a low chuckle escaping his throat.

"But—"

"I love yours," he says, nipping it again. "And before you say a damn thing, this thing, the you-on-your-knees thing, the my-face-between-your-thighs thing, the your-perfect-ass-bent-over-in-front-of-me thing—that's gonna happen again and again and—"

I stand up and turn to give him a soft dose of reality. However, he grabs the back of my head and kisses me relentlessly. When he finally pulls back, leaving me wanting more, I look up at him as tears sting my eyes.

"It's not realistic. You're touring."

"You're schooling."

I flinch when he mentions school.

"Spill it, Tales."

I shake my head. "Everything's fi—"

"You are an easy read, Tales." He cups the side of my face.

"How so?" I hold my hand against his.

"I'm not going to give away all my secrets,"-he smirks as his eyes rake down my body—"but your body talks. Your eyes, Tales… They talk and I'm listening, so spill it."

I pull my hand away, "You can't tell Madison. You just can't, okay?"

"I'm thinking, after the past few days, she kind of has an idea."

I shake my head as I fist my hair in my hands.

"I'm not going back to Julliard. I'm not, and it's totally okay. I mean, things just weren't meant to be. It's perfectly fine, and—

"It's your dream, Tales. Hell, my mom knew that when you were—"

"You need to just stop talking and get into the bath. I won't …" He grabs me and hugs me. "It was a foolish dream," I whisper, "and I don't want to talk about it."

"Tales, I've seen you dance. I know you're amazing, so whatever they said that made you decide not to go back—"

I pull back, needing distance, needing a change in subject.

"Bath. Please, Memphis. I've made up my mind, and I won't be returning."

"Tales …" He uses that tone that all those people at my dad's funeral used.

"Don't. Just … go." I point to the tub, and he steps in, holding his hand up as if to retreat. "Thank you."

"Join me," he says, resting his elbow on the side of the tub.

"Your mom, your sister, your—"

"Beautiful. You're so fucking beautiful." He is staring at my mouth, and I've read enough Cosmo to know what to expect after sexual intimacy. He's feeling the afterglow, but heck, so am I.

"Do you need anything more?"

His eyebrow shoots up. "What are you offering?"

I cover my face and laugh.

He grabs my skirt and pulls me toward him.

"Just sit for a minute, okay? Just sit here and don't think, Tales. Just—"

"You're beautiful, too," I say, shaking my head from side to side.

"I like that you think so."

"You make me laugh, like a lot."

"And come," he says. I uncover my face and roll my eyes. "A lot."

"I am so sorry about all this stuff—the past couple days, your dad … and all those horrible things that happened to you."

"It got me sympathy dome from Tallia Annabelle Priest." He winks.

I now know what dome means.

"She also stuck by me when I was a dick, lying out in the hospital—"

"And endured your sexual harassment for days," I add.

"And is still sitting here now."

I look into his eyes as he looks into mine.

"You're in pain."

"So are you. I'm so pissed at my father, Tales. So fucking pissed. But you, well, you lost yours and I—"

"I'm pissed at him, too," escapes my mouth.

"Why?"

"I didn't mean to say—"

"But you did, Tales, so tell me."

"You just got out of the hospital. You just—"

"Look, Tales, I'm gonna tell you a little secret about men, okay?" I nod. "After a blow job, ending the way the one you gave me did, a man is on cloud ninety-nine for a good half hour. I'll be pissed off soon enough, so right now," he pauses and smirks, "you should suck it up, okay? Talk to me."

I don't want to say any more, so I lean down and kiss him.

"I'm going now. Remember, Mads doesn't get to be part of this" —I motion between us—"*thing,* okay?"

"Whatever," he rolls his eyes and leans back.

I stand up and walk out, saying, "Text me if you need me."

"I plan on it."

***

After helping with dinner preparation, I decide to give Madison, Memphis, and their mom some time alone. I go into the guest room, lie back on the bed, and look at my new phone. I'm not going to lie and say I hate it, because I don't. I love it.

I have a message from Jane, my school roommate, one of the few numbers I recognize. I click on the green app and it opens.

Are you in Florida?

Yep. How are you? I type out.

Are u prego?

Holy cow! What?

NO! What are you talking about?

STD lead singer? You and him. I swear it was you in the picture on Twitter.

No. Memphis is my best friend's brother, and NO. Still no.

Maybe you should get that way. He's hot!

I don't reply. I do get on Twitter and search

Memphis.

@thelocofamily tweets @stdrock1 MB, she's not your type. #rockmebaby #foreversteel

@clofton1 tweets @stdrock1 MB #rockerbabyonboard gimme 1! #foreversteel

@m_migliaccio tweets @stdrock1 MB, is she even from #jerseyshore?! #foreversteel

@ TE1998 tweets @stdrock1 MB, you + me = screaming O, not screaming baby. #foreversteel

@michelledrew962 tweets @stdrock1 MB, I'll rock you regardless! #foreversteel

Pregnant! Dear Lord. *Memphis, you ass!* Thank God my mother doesn't have Twitter. I wonder if his mom does.

I keep reading through the feed.

@nikkirives1 tweets @stdrock1 MB, YOU ARE SO NOT @ZacEfron ... but you are hot. I'd swallow. #foreversteel

@triciaann322 replies under the thread

@stdrock1 MB, even hotter than him. I'd try anal. #callme #foreversteel

@mischellyb tweets @stdrock1 MB, my pussy, ur face.

@lita08 tweets @stdrock1 MB, saw you at LIV. #yourockedhisface Get well dome *<3 #foreversteel*

@Jeana05816262 tweets @stdrock1 MB, #getwelldome hahahahaha #imin #foreversteel

@DannielleJeffer tweets @stdrock1 MB, Get well <3 #foreversteel

@ ttantonelli tweets @stdrock1 MB, is the news true? If yes, give me one night before baby. #justonenight #foreversteel

The bedroom door opens and Memphis walks in, locking it behind him.

"What are you doing?"

"The guys convinced Mom and Mads to go out on the boat." He smirks. "I just took a pill, so I was gonna try to convince you to do a little—"

I hold up the phone. "Do you know what they're saying?" That makes him stop.

"Who?"

"Your gaggle of groupies on social media."

He sits down next to me. "Haven't been on since you got here." He runs his hand through his hair before he takes the phone and looks at it, "Oh, wow, I'm having a baby, and I am hotter than Zac Efron. Not bad." He laughs. "No pictures, that's a plus if that's what you're worried about it."

I take it and scroll through. "At jamiesexton1 posted a picture … of her panties." I shake my head. "She says 'no STDs, but my panties are soaked'."

"Is that so?" He laughs.

"And @lizziestevens wants four STDs at once."

"She's not fucking around, huh? Just going for it." He takes the phone and throws it on the bed, then kisses me.

Soft, wet, and urgent lips cover mine. He sucks on my lower lip, then runs his tongue across mine.

"I'm not gonna try to fuck you, Tales," he says as he holds my bottom lip between his teeth. "Just wanna do some of this and talk."

"Mmm-hmm," I moan.

He pushes against me with his chest so I am lying down on my back, and he is holding himself up with one arm.

After he explores my mouth with his tongue and ignites that part of me that only he has, I pull back and push against his chest.

"How about you lie down?"

His eyes are dopey and his smile is sloppy, but he is beautiful and makes me—for the first time in my life—feel that I am, too.

"You think you can keep me down?"

"Wouldn't want to." I kiss him as I turn him so he is the one lying down.

"No?" I shake my head from side to side. "Why not, sweet cheeks? I wanna keep you down."

I smile. "I wouldn't mind it for twenty minutes or so."

His hand covers his chest. "Wow."

I grin, thinking I just pulled off some naughty talk and he laughs.

"Tales, twenty minutes is for teenage boys and married men if their wives are lucky. I gotta come at least once and get my cardio in. Forty-five minute minimum for this ride."

"Is that so?" I laugh as I lie across his chest.

"It is. I swear. Scouts honor and all that good stuff. You wanna try it out?"

"I do, but I think you have about ten minutes in you before you fall asleep."

"Not gonna lie, I'm feeling tired as fuck."

"Then go to sleep."

He looks at me more seriously now, fighting to stay awake. "I really, really like you, Tales."

"I really, really like you, too."

"I really do, though. I'm not kidding around."

His eyes close for a minute, and I see him fighting sleep before he half opens his eyes and smiles. "Emerald City. I wanna live there, you know."

"Yeah, I kind of like Care-a-lot better."

"I care-a-lot about you, Tales. Never hurt you." His eyes close. "Never."

I watch him sleep for a long time. I just lie with my head on his chest and watch him.

I would pinch myself, but I know it's not a dream. I know, when I leave here, he is going on tour with all those … women, like … I grab my phone and look at Twitter. @lauriesuz, @rhik1986, @pitjada, @harleygirl105, @daydeamin_nerd, @mamabear824, @melissaq824 @TiltheLastpage, @NEPatriots4ever,@AmyD159, @xsandyra, @momsnaughtyplay, @Fallowill79, @mambrum78, @hwngirl109, @tcoleman1210, @richellgg, @CasBraithwaite, @rholub1, @melissagratton1, @ajsbookreviews…

I can't keep looking at all the women's tweets, women who would do anything—including seducing a sexy, talented, half-drugged, and injured rock star by giving him oral sex in a Miami mansion—to try to gain his attention and affections. All those women who … are just like me.

I could never compete.

Not ever.

He groans and moves beneath me. I am sure I am making him uncomfortable. Even though I would like to stay like this for as long as I possibly can, I move so he can rest and recover because Memphis Black is about to become a rock legend of epic proportions.

My eyes travel down his body and I sigh. Definitely epic proportions.

I take my phone and click on the mail icon, trying to distract myself. I enter my email information, log in, and find thirty-eight emails. One is in response to an ad I answered. The subject reads, '*When can you start?*'

I read through the message and smile. It's a paid gig, twelve weeks dancing with a traveling dance company. They also offer me an instructor position at one of their schools when the tour is over. The more students I have, the more I make.

I keep reading and see that they are very impressed with the fact that I attended Julliard and offer me a thirty thousand dollar a year position with health care and the possibility of retirement, should they decide to keep me past the six month mark.

I respond immediately since the email was dated three days ago.

With thirty thousand dollars, I can afford to get a bigger apartment for my mother and me as long as I ride the train into the city every day, and I will. I will do it because I take responsibility for my actions, even if I can't ever divulge my darkest secret, my biggest sin.

I wake up, seeing Mads looking at me funny, and not funny as in ha, ha either. She looks kind of pissed. I look around for Tally, who is curled up at the foot of the bed in a little ball, sound asleep. Crap, I fell asleep in their room.

"Don't be like him, Memphis," Madison says quietly.

"Huh?"

"Like Dad."

"You serious right now, Mads?" I'm beyond pissed right now and in some serious fucking pain. Then I sit up quietly and shake the urge to pat POW! She's got to be drained, too.

Mads puts her finger over her lips, telling me to be quiet and nods to the door.

Begrudgingly, I walk out and stop when she walks out the door.

"Why was the door locked?" She sneers.

"How the hell do I know?" I ask.

"She deserves more. She is kind and—"

"Why don't you just ask me what it is you've already got concocted up in that head, Mads?"

"Have you slept with her?" she spits out.

"You know we've slept together. She's in there

now, sleeping," I emphasize the word sleeping.

"You know what I mean, Memphis," she says in an angry, yet sad tone. "Did you fuck Tally?"

"No." She looks at me like I'm full of shit. "Never been a liar, Madison, and again, no, I haven't fucked, banged, stuck my dick in her—"

"Fine," she says, shaking her head. "Now answer one more question."

"Then you'll leave me alone about it, Mads. Not another word, understand?"

"Yes."

"Then shoot."

"Do you wanna?"

"Fuck, yes," I say without hesitation. "She's beautiful and good and—"

"She's good; don't forget that."

"Never could. Now how about you answer me a question?"

"Shoot," she throws my word back at me.

"Which one of my band mates do you wanna fuck?"

"Every single one of them." There is no hesitation in her answer, and it's like a knife to the gut. "Don't ask questions you don't want the honest answer to, Memphis."

"Lose the 'tude, Gertrude. I am warning you now: you fuck one and I am going through your high school yearbook and banging every bitch in it." I grab the back of her head, pull it toward me, and give her a loud, sloppy kiss because I know she hates it. Then I walk away.

"Pig."

"Oink, oink, Mads. Oink fucking oink," I say

as I think, *just like Dad*. "Now feed me. I'm fucking starving."

I walk around the corner, where Mom eyes me suspiciously. "Good evening, beautiful lady." I give her a one-armed hug and kiss her cheek.

"Did you have a nice nap?" she asks, giving me the mom eye. It's like the stink eye, but for moms.

"Yes. And, Mom, I'm not banging Tales."

"Sit and eat," she says, wiping her hands on the kitchen towel. "No more talk like that, and be nice to your sister."

"She started it." I know I'm whining, and when I hear snickering and look over, I see the entire band trying not to laugh. "Mind your business."

Tales is quiet when she and Madison walk out. She's even more off than she was before. I promised I wouldn't say anything to Madison, but I hoped she would. Girls need to talk to each other and shit.

After dinner, I get another pill, which makes me really tired immediately. When no one is looking, Tales sets a bottle of water beside me, not just once, but three times. I give her a wink. She looks around to make sure no one sees it, and then we go about our business.

Our business is kind of boring in all actuality. Finn is spending most of his time hunched over a notebook, writing, and Billy is playing guitar. He's not bad at it, either. River—well, River is like a little cockroach. He scurries away when Mom walks in a room, like she's a damn burst of light, and trust me, she's not. She is all gloom and doom, and when I get ahold of that motherfucker, he's gonna see darkness for sure. Mads and Tales talk. Well, Mads talks; Tales interjects once in a while. As much as I strain to hear what is being said, I can't. Then I fall asleep.

***

I wake up in my room, where Tales is standing beside the bed, looking at me.

"You taking a walk again, Tallia?"

She shakes her head and pulls her nightshirt over her head.

"You know what you're asking for?" I ask as my dick hardens immediately.

She nods and drops her shorts.

"Say something so I know for damn sure you're awake, sweet cheeks."

With her voice full of desire, she asks, "Do you have a condom?"

"Would it offend you if I said I had enough to last for a long fucking time?"

She shakes her head, crawling up onto the foot of the bed as I reach over and grab a condom out of the nightstand.

I rip it open with my teeth and roll it on.

"You sleep naked all the time?" she asks as she straddles my thighs.

"Only when I know there is something I want that wants me as badly."

"Right," she says as she reaches up and takes me in her hands.

"This isn't how I wanna rock with you, Tales. I want a little more control."

"You want me to stop?" she asks as she strokes me.

Teasing, taunting, and not at all the Tally I knew growing up, but she is not a kid anymore. She is all woman.

I sit up and grab her hair, tugging it so Emerald City is shining in the moonlight coming through the window. I kiss her, lick her, and like always, she tastes addictive, more so every time.

I let go of her hair in favor of gripping her ass and pulling her up against me. "My show, Tales. I'm gonna rock you my way."

"Please," she says, wrapping her legs around me, and then her hands fist in my hair.

I love and hate this. I want her on her back. I want her on the wall. I want her ass in both my fucking hands. Right now, though, I'll take her any way I can get her.

I reach between us and rub my cock against her hot, soaked opening and push in.

"Fuck!" I roar. "Fuck fuckity fucking shit, you're tight, Tally. So fucking tight."

She doesn't say anything, only bites my shoulder as I push in more. "Fuck, I need like a shoehorn or some motherfucking—"

"More," she says, and hell yes, I give her more.

Her body shakes as she bites down harder.

"Sweet cheeks, I don't want to hurt you. You're soaked, I wrapped, and —"

"More," she growls at me.

I push in farther, then reach between us and play with her clit. She pushes against me and whimpers.

"Memphis, please just—"

I grip her ass, flip her over, and I know I am

smashing her into the sheets until I can get my good arm to hold my weight.

"Three, two …" I can't take it anymore. I want in, and I take it.

She cries out my name as if singing praises to the stars.

"You okay?"

"No. God, it's … it's …"

"Yours, Tales." I roll my hips, stretching her because she is so tight I am ready to burst from days of need and the pressure. "Relax, sweet cheeks. Feel; don't think."

I'm fucking this up. She is inexperienced, and the only foreplay I performed was this afternoon.

I roll to my side and bring her leg over my hip. "Sorry." I kiss her neck, her cheeks, and then her mouth. I suck on her tongue, reaching around to grip her ass. I spread her wide, and thank fuck she's flexible. I rub my finger around the back entrance of her pussy, and she moans.

"Good, isn't it?"

"Yes." She kisses me now, sucking my tongue like she did my cock earlier.

I grip her ass and guide it back and forth slowly, making sure not to give her too much or too little. Her muscles inside relax as I begin to thrust in and out, taking her further when I feel she's ready.

"That's so fucking good, Tallia. So. Fucking. Good." My dick is now sliding in and out easily as I fuck her slowly, but still give it to her hard.

"Yes," she moans. "Oh, yes."

I love the sounds she makes when I am almost

all the way in. It's like I am stealing her breath.

"Take me how you want me, Memphis. I want you to."

"I'll take it just like this. Fuck, Tales, my jam is usually harder, faster, but this, this is fucking heaven. I am inside the closest thing to heaven I'll ever feel. You … Fuck, Tales, you are the closest thing to—"

"Oh, God."

I feel her walls contract and squeeze me.

"Come for me, Tales. Come for me now and then do it again."

We rock, we sway, we stop, we kiss, and then we start all over again.

"I don't ever want out. I'm in so deep, I don't ever want out."

Gently, she pushes me so I roll to my back, and she follows, my dick never leaving her. I have one hand behind me, resting on a pillow, and the other spreading her so I can see her tight, little pussy milking my cock.

I run my thumb between her folds and press her little, pink clit. She whimpers, so I do it again and again. Each time, she rides me harder and faster until she is finally exhausted. Then she leans down, and I cup her perfect little B cups and bounce her up and down. I pinch her nipple, and she grips my hand with both of hers, holding on as she falls apart on top of me.

"Can't hold back when you're riding me like that, Tales," I warn her. "I'm gonna come, Tales."

"Me, too," she pants. "Oh, God, again."

My cock twitches, and I grunt as the force of

my orgasm sends aftershocks through her. "Fuck. Oh, yeah, fuck!"

I slowly bring her down onto me. She lies there, head to chest, bodies moist with sweat, and panting like we just ran a 5K.

"Best I ever had, Tales." If I had a gold star to give her I would.

"You, too," she pants.

After a few minutes, she tries to sit up, but I hold her down.

"No."

"No?"

"No, just stay right like that," I don't want her to leave.

"Okay."

***

I wake up to pain and an empty bed. She wore my ass out, and I liked it. She gave me the pill Mom left on my nightstand after round two. Either she was too exhausted to deal with me or she knew I was in pain before I did. Either way, I had Tallia Annabelle Priest for two rounds, the second even better than the first. And right now, I am waiting for round three. Maybe the boys will take Mom and Madison out on the boat again.

I grab my phone and shoot her a text.

Good morning, sweet cheeks. When can you come back in here? I miss your ass already.

Then I put a flower emoji and hit send.

I hear a phone sound off, sit up, and look across the bed. Her phone is on my nightstand.

I laugh because I now have even more confirmation that I indeed fucked her brains out last night.

I get up and decide to take a shower, secretly hoping she comes in to get her phone and decides to join me.

After the disappointing shower, I walk out into the great room where Mom is sitting on the couch.

"No, I don't want to discuss it. The kids know, Dale. I won't pretend anymore, okay?" I hear him yelling and want to tear his head off, but Mom is being so strong. "Well, I'm pretty sure our son and Tally have something going on." His voice is loud again; however, I can't hear a damn thing he's saying. "Really, Dale? Is that all you care about, you self-centered, self-indulgent, prick? You know what? Screw you. You go right ahead and live whatever way you want. I'll continue taking care of the two people who matter the most to me." I hear him cut her off. "I'm done lying for you. You made your bed; now lie in it." She hangs up, then pulls her knees up and hugs them as she cries softly into them.

"Mom?" She jumps at my voice and looks up, startled. "You okay?"

"Sorry you had to hear that."

"No, I'm sorry you're going through this." I sit next to her on her right and wrap my arm around her, hugging her. "Fuck him. He never believed in me, anyway. I will take care of all of us, you understand?"

"I'm your mom; it's my job to take care of—"

"You take care of you. I've got the rest. Things

are changing. I've got us now."

We sit for a while, and as much as I want to tear Dad's head the fuck off for doing this to her, I want more to become the man she raised. And she didn't raise a fucking piece of shit. She raised me.

"Morning," Madison says as she walks out and looks around.

"I'm gonna have breakfast delivered." I grab the phone from my pocket and dial the staff number. "Morning, sunshine," I greet over the phone. "How about breakfast for seven? Starving—"

"Six," Madison whispers.

"Yes, seven." I look at Mads, wondering how the hell she graduated when she can't add for shit.

"Tally left this morning, so six," she says, rubbing her eyes.

"Ha, ha. Very—"

"She did," Mom whispers. "She didn't tell you?"

"Six," I say with more of a bite than intended. "Yes, I'm sure."

I hang up and try to take slow breaths, count some fucking stars, look off into the distance, anything that will calm me down, but I am pissed.

"Are you pissed?" Madison looks a bit shocked.

I shake my head. "Just think it's odd she didn't say goodbye."

Mads yawns. "She didn't want to wake you."

"She left her phone," I say, knowing it comes off pissy.

"You also know how she hates to feel like a

charity case."

"Why the hell would she feel like a charity case? And is she that fucking stupid that she'd travel without a fucking phone? She's a fucking girl, by herself, no phone and—"

"She grabbed one of those pre-pays on the way. Chill out."

Chill out? Are you fucking kidding me? Chill out?

This is what devastation feels like; this is how Tally makes me feel and how I feel for her. This is how you're supposed to feel, and those other women meant nothing.

How am I going to be better than my dad and get Tally to understand?

Fuck, she better not have used me. Would Tally do that shit? Why the fuck would I question it, she's not here now. She didn't even say goodbye for fuck sake.

"I need a pill." I need the shit in my head to go away.

"You need to eat something first," my mother scolds.

"Right. Fine. And when is my doctor's appointment? 'Cause I also need to get back to work. I have a tour to prepare for."

A week after I returned was the first time I heard from Memphis. He told me he was on his way home, and we needed to chat. I told him we didn't, and he needed to shine. I threw my phone away the next day and got a new one. No, I couldn't afford it, but it wasn't an indulgence, either; it was a necessity.

Necessities should also be categorized. Although I needed new ballet slippers because mine were so terribly worn that my feet ached, I needed a thirty dollar pre-pay more. The soul's health was much more important than the feet's. Feet don't take as long to heal.

A week after his first call, he showed up at the old apartment. He was angry, so angry at me, and I tried so hard to make him understand that I left for him. I wanted him to focus on his career, but he didn't buy it and demanded an explanation. When I wouldn't give him that, he took something else—my lips.

I have decided lips are even more intimate than a vagina. His kiss was impossible to pull away from, so I didn't. He did, and then he told me when

I came to my eff'ing senses to call him, because *he hadn't changed his fucking number*.

I smiled and hugged him. "Soar, Memphis," I whispered, then turned and walked into the apartment, leaving him in the hall.

He banged on the door for a good ten minutes, and I fell to my knees and cried.

Crying is soul cleansing. Well, ugly crying like I did is soul and sinus cleansing, though not something anyone should ever do in front of another human being they love or want to return your love.

A week later, he called my new number from Madison's phone.

"Tell me what the fuck I did. You owe me that much."

My response: "I owe you even more than I can ever give you, Memphis. Forget about me. Move on knowing I will always have a little girl crush on the boy next door. Soar, Memphis."

Apparently, that made him angry. He tried to call back several times, and he left messages, a lot of them. Each one made me cry, each breaking my spirit, and each making me realize that Karma really is a bitch.

A day later, I am walking around the corner to my apartment, and he is leaning against the brick wall.

I force sunshine. I smile. I dig down deep and do what I was raised to do: be polite, be kind, and be a good girl.

"My hand is healing." He pushes off the wall. "I can use it now."

"I knew it would. That's a God-given talent you have." I smile, though the threat of tears is burning my chest and moving up my throat.

"You aren't talking to Madison anymore, either?" he says, as his eyes rake my body from head to toe.

I swallow down my tears and give him more sunshine. "Just been busy."

He looks in my eyes. "What the hell happened? For the life of me, I can't figure it out. Did you not come to my bed, strip naked, and fucking climb me, basically begging for my cock? Tell me, what the fuck did I do?" He beats his left hand against his chest, and I see the pain it causes him. He yells again, "Tell me, goddamn you!"

He draws his fist back as if he's going to strike the brick wall, and I yell, "No!" Then I grab it and cry.

"Tales, come the fuck on. Talk to me."

I strangle the sob and shake my head, releasing his hand. That's when he grabs my face and pulls it to his.

"Talk. To. Me."

When I close my eyes, he grabs me by the ass and lifts me, walking us to the door of my apartment building. "Your mom home?"

"No."

"Apartment number?"

"No."

"Fine, then right here." He pushes me back against the wall under the stairwell, pulls a condom out of his pocket, and tears it open with his teeth. "You fucked anyone else?"

"No," I cry. "No, I haven't."

"You gonna tell me no?" he asks as he unzips his jeans and sheaths himself. "Tales, say the word no, or I am gonna give you something I know you want. I can fucking smell your desire. I can see it lighting up in Emerald City. You know who the fuck I am?"

"Memphis," I answer as my head drops to his shoulder while he rips my panties and pushes, not one, but two fingers inside me.

I cry out as his fingers move and twist swiftly in and out, feeling the burn immediately.

"No. I'm the fucking Wizard of Oz, Tales." He rubs himself against my wet flesh, then pushes in. "The wizard controls Emerald City, you feel me?"

When he shoves inside of me again, I immediately feel an orgasm's tug.

"God, yes." I bite his shoulder as he rams himself in and out of me over and over as I tremble, shake, and contract everywhere.

He doesn't stop; he fucks me hard and unforgiving as he sucks on my neck and bites it harder than ever before.

"You." He rams into me again. "Don't." And again. "Get." And again. "Two." And again. "Hours." And again. "Of my cock." And Again. "Until I know." And Again. "Why you're doing this!" He growls right before he comes apart.

His dick twitches inside of me as he comes. I feel each burst, absorb each thrust, take it because I want him so badly.

As he sets me on my feet and leans in, I am shaking and breathless.

I lean up to kiss him, but he pulls back.

"You don't get my mouth again, Tales. Yours is for either sucking my cock or answering my questions." He pulls the condom off, takes my hand, and drops the used rubber into it. "Get on the damn pill. I'm sick of using these fucking things." He pushes his thick, semi erect dick inside his black jeans and walks away.

On shaking, post orgasm legs, still quaking inside, I walk down the hall and toss the used condom in the trash, walk up three flights of stairs, trip into my apartment, and then fall onto my bed and cry myself to sleep.

***

A month later, I walk out of the dance studio and onto Broadway. If I hurry, I'll catch the early train back to Hoboken and get home to soak my feet.

I am exhausted. Since my return a month ago, I picked up two classes a day at Classic's Dance Studio. Six days a week before and after, I dance with my tour crew, and we practice anywhere from five to seven hours, five, sometimes six, days a week.

Mom and I have a two bedroom that I love. She was against it at first, because it was more than her social security check from dad's death every month, and she felt it was indulgent. I told her a moderate indulgence was acceptable.

Everything should be in moderation, even indulgences. Anything else is either gluttonous and will fill you until you burst or starves the soul and kills you. That's my new way of looking at life and also the only reason I can still look in the mirror.

When I round the corner, I see Madison. She looks like she wants to smile, like she's ready to burst. Her long, straight, black hair is piled high on her head, and her eyes are covered with some ultra-chic sunglasses that are too big for her face but look amazing, regardless.

I stop in front of her and give her sunshine, and then I give her rain.

She reaches out and pulls me tight. "I am so mad at you right now, Tales. You're breaking his heart."

"I just can't be with him. I just want him to do his thing and become who he is meant to be."

"And what about you?" She looks around. "Is this who you are meant to be? Where you are meant to end up? Fuck, Tales, from Julliard to …"

"Broadway." I shrug. "I really like teaching. I'm content." I wipe the tears from my face. "What about you?"

"I'm not ready to go back to school. I think I'm going to take a year off, maybe do some online stuff. I just want to be with my mom right now. You know how it is." She points to the building. "You like it here?"

I nod because, if I tell her in words, it'll feel more like a lie than it is.

"Tales." She looks dead serious. "You have to talk to him. He's doing some really fucked up things lately." She laughs nervously.

"Like …?" She shakes her head. "Not drugs,

right? He's not—" I can't even ask if he's addicted.

"Well, he really likes his pain pills, and he actually fell asleep during recording last month."

"When last month?" I wonder if it was before or after our encounter.

She smirks and shakes her head. "The stairwell day." I gasp. "Tales, he isn't really quiet about the way he feels. He's also adamant that he's gonna wait you out."

"Wait me out?" He hasn't let go. Immediately, I feel happy, but I shouldn't. And, oh, my, goodness, he told her!

She looks at me, not answering. After a few minutes, she sighs.

"Look, come have dinner with me."

"My mom …" I start.

"Don't give me that shit. It's Wednesday; she's at a woman's church thing, isn't she?"

"Madison, it really is best if we just—"

"I know, okay? I fucking know, and I'm sorry, but shit happens, and—"

"What do you know?"

"About your dad. About my dad. It wasn't a woman in his bed at that hotel, Tales. I didn't see his face, but fuck … Do I even need to keep going? I mean, it's really not something a girl wants to remember."

"You knew, and you didn't tell me!" I yell at her. She looks stunned.

"You didn't tell me, either. It's really not a fucking conversation you ever expect to have with anyone, let alone your best friend whose father is a fucking minister and apparently a bottom—" I cover her mouth with my hand and scowl.

"Shut your face," I hiss at her.

She starts laughing and hugs me. "Oh, Tales. To think, we could have been step—"

"You really have to be quiet. Imagine the scandal. Imagine what they would say about Memphis."

"Oh, my God, that's why you won't admit you're in love with him. That's why you're pushing him away. Tales, that's so gallant of you, but you're the chick. Let the one with the dick figure that out."

It feels good that someone else knows, but it shouldn't. It should feel good that it is Mads and not a random stranger, but it doesn't. It feels awful that Memphis might have to face this, but if I open my mouth he will…He will hate me.

"Does your mom know?"

"Not sure. You're the only person I've talked to. Does yours?"

"No, absolutely not. I think she would die."

"Or join a cult," Mads says, smiling sadly.

"Or that." I smile back in the exact same way.

"Come to dinner with me?"

I nod. "I would really, really like that."

"Me, too. I've missed you."

"I've missed you, too." I just didn't think I should be allowed to feel that way after keeping the secret from her, but she did the same. What a mess. What a complete and total mess.

"I've missed you more than my brother has."

"I've heard from him more," I joke

"I don't swing that way, so back off." She laughs as she jumps in her little, red Beemer.

I get in the other side and close the door. "New ride?"

"Father is feeling guilty."

"Well, guilt looks good on him," I attempt to joke.

"Your father didn't," she throws back at me, and I fall into a laughing fit. Both of us do. "Hashtag: white girl problems."

"Oh, wow, we're like the Kardashians."

"Oh, fuck no, we aren't! Hell to the no. But Brody Jenner … Damn, I would like to cry on that shoulder. You know, bond over a little dysfunction and then get all dysfunctional in his sound booth. He could spin a record. I could spin on him."

"You gotta keep it a secret for Memphis." I state the obvious.

"You love him, Tales." And so does she.

"I think I do." That's another lie. I know I do. Without a doubt, I know I do.

"It wasn't a question. You love him, Tales."

I shake my head. "I don't want to. I really, really don't want to."

"Why?"

I look at her and roll my eyes. "Why would you even ask that?" He's going to hate me when he finds out, I say to myself.

"Because he loves you, too."

"Did he say that?"

She looks over at me. "No, I did, and no one knows him like I do."

I nod and she hugs me.

I sit in the sound booth at Forever Four in a fog, wondering what the fuck happened to me. *Soar, Memphis*, runs through my mind like a fucking freight train. How does one do that?

"You sound good, Memphis." X-man walks in and sits behind me. "'Bang Bang' is a fucking epic jam. It's your first chart topper."

"We'll see," I say with a nod. "We all set here for the day?"

"You're kidding, right? You have two more songs to get nailed down." He shakes his head. "Let me give you some advice …"

"Not being rude, man, but I don't fucking need any. I've got this."

"Really? What is it that you've got? No, don't answer that. Let me tell you what you've got." He stands up and leans against the wall. "You have one of the best voices in the industry, yet that guitar is more important to you. Your raw sex appeal that makes the girls fucking crazy, second best in the industry—"

"Second to who?" I half-laugh, half-snarl.

"Me," he says as if it's gospel.

I can't help laughing, and so does he.

"You lead this crew from the front. You don't get pissed when River gets fucked up like Finn does; you don't get pissed when Finn doesn't talk for days because he is so deep in his head. He is a total D-bag to everyone around, like River and Billy are. And you don't get pissed when Billy spouts off all the knowledge in his fucking enormous head and makes everyone around him feel fucking stupid, including me." He chuckles, shaking his head. "You are the lead here; don't get hung up on a set of strings."

"Not gonna feel natural on stage without it."

"Believe it or not, I didn't snatch you up because of your ability to finger fuck the six strings. It's the voice and your natural leadership ability."

"And because your wife—"

He glares at me. "My wife what?"

"She found me at Rockin' Joes."

"She knows talent." He grabs his package. "And she is mine forever."

I nod. "Forever Steel."

"You're part of that, too, man, although you put your own twist on it." He tries to look pissed, but I know the name amuses the shit out of him. "You're family now, and that means, if you need a kick in the ass, you'll get it."

"That mean I can get the ink, too?"

He laughs and nods. "You want the ink?"

"Every one of my tats means something to me. And with each one—"

"You gained some sort of clarity or a moment of self-realization."

I nod. "Exactly."

He muses for a minute before nodding. "I could use some fresh ink, maybe a piercing to surprise my Irish." He looks at his watch. "Fuck it, let's blow off and head down to Forever Steel."

We walk out to where Taelyn is holding their son.

"I'm gonna go with Memphis down to Forever Steel. He's gonna get some ink."

"And you?" She smiles at him.

"I'll surprise you."

She laughs and nods. "I'll see you soon."

"Prepare yourself, Irish," I hear him whisper as he bends down and kisses her, then kisses the baby.

"Will do." She blushes. Fucking blushes, just like Tallia Annabelle Priest.

I can't believe I've left her alone for so damn long. Fuck, I can't believe I haven't gotten laid in that long.

But I can't. I'm now like that little chick with the golden hair; except, I'm not sampling porridge. I don't need to know which one is just right. I already fucking found it.

"You ready, man?"

"Yeah." I nod.

When we walk into the shop, I look around. The storefront tells a story of Xavier's family. The outside doesn't match the inside, not one bit.

The white walls display thin, black, framed works of art that are lit with track lighting. They are not pictures of tattoos, but art. One wall is full of black and white photos of people and places. It's unbelievable how the artist caught stolen glances, private moments, and older buildings that no doubt tell stories of history and life.

The next wall holds paintings that pretty much sing. Each showcases an instrument or a stage. I notice X-man wearing a fedora and playing a saxophone in one.

"That's you, isn't it?"

"Yeah, seems like a lifetime ago." He pats my back. "Let me get Rico."

I look at another wall. There are white, lighted pedestals lined up against it, all holding sculptures. Nothing whimsical or cute. Whoever did this was in a dark place. I look at the dates. It's the same year as hurricane Sandy hit the shore. I wonder if this twisted steel is from the havoc that bitch wreaked.

There are more pictures on another wall—photos and paintings—and I recognize all the people in them. Cyrus, Tara, and their two kids; Justice, Truth, and at their feet is the ugliest dog I have ever seen; Jase, Carly, and their girls, little Bell and Kiki; Zandor and Bekah, and she is on her knees next to him; Xavier, Taelyn, and baby Patrick in front of the Red Socks stadium, him and the baby sporting Yankee's gear, but she isn't. Next there is Abe and Nikki; someone who looks familiar; a woman in a vineyard; and Sabato, whom I have seen around Forever Four a handful of times; and the girl, Mel, who looks at him like he's a god. The shit kicker is he's looking at her like that in this picture, too. Then there is Momma Joe, surrounded by all of them.

"Right there is Forever Steel, man," Xavier says from behind me.

"Who's this?" I ask, pointing to the vineyard

picture.

"My cousin Dominic and his wife, right before she started showing."

"Showing what?"

"The kid growing inside of her." He laughs. "Come on, man; he's ready for you."

When I walk into the back room, Rico stands up. "You sure about this?" he jokes.

"I'm sure." I pull my shirt off and lie down.

"The pain is only temporary," Xavier says, patting my shoulder.

"But the commitment is forever, man." Rico winks. "You sure you want to commit to this?"

"Yeah, I am."

"Just like the brothers?"

"No," I answer. "I'm gonna rock it my way."

"I knew you would, man." Xavier laughs. "See you on the other side."

Xavier leaves as I roll to my stomach. "Across my shoulders. Forever faded, grey in the background. Steel bold and black."

"Bold and black is pretty damn close to heaven, man. Throw in some curves, and I am on it like white on rice." Rico smirks.

"We ain't just talking ink, are we?" I laugh.

"No, man, we ain't."

I lie down and feel the sting of the needle. I don't go to the place in my head I've gone to before. No hiding from the pain. I feel it. I want to feel every damn inch of it. I embrace the pain, relish in it. I accept it, and I appreciate it.

"I want an emerald centered below it, tinted green. Light enough so that, when I want to add to it, the addition won't get lost."

He chuckles. "Whatever you want, man."

"I may want something else, too."

"I get paid by the piece, and I got all night."

I walk out of Forever Steel with Xavier laughing.

"You didn't just drink the Kool–Aid, man; you fucking did a keg stand on that bitch."

"Thanks for bringing me. I needed that." I nod.

"We all do once in a while." I look down at his arms covered in ink. "Some of us more than others."

"Yeah, true, true."

My phone rings and his immediately follows.

"The wife." He holds up the phone.

I hold up mine. "The queen."

"See you tomorrow."

"I'll be in early," I tell him as I walk away.

"Sup, Mads?" I answer my phone. She wants to see me. "Yeah, I'll be there in twenty."

***

I pull onto River Street and throw the keys to my new ride to the valet. Dad bought Mads a little, red Beemer, and she kept it. He bought me one, too, and I traded it in for an Escalade. It's identical to the one I drove in Miami where I purposely fucked with Tales because making her squirm was second best to fucking her raw. Now I know better. There isn't a second best to her, and no matter what the fuck is going on, I won't try to find out if there is for a long time.

"Keep it close. I won't be long."

I walk in and bee line it for the hotel bar, but as soon as I walk in, I see her sitting there, and she sees me, too. This is no surprise to her, though; it's not me waiting for an hour outside her apartment so I can remind her I'm still fucking breathing. This is her knocking the wind out of me, so I can't.

Madison turns and gives me a sad smile, and I shake my head as I walk up to her. I kiss her on the head, turning my back to Tales.

"Where's the car?"

"In the parking garage."

"No flat, huh?"

"No."

"So you lied to me to get me here." She shrugs. "Don't you think you should have given me a fucking heads up, Mads? Fuck."

She nods toward Tallia. "You gonna say hi to her?"

I turn and do my best to act unaffected as I give her a nod. "Tales."

"Hi," she whispers, her lower lip popping out a bit.

I look away before I can't. "So why am I here?" I ask Madison.

"Geesh, you don't have to be a fucking assh—"

"Madison, don't," Tally says sadly.

I look back at her.

"We need to talk."

"Yeah, well, I'm kind of not in a place to talk right now." I stare right at her pouty, little lips, remembering the last thing I said to her about them.

I think of her dad, hoping it keeps the impending erection at bay.

"I need to tell you something," she says, looking down at her hands. She's wringing the hell out of them, and quite frankly, I'm nervous.

"You pregnant?"

She smiles and shakes her head. She then lets out a cute as hell, nervous, little chuckle and looks up at me.

Emerald City has a storm brewing, and it ain't just a sprinkle.

I pull a barstool up and sit.

"First, promise me you won't hate me. Even if you do, tell me you don't so I don't have to live my life thinking any worse of myself than I already do," she says as the first tear falls.

"Keep talking, Tales, because right now, I'm ready to rip his fucking head off."

"Memphis, you asshole, she isn't fucking anyone."

I don't look at Madison. Quite frankly, I wish she would walk away and leave me alone with Tales. Whatever she says to push me away is gonna hurt, and I don't need the little queen to see that shit.

"Tales, she need to be here?" She nods. "Okay, so you need her for moral support? Just spill it, would ya?"

"I caught Dad in bed with someone when he visited me in Chicago."

"Right, our dad's a low life cheat. I get it."

"I caught my dad kissing someone right before I left for Julliard," Tales whispers.

"Seriously? Your dad was fucking around,

too? Tales, if that's what this is about … if you're worried all men are fucking scum, I can promise you—"

"It was your father," she whispers.

"The person I caught Dad with in Chicago was Tally's father."

I feel like I have just been punched in the gut. Like the blonde kid in the movie with the green lighted sword—Luke, that's his name—when he found out that fucked up black, robot-looking, evil thing was his father. Yeah, I know how the poor son-of-a-bitch felt.

"This is a joke, right?" It has to be. "This is a prank. This is—" I stop when Tales grabs my hand and shakes her head.

"I am sorry for what I did by not telling you."

I pull my hand back and stare at her. She's not fucking around.

I look at Mads. "You caught them playing hide the fucking salami?"

Tales giggles, and I whip my head around to glare at her.

"Sorry, it's just—" Then the storm hits. "I should have told her. I should have told you."

"But you didn't, because you wanted the fucking fantasy, just like every other fucking chick I've fucked." I stand up and throw a hundred on the bar. "I'm out."

I leave, feeling sick to my stomach, pissed off, I wanna destroy something! Then I feel a tug on my hand. Just by a touch, I know it's her.

"Don't walk away from me until I have given you the entire truth. If you're going to hate me, you're going to do it forever, but don't you walk—"

I turn, tug her arm, and then walk as quickly as I can to the entrance. People are starting to look, and I don't need that shit. Don't want it either. I wanna be left alone to process this, this fucking mess.

Outside, I give the valet my ticket.

"Give me just a minute, sir," he tells me.

"No, he's staying for dinner with his sister. Call me a cab."

My fucking jaw drops at her audacity.

"You think you get to tell me what to do, Tales?"

She shakes her head vigorously. "I don't know. I don't know what I am to you. I do know she's your sister, and she always will be, and …" She stops and grabs my hand. "Two minutes, that's all."

When she pulls hard at my hand, I decide to hear her out, just hear what she has to say. I want to know the what she thinks will make me hate her.

Once we're around the building and in the alley, she turns and looks at me. "After I saw them"—my stomach turns—"I kind of got angry and, I guess, confused, too, just like you right now. I … I'm sorry. I don't know how to say this. I mean, so what, right?" She drops my hand and throws hers in the air. "God, I am so selfish. I—"

Nope, I can't do this right now. "I need to leave."

"No! No, you don't." There is panic in her voice, and she is fisting her hair in her hands.

I hold back from comforting her because I

don't know how to process all of this.

"Mads … Mads knew and didn't tell, because she was so afraid you'd lose focus on tour. She was afraid your mother would fall apart, but Memphis, *she* fell apart. Mads fell apart, and she is still falling." She slaps her hands on her thighs and starts pacing back and forth. "None of this is fair, and she needs you, and you're gonna need her, too."

She spins on her heels and looks at me. "And you starting a tour … I mean, all press is supposed to be good press, but can you handle it, or will you have to prove your sexuality for all of the country?" She squeezes her eyes closed. "Not that it's any of my business, but please don't do that to yourself."

She takes in a deep breath. "I didn't know who to talk to. I couldn't talk to Mads, and I sure as hell couldn't talk to my mom, still can't. So I just shoved it down deep and let it soak. And, well"—she covers her face—"I got mad that I would never be able to think or even hope that maybe someday you would kiss me again for real and not just because you were drunk. I fantasized about that kiss for years, Memphis, and it just wasn't fair. God, I must sound so stupid to you." She resumes her pacing. "So I slept with Jones."

Hearing her say the name of some guy she banged pisses me off.

"I slept with him because I knew, at seven ten p.m. on Sunday night, my father would call."

I have no idea what the fuck that has to do with anything. I look at her as she peers up at me, Emerald City hidden behind a curtain of dark brown locks.

"I told Jones to answer my phone, and he did, and then … Well, then my father flipped, and I didn't deny what a sinner I was, because I didn't care. I didn't care, because everything he said to me was a lie. And then do you know what happened, Memphis?"

God, the need to comfort her is overwhelming. "I think so, Tales."

"He died. He died a week later of a heart attack because of me."

"He didn't die because of you."

"Did so." She starts pacing again. "So I'm a terrible person. Even worse, because then I agreed to a vacation, knowing damn well you'd be there, and I basically prayed you and I would … you know."

I needed a better fucking explanation to what she was talking about. Was it was revenge, was it the fucking fantasy? "Because I'm getting famous. Because I'm a bunch of chicks' fantasy, because—"

"Because you've been mine since the day you pushed Johnny Stone down when he was picking on me, then just kept walking. Because you always did things like that. You were merciless at times, but I always made myself think it was because maybe, just maybe, I was your fantasy, too. I know how stupid that sounds, but you were nice to me. You didn't judge me; you stuck up for me. When everyone else picked on my clothes, you complimented them. You watched cartoons with me and Madison. You still call my T-shirts vintage and make them seem cool, but they are not,

Memphis. They're hand-me-downs or thrift store finds. Did you know that the only clothes I have ever worn that were new are my underwear?"

I shake my head no in answer.

"In my very lonely childhood, you were ever-present. You were my fantasy first, so yes, yes, I knew. Hell, I even pretended I didn't know you were going to be there so Madison didn't see through me, because she has a tendency to do that, you know."

I nod.

"But when you came out with those two girls, all I could think about was my mother and how disappointed she would be in me, and I don't like to disappoint people; did you know that? Did you know that, Memphis?"

"Yeah, Tales, I knew that." Even as a kid, being the better dancer between her and Mads, she stepped aside and let Mads play lead in every little backyard production they ever gave my mom. Same thing with her parents, Tally toed the line. She was the perfect kid.

"Then I couldn't stop myself. I couldn't, because my fantasy—the Memphis who was always my knight in black leather and ink—said things to me that, even though I didn't know I wanted to hear them, affected me."

"Tales—"

"Please don't say anything. Just kiss me or push me against a wall or let me go down on my knees for you again, because I don't wanna think. I want to feel." She steps forward and grabs my shirt. I see her mustering up courage before she pushes herself up on her tiptoes and leans in.

"Can't kiss you, Tales." I step back regretfully.

"Then let me kiss you," her eyes and voice plead in unison.

"No, I can't allow that, either." Someday I will laugh at this, but not now.

She nods. "I understand. I do. I understand. I mean …" She turns her back to me, and I hate it. I want to see her eyes.

I grab her hand. "Look at me, Tales."

"I don't need you to make this okay for me. I just need you to be okay and accept my apology. I need you to soar."

"Turn the fuck around," I growl. "I won't soar alone, and I sure as fuck can't do it with you right this minute."

She does, very slowly, asking with a whisper, "Can you forgive me?"

"Tell me what you want from me."

"To forgive me."

"Done, but I need time to process it all. What else?"

She shakes her head, her face flushed red.

"Need time for that, too."

"I understand. Be happy, okay? Be happy and be safe."

"Tell me, Tales." I see it in her face, I just need to hear it and I really need her to say it.

"I did."

"Fuck that. Tell me the truth about us, Tales. At the very least, tell me the truth about what you want from me."

"Fine!" She slaps the tears now falling down

her face. "I want you to trust me and know I would never avoid telling you the truth again. And not just for you, for me, too, because it hurts right here." She holds her hand over her chest. "I wish I had kept you a fantasy because it hurts too much right here." She hits her chest harder now.

"Don't do that, Tales. Jesus." I grab both her hands in one of mine.

"I love you. I love you, and I want to be with you, and—"

"Don't you say that shit to me right now," I snap at her, and she looks scared. "Fuck!" Forever Steel equals forever fucked right now. Dammit!

"Sorry, but I had to tell you, or if you'll let me, I'll show you." She has just opened up completely to me, and I can do fuck-not about it.

"Can't let that happen now, either."

She nods and sniffs loudly. "Okay. I'm sorry. I just—"

I take her hand and shove it down the front of my pants. "Feel this, Tales, but be nice." I push her hand farther in, and she gasps.

"What happened to you? Do you have a—"

"I liked it, so I put a fucking ring on it."

"What?" She almost laughs the nervous laugh I enjoy so much.

I pull her hand away. "It's a dolphin"—I almost smirk—"topped with a prince. Google it then call me in about four to six weeks and tell me what you told me a few seconds ago.

"Fuck fuckity fuck!" I turn to walk away and stop. "Go eat dinner with my sister!" I bark "Fuck, Tales, I have to get out of here." I turn back and kiss her. Can't help myself, but it's quick. "Don't ever keep shit from me again."

"I won't, not ever."

Damn right you won't, I think. "Tales?"

"Yes?"

She is smiling, and I know she expects me to say the words back, but that's not going to happen right now. I have got to be pissed, or I'll never have the upper hand.

"Next time you see me, you'll be on your knees, and I'm gonna be so backed up you're gonna have to chew my come before you swallow it."

I Googled dolphin and prince as soon as I got home from dinner with Madison, which was a couple of hours later. We had a lot to talk about.

Offensive!

Intimidating!

Interesting …

And …

Intriguing.

Madison sends me a text three days later. Memphis doesn't.

It's a partial tour schedule.

STD AMERICAN TOUR

DATE	VENUE	LOCATION
SEPTEMBER 8TH	BBVA COMPASS	HOUSTON, TX
SEPTEMBER 9TH	TOYOTA STADIUM	DALLAS, TX
SEPTEMBER 16TH	AMWAY CENTER	ORLANDO, FL
SEPTEMBER 17TH	AMERICAN AIRLINES ARENA	TAMPA, FL
SEPTEMBER 18TH	PHILLIPS ARENA	ATLANTA, GA
SEPTEMBER 20TH	XCEL ENERGY CENTER	ST PAUL, MN
SEPTEMBER 22ND	RIVERBAND MUSIC CENTER	CLEVELAND, OH
SEPTEMBER 23RD	BLOSSOM MUSIC CENTER	CLEVELAND OH
SEPTEMBER 25TH	GILLETTE STADIUM	FOXBOROUGH, MA
SEPTEMBER 26TH	GLOBAL CITIZENS FESTIVAL	NEW YORK, NY
OCTOBER 3RD	BADER FIELD	ATLANTIC CITY, NJ

I swallow hard and have to sit down as I read over it, then send back a text.

That's amazing! He deserves this and so much more. Is his hand okay? Is he healing well? Is he resting? That schedule looks grueling.

She doesn't respond. I look at the phone for a good two hours, waiting.

There's a knock at the door, and I open it.

"Tales?" the deliveryman with a huge basket full of white Gerber daisies asks.

I nod and smile. I even laugh as I take them.

"Thank you so much." Then I hug him. Why? I have no idea.

"You do know they're not from me, don't you?" He looks confused.

"Yes, yes, of course I do. Sorry." I shut the door because he starts to look at me funny, and not funny as in ha, ha. Funny as in *creepy*.

I carry them to the table, set them down, and grab the card.

It reads:

> *Heads, you stop worrying. Tails, keep that shit up. It makes me happy. Either way, Tales wins- MB*

My mom comes in and sees the flowers and looks at me suspiciously.

"They're beautiful, right?" I ask.

"Yes. Who are they from?"

"MB, so it's either Madison or Memphis."

"Memphis Black?" She looks at me strangely, and I nod. "Be careful, Tallia. He lives in a much different world, honey."

A week passes, and the dance tour company hands out the travel schedule as we leave rehearsal. It's more than seventy-five percent West Coast cities. My knee-jerk reaction is to take a picture of it and text it to Madison, but right now, I have thirteen seven-year-olds who love ballet stretching and waiting for their class to start. They make my day brighter for sure. They actually make three days a week brighter, and they are my absolute favorite class to teach.

The hour flies by and ends with a circle, all holding hands, all smiling, and all ready and excited for the next day.

The last part of my day is my least favorite class, but it pays well. It's also three days a week, and an adult aerobic-dance class.

Nine hours of dance today, and I am exhausted. Exhaustion is something I welcome with open arms, though.

I walk out and punch the code to lock up for the night.

"Tallia?"

I look back to see where the raspy voice is coming from and see a blonde woman. She's beautiful, standing in front of a black town car.

"Can I help you?"

"I sure hope so. I've been watching you for the past couple days. Two of my dancers take your class. You're phenomenal." She steps forward and extends her hand; I shake it.

"Thank you."

"One of my dancers fell and fractured her

ankle during a practice last week. They mentioned you may be a perfect match to do a gig for a month, more if we mesh."

"Sounds intriguing, but I am already part of a dance team, and we're touring for three months."

"I'm not gonna beat around the bush here, but I do my homework. I know what they pay, and I can double it."

I look at her skeptically. "Nothing illegal?"

She smiles, which puts me at ease. "This isn't normal for me. I don't go looking for the talent, but when they talked you up, I had to make an exception. One month, double pay. Google me: I manage a band. When you see who I am, I know you'll want in. It's a good gig." She hands me a card. "Give Jane a call; I need a decision tomorrow. If you don't want in, I need to find someone fast."

I take the card. "Thank you."

"Double the pay, five hour days, and a fifteen hundred dollar bonus"—she looks down at my beat-up dance shoes hanging from my gym bag — "and I'll throw in a decent pair of shoes."

I start to walk away.

"Tallia?"

"Yes," I say, turning around.

"I don't need this getting out. There are people who love to talk shit about me, and I require anyone who works for me to sign a confidentiality agreement."

"Understood."

I finally make it home, thinking how nice it would be to buy a car and avoid the train. I normally don't mind, but the three days a week that are long days kill me.

Mom is asleep. She has a long weekend planned with her church group. She seems happy now. She is smiling again, spreading sunshine.

I hear a light knock on the door as I smell the flowers. I walk over and look through the peephole.

My heart skips a beat and then another. He looks beautiful … And now he's running his hands through his hair and turning around.

Quickly, I unlock the chain then the deadbolt, and I open the door.

"Hey," I say, trying not to act like I am over-the-moon to see him. He turns around.

"Hey, back," he says, looking down.

"Do you want to come in?" Dear God, he is beautiful even in cargo shorts, a tee shirt and that beanie.

"No." He shakes his head slowly and then finally looks at me.

"Did you come to tell me you hate me?" My voice betrays me, showing the pain from the thought. He looks at me like I'm crazy, which makes me feel stupid. "'Cause you could have just sent a text." I step out in the hall.

He sighs. "Did you get the flowers?"

"They are so beautiful. Thank you. Thank you so, so much." This is a good sign, right?

"They still alive?" His nose scrunches up as he runs his hand over his black beanie.

"Yeah."

He starts to take a step forward then stops himself. "They smell good, Tales?"

"You can come in and—"

"Nah." He shakes his head. He looks in my eyes and groans then slowly grazes down my body with his eyes, and I feel my nipples strain against my leotard. "Tales?"

"Yes?" I say as I step back against the wall, seeking its cool comfort on my very warm body.

"I'm gonna be touring for a long time." He may as well have thrown a bucket of ice water on me.

I open my eyes and look at him as I cross my arms in front of me.

He smirks, noticing the change in my demeanor. "You still gonna be here when I get back?"

"Is this where you want me to be, Memphis?" I feel my lip quiver. "Here?"

"Tales."

"Have you forgiven me yet?"

"Yeah. Have you forgiven yourself?" I shake my head. "His death wasn't your fault," he tries to tell me.

I blow upward, trying to cool my eyes to stop the tears, to keep myself together. I don't want to push him away by acting too needy.

Wanting to change the subject, I ask, "How is Madison?"

"Busy." He chuckles. "We put her on travel detail."

"Travel?"

"Find hotels, and book flights to tour cities. She works about thirty hours."

"Will she travel with you?" I ask.

"Does she have to?"

I give him a confused look, suddenly feeling

insecure, "Why are you asking me that?"

"Will you feel more comfortable if your best friend is hanging out with your … me?"

"Is she still my best friend? I mean—" I am all emotion right now and I don't like it. I push myself back against the wall, wishing I could sink into it so I don't reach out to him. All I want to do is hang on to him, any part of him.

"Damn, Tales."

"I miss her. I miss you. I miss—" I finally admit.

"I miss you, too, but we have another three weeks before—"

"Three weeks?"

"I'm healing." When I look at him without expression, he says, "The fucking dolphin prince needs to just chill the hell out for—"

"Your penis piercing?" I whisper.

"Yes," he whispers back mockingly.

"Because of that … thing."

"The Great and Powerful Oz?"

My jaw drops, and I have to cover my mouth so I don't wake the entire building with my laughing.

He smirks. "Tales, you don't laugh when a dude talks about his dick."

"Do you regret it?"

"I don't know. I'd like you and me to figure it out together."

"Together?"

He looks around as if he's lost something. "Were you not the one I nailed under the stairs? Do you have a fucking doppelganger? If you do, before

I make any sort of commitment, I really want the three of us to get together at least once."

"You still want me?" my voice squeaks with excitement and emotion.

He smiles and nods. "Yeah, Tales."

I walk up and hug him, taking care not to push against him. "Does it hurt?"

He wraps his arms around me, returning the hug. "What?"

"When you're hard?" I whisper in his ear.

"Wow. Shit, apparently not. It's gonna when I can't be up in you, though." He grinds against me.

"Why did you do it?" I ask as his nose runs across my hair, and he inhales.

He pulls back to look me in the eye. "I was pissed at you, pissed enough that I was afraid, if I went on tour, I would fuck whatever I could to feel something other than angry for a while."

"You were going to have sex with the—"

"Gaggle of groupies," he confirms with a nod, "until I stopped feeling sorry for myself and realized I'm not just Forever Steel. I'm kind of forever Tales, too."

I look up at him, wishing, hoping. I know I'm pleading with my eyes for him to tell me what I desperately want to hear from him.

"All that shit you said to me the other night." I frown at him, and he corrects himself. "I mean, stuff, Tales, not shit. Shit, you know that." I nod. "All the talk about me being your fantasy has sent me into my head so deeply I can't even begin to understand it all myself. But I do know that, for years—and when I say years, I mean it—I have been drawn to you.

"When we were kids at church, your old man saw me looking at you. It wasn't like I wanted to bang you; I was just watching you and how you acted, how the girl who smiled and was kind to everyone held herself together. I suppose I have been in awe of you since then.

"One day, your father caught me watching you and said, 'Do you know what happens to sinners, young man?' I told him no, I didn't. I was a fucking kid! He looks at me and says, 'They burn in hell.'

"I fucking laughed in his face. Hell, he preached God's love and was pegging me at ten years old as a sinner. He didn't think that shit was funny. I wasn't thinking about banging you back then, Tales. I was fucking ten.

"He told me, 'If you have sexual desires for her, you best get down on your knees and pray, young man.'" Memphis shakes his head. "I had no clue what he was talking about. Sex was far from my mind. I was into Legos or some other shit my old man bought, promising he'd spend time doing it with me and then bailing.

"I figured out about sex really quickly after that, and you, Tales, were my first fantasy. I mean, I'm not sure it was planned, but I thought about you, and I thought about sex. I thought about sex, and I thought about you. You understand what I'm saying?"

I nod and he continues, "You were also untouchable, too good for me: sweet, kind, innocent, all the things I never was. I also wanted to protect you from the little fucks who picked on you, but you would just smile in their faces like an angel. I was never gonna be good enough, so I didn't even give it a second thought until Miami."

I push up on my toes and grab his face in my hands. His admission, his confession, makes me not only love him, but want him even more. "I hope you know better now. I'm no angel."

"And … that's my cue," he groans and steps back, his massive erection prominently on display. "I'm out, Tales, like a boner in sweatpants." He takes something out of his pocket and hands it to me. "Don't give this up again."

I nod, watching him walk away. Then I open the apartment door, and as I shut it behind me, I whisper, "I love you, Memphis Black."

I look down at the phone in my hand where I have a message already from him.

See you soon, sweet cheeks.

When, I want to ask, but I don't.

Morning comes too early. They all have lately. I toss and turn and think of what commitment and being on the road means.

I got Mads a job, hoping it would give her something to do. She and Mom are all sorts of emotional lately. Mom, she, and I aren't on bad terms, but when I found out Mom knew for a couple years that Dad was all kinds of freaky, I was kind of pissed.

She was unapologetic and told me, when I had children someday, I would understand her choices. I'm not sure that's true, not even sure I want kids.

Kids? I grab my phone and send Tales a message.

You on the pill yet?

I get a response twenty minutes later.

I have an appointment next week. <3

Chick doctor?

Does it matter? <3

Does a bear shit in the woods?

Some do it at the zoo. <3

Dolphin be damned, I need to see her. It's not like I can sleep, anyway.

Dinner tonight?

You sure you have time for me? <3

I call her immediately, and she hangs up. What the fuck?

You fucking kidding me right now?

It was meant as a joke. I'm sorry. I know you're busy. <3

I'll pick you up at eight.

I won't be back until nine. <3

My bad. It's Wednesday, right? You teach the kids.

Shit, did I really just send that? What the fuck!

Stalking me? <3

Nine p.m.

***

"You're early," Xavier says when I walk in the front door of Forever Four.

"Yeah. I have another song."

"Is it good?"

I look at him like *what the fuck?*

"What? Is it? You know whether you write shit and whether you write something good."

"Everything I write is—"

"No, man, how about "Come fly with me"? That was shit." He shakes his head. "Then you follow it up with "Soaring," and that was shit and—"

"Fine, just have a lot on my mind; that's all."

"Spill it," X says, pointing to his office.

We head back, and he sits down behind his desk.

"I left my vagina at home. Maybe—" I start to

walk away.

"Shut the hell up and sit."

"No really—"

"Tallia Priest, sister's best friend. You—"

"What the fuck?" I snap

"Billy," we both say at the same time, and Xavier laughs.

"And your parents are having problems. Add all that plus preparing to take STD to the top, and it's hard. I get it, so spill."

I sit down and shake my head. I tell him damn near everything, even about my dad.

"Okay, well, that's ..." He runs his hands through his hair and shakes his head.

"Fucked up? Yeah, it is." I feel my blood boil.

"Have you confronted him yet?" Xavier asks.

"You want me on stage or in jail?"

"I hear ya. Maybe he's not gay."

"Well, what the fuck, then? Was he just holding it in his mouth till the swelling went down?"

Xavier sucks in his cheeks and tries not to laugh.

"Laughing won't offend me. I've been between rolling fits of laughter and ready to knock him out. The shit kicker is I say he's a piece of shit out loud or joke around to the wrong person, and I'm labeled as some fucking gay basher when I'm not. I am bashing the fact that the asshole who raised me is a fucking heap of shit who lied to his family and ruined our lives and the life of a girl who means a lot to me."

"I feel you." He sits forward in his chair. "I'm

also pretty damn proud that you are thinking of the backlash it would have on you."

"And the band. Fucking wackos everywhere would be following us and ruining us before we even really get a chance."

"And the girl?"

I look up and shake my head. "She's the most down-to-earth chick in the world."

"And you like her?"

I stand up and walk to the window that overlooks the parking lot. "Yeah. Known her forever, but this life … I don't know."

"I understand," he says, "but how are you gonna know if you don't try?"

I turn around and sit against the windowsill. "I just want her to stay her. How fucked up is that? I should want to shower her with gifts, help her get a place for her and me when I'm home, buy her some damn clothes that aren't second-hand."

"Look, it sounds to me like you want a kept woman. That's not fair to her," he begins, but I cut him off.

"Are you fucking kidding me right now?"

"No. You don't want her in second-hand clothes and to have a place to tuck her away when you're on the road."

I laugh, and he scowls at me. "Sounds bad when you say it like that," I admit.

"Not my words, yours." He waits for me to explain, and when I don't, he says, "Oh, I see how it is."

"You see how what is?"

He stands up and walks toward the door.

"That's it?" I yell behind him.

"Sure is, man." He chuckles. "Sure is."

I follow him out. "I don't want this life to suck her in and change a fucking thing about the girl I love."

He turns around and smiles. "Yep, I saw how it was and I get it. I also know you gotta figure it out for yourself. If it comes easy, it doesn't always stay. You've got this, but like everything, you gotta work to find a way to make it happen. Now, go give me a song, not some shit."

I walk out of the sound booth an hour later.

Nickie D pats me on the back. "Platinum in six months."

"Hey," Xavier calls from behind. "Band chat."

"Band chat?" Nickie raises his eyebrow. "Which one of you did some shit I'm gonna have to get you out of?"

"You were with me, so my buck's on River." I laugh.

We walk into the conference room and sit. Finn is chewing on a pen cap, staring at his notebook; River is baby talking to Xavier's kid, who's in some jumpy thing; and Billy is messaging on his phone.

"Okay, listen up." X-man starts. "The talk about the opening act contest has gone fucking viral. We aren't just getting rock bands; we're getting *Americas Got Talent* shit. So, Taelyn, Nickie D, and I have decided we are going to step in until we get this record produced or find some people who know talent."

"Groupies know talent." River laughs, and so does the kid. "Yeah, they do. Huh, little buddy? Fist bump." He holds up his fist, and the kid literally taps his fist with his hand. "We'll work on that."

"Or until Patrick understands what the hell is going on, which looks to be any day now." Xavier looks at Taelyn and shakes his head. "This is happening too damn fast. It's your fault."

"My fault?" She laughs and picks the kid up. "Lunch time."

"See? Your damn fault," he scolds her, but when she walks away, he smiles.

He returns the focus to the task at hand. "As much as you all are dying to be involved, we've got it for the first few dates. Shit's subject to change, and I really would like you guys to be part of this. It's good for your image. Show support and love for the community, and they'll show it for you. We all on the same page here?"

"I'll help whenever, X," River offers.

"Sober?" Xavier asks.

"Right now I am, but not gonna promise that in a couple hours. Besides, I'm at my fucking best when I'm in my own head."

"But not passed out on stage, River," Xavier warns, looking at him and trying his best not to yell.

"I kept my shit together for the Burning Souls tour; I will be doing the same for ours."

"Travel is booked. Madison has done really well at that, and she's working with Taelyn on social media promotion of the band. Nickie and I are trying to set up interviews and radio spots in cities where we are playing. And the album," he pauses and smiles, "fucking insane."

"Epic," Nickie concurs.

"Orgasmic." River laughs.

***

There's a man here with a car, and it's not you. <3

He's gonna bring you to me.

So I should trust a man with a black town car who may possibly resemble someone from an Italian mafia movie and not an OBGYN who works in an office surrounded by people because he has a penis? <3

Enough finger tapping. Get in the car.

A little while later, I see her get out of the car and look around. Her shoulders sag a bit, but there is no regret on my end.

I'm sitting outside my mom's home by the outdoor fire pit with my acoustic when she walks up.

"Come on over here," I say as I put a foot on the bench and pat between my legs.

She smiles a little. "Is that safe?"

"I'm not sure. I guess we'll find out."

She walks up, sits between my legs, and leans back. "If you get uncomfortable, let me know. I've sat on this bench a million times, for hours on end."

"Listening to a dumb kid strum his guitar and watching him dream."

"He wasn't dumb."

I laugh. "Are we going to argue about younger me, Tales?"

"No. I just wanted you to know that I'm perfectly comfortable on this bench."

"I wasn't talking about the bench, Tales. I was talking about the harpoon that will very possibly be poking you in the back any second now."

She looks up and smiles. "I see."

I lean down and kiss her, and she gives it right back. After a couple of minutes, I pull back and groan.

"Does it hurt?"

"What, Tales?"

"The wizard." She blushes

"No. I was thinking about a new song. Mouth open, tongue in … I better stop there."

"Sounds very interesting," she says.

I reach behind the bench and grab the bag I brought for her. "I hit Yelp up and found a couple vintage shops, so I got you some things."

She smiles and takes the bag, not opening it. "You didn't have to do that."

"Aren't you gonna look at it?" She leans against me fully and looks over her shoulder.

"I'd rather look at you while I have you."

"Play along, Tales." I kiss the top of her head and push the bag toward her.

I watch her open the bag and smile. She pulls out the first one—a Kermit the frog T-shirt.

"When I look at you, I see cartoons and everything in vivid color," I tell her.

"Cartoons?" she whispers

"Yeah." I laugh. "You used to come over after school and watch them with Mads. You would laugh at the same damn jokes over and over."

"They were funny."

"Maybe. I wouldn't have noticed; I was too

busy being amused by how damn easily you smiled." She looks at me and smiles. "Like that, Tales."

"I like smiling."

"Thank God, because I love your smile."

She pulls out the next. "*Star Wars*?"

"Vintage, and Billy went with me. He likes that shit."

"Do you?"

"I did as a kid, and so did you. Mads hated it."

"Thank you."

"There's more." I point to the bag.

She reaches in and pulls out another tee—Rolling Stones.

"It's vintage, but new."

"I like it." Her smile is bigger now as she reaches in for another one.

Pearl Jam, The Doors, The Who—one after another, she pulls out the T-shirts, grinning from ear to ear. She then pulls out the long skirts, all thin material and flowing.

"So, I was thinking … I don't want you to change because of me, I want you to be the same girl I have been drawn to since forever. I want you in clothes that don't scream groupie, and I want you naked in my bed. I'm scared to death that my lifestyle will change you, and I want nothing to do that. Not me, not the road, not a damn thing, Tales."

She turns and looks at me. "I'm not changing."

"I need you to soar, too, Tales. Follow your dreams, not mine."

"I am."

"I know." I push her hair away from her eyes

and then pull her toward me, just so I can smell her. God, she smells good all the damn time and everywhere, too.

"Look, I found a little house on the shore. I want it to be a place where you and me, you know …"

"Have sex?"

"Well, yeah, but maybe … I don't know. Fuck, Tales, live together?"

"I live with my mom, Memphis. She needs me."

"I need you, too."

"I'll be there for you anytime, anywhere."

"Good. Then you'll move in."

"Memphis …"

"Tales, I'm serious. I'm gonna be on the fucking road the whole damn month of September, and that's just a start. If I can grab a plane and get home, I want your ass there, ready for—"

"I'm going on tour with my dance company, Memphis. When we're in town at the same time, I will be—"

I'm still trying to swallow that pill- her being on the road and shit- but this whole 'Soar Memphis' has me tripping.

"I love you, Tales. What the fuck? I'm asking you to—"

"You what?" she asks, stunned.

"I love you, and—"

"Stop. Just stop at that and let me enjoy that before you go and attach strings to it, okay?"

"Attach strings? Wow, Tales, that's fucked up." She's acting like she didn't say she loved me, and she fucking does. I know it.

"No, Memphis. Love is not fucked up."

Insta-tarpoon. Tally said fuck, and she knows I'm hard because I am railing her in the back right now.

"It's new. We are going in two different directions and—"

"Cut the shit, Tales!" I snap. "Tell me what you want." And do it now, I want to scream.

"You. Just you and me and every second we can get together, without"—she smiles and moves her back from side to side slightly—"obstacles in our way. I want you, but I want me, too. What you just said"—she holds up the clothes—"what you did … You want the same thing."

"All right, then." I put my guitar on the ground.

Fucking head-trip. A motherfucking head-trip. I need an answer or duct tape and cuffs. Either one would work right about now, so I'm gonna step away to figure out what defensive move I'm gonna need to take.

"Look, I need to get some sleep—"

"Memphis?" She stands up slowly. "I love you."

"I love you."

She giggles as she turns to walk away.

"Tales, don't go."

She looks back.

"Go with me."

"Where?"

"Doesn't matter; just come with me."

And here we go again. Fuck!

I walk up to his vehicle and smile. "Want me to drive?"

He opens the passenger door. "No." I turn and wrap my arms around his trim waist and hug him tightly. "You're a pain in the ass," he tells me.

"We're both young," I respond.

"And talented. I get it; we both have a dream, so why don't you go back to school? I can—"

"I like teaching dance much more than I like dancing on stage for the applause."

He leans back and looks down. "Really?" The way he says it makes me laugh.

"When have I ever wanted the spotlight?"

"You should be in it, Tales."

"No. I like seeing others in it, like you, the kids, the dance team, but as a whole …" I make a face that shows my distaste.

"Then come on the road with me. Teach us some moves." He squeezes my ass.

"There isn't a move I could teach any of you. The talent's there; the skill is honed. It's perfect."

"Not true. Me up there without a guitar—"

"I'll tutor you."

"You will, huh?"

"In what, three weeks?"

"Two," he says quickly.

"But you—" Has he been holding out on me? Why the hell do I wonder that? Good Lord we both just need to stop and enjoy a moment.

"Two."

"Right." I step away and get in the Escalade.

He gets in the driver's side and asks, "Where to?"

"Feed me," I say then decide to say something to change the darkening atmosphere. "Something salty and warm. Maybe a cream—"

"That's enough, sweet cheeks."

"You could have just talked to me," I say, pointing to bulge. I still don't understand why he would go and mess with… that.

"You'll like it. Now enough talk about—"

"Fine." I bet it hurts. Well I think it must I mean, hello!

It's quiet for too long.

"My mom is going out of town for the weekend." I turn in my seat and look at him.

"Is that so?"

"It is."

"Come stay with me, then?" he says.

"Where?"

"Our place." Grrr. He's being so stubborn.

"Or you stay with me."

He looks at me out of the corner of his eye.

"More privacy," I allude.

He doesn't reply. He pulls into the pizza place he used to take his dates to in high school, and I laugh.

"Old faithful?"

"What?" He looks at me confused.

"Nothing." I open the door and get out.

"Oh, I see now. I like the pizza here, and I know you do, too." He takes my hand and links our fingers as we walk in.

"Tony, what's flying, man?"

"Well, lookee here." Tony, the older Italian owner of the shop looks over at me and laughs. "And Tallia Priest."

"Hey, Tony." I feel my face heat up.

"Did he kidnap you, or did you come willingly?" Tony jokes.

"Kidnapped me," I say, grinning at Memphis.

Memphis rolls his eyes then orders his favorite pizza. "Chicken, bacon, ranch, a medium."

We then sit in a booth where he sits across from me.

"Ever think about leaving this place?"

"We both kind of have." I answer.

"I mean farther away."

"Of course. And you?" I take off my sweater and sit back.

"No, not really."

***

The weekend plans were cancelled. Memphis and the band had to travel for some interviews in Texas, hoping to sell out the shows there. He was apologetic, and I was understanding, even though it stung.

The next week was busy, and something interesting happened. Ted, a member of the dance team, ended up spraining his knee. I talked to the manager of the dance team and learned that Ted's partner, Anna, would be asked to leave the team. They just didn't have time to train a replacement for Ted and all of our dances use partners. I offered to leave, instead, despite being afraid I would lose the classes I had and nervous that I was taking such a risk, but she didn't accept. She asked that I stay on.

I decided that I should call and find out if the Stevie Danielle's offer was still good. She said she was just about ready to fill the position, but she would still prefer me. I told her I was still interested and asked for another day to think about it.

I explained my situation to the manager, and she asked if she could change my mind, I told her no. This is a big deal for me. I hate disappointing people. I also hated telling Memphis to soar when I myself wasn't even considering taking a step to do the same myself.

I walked out and grabbed my phone out of my bag, ready to call Stevie Danielle's back when a message appeared.

Stevie was willing to give me an extra thousand-dollar bonus.

I messaged, asking if I could continue teaching my classes, and she responded immediately with yes.

Fate? I believe so.

I met with her assistant that evening and signed the confidentiality form after reading over my obligations. Four shows that were weekday, state fairs: New York, Connecticut, Massachusetts, and New Jersey. Expenses were paid, meals included.

I couldn't talk to Memphis about it, because of the confidentiality form, but that was all right with me. I am going to get a taste of what traveling with a rock and roll band is like, even if it isn't with Memphis. Then maybe, just maybe, it won't scare me so much to admit that I would love to someday work side by side with the man I love.

I wasn't lying when I told him the band had great stage presence, but it could always be better.

I wasn't putting all my eggs in one basket, not at all. I was simply testing the waters.

***

It's been over two weeks, and I have seen him once. We talked about the classes I have been teaching and his crazy schedule while at Tony's for pizza again. He always wants to go there, and I thought it was because the road made him homesick, but he wasn't even gone long. I worried about him. We kissed and cuddled in the car, though he seemed to be exhausted all the time.

I have stayed away from the band's Twitter and other social media pages. I remember how it felt the first time, and now they were actually out there on their own and not fronting for someone else.

I honestly love working for Stevie. She is outrageous and the total opposite of me, and I am entertained all the time. She often asks about our private lives, but I never talk about Memphis. I got this gig based on my talent, and I will not use his name now nor in the future.

Shaunna is bass, Courtney acoustic, and Kellie plays the drums in the band. They are just as cool. They aren't around a lot, but when they are, it's a laugh a minute.

Cassy, Ivy, Joely, and Christi sing back up, while Christa, Liz, Dani, and I are the dance crew.

Cassy, Ivy, Joely, Christi, Liz, Dani, Christa, and I often work together.

I never really fit in anywhere when Madison wasn't around, but here … Here feels good. I now understand why Memphis loves his career so much.

We are all packing our bags up and ready to leave when Sonya, Stevie's assistant, comes in and hands us all an envelope.

Payday! Oh, how I love payday.

On my way to the dance studio, I send Memphis a message.

Tomorrow night? <3

I wait for his reply until it is past time to change into my ballet outfit.

The smiles, laughs, and dedication make everything better until it's time to do our circle goodbye, and the last little, pink tutu scoots out the door.

I laugh as I change into shorts and a tank top. It's hot and humid in New York City in the summer.

My life is busy, and I love my work and am dedicated to Memphis and my relationship, yet I have never been lonelier.

I gather my things and look one last time at my

phone. Still no reply.

He's busy, I keep reminding myself. It's less than two weeks from his very first concert as a headline band, right here in New Jersey. My heart swells with pride, but it also aches, something I need to get used to, and for him I know I will.

I lock the studio door behind me and start walking to the train station. A year ago, I was here and scared out of my mind when walking alone, but now I know I am not alone in the city. There is a cop on every corner and dozens of people walking in the same direction I am.

I walk to 49th Street to catch the N, taking in the lights and the people around me. My timing is perfect, and I get on the subway and find a seat with no one sitting on either side. In three minutes, I am at 34th Street in Herald Square. From there, it takes one minute to catch the train back to Hoboken in less than fifteen minutes. After twenty-six minutes, I am off the train and walking the two blocks to my little apartment where I can soak my aching feet and shower off the day.

I walk into my apartment to find a note. Mom is anti-cell phone, so notes are a common thing to find on our little table.

I pick it up and read that she is with Susan, a woman from our church, at the hospital. Emergency appendectomy and she will be home in the morning.

I kick off my sneakers, and I'm pulling my hair out of the elastic band holding up the not so perfect ballet bun when a knock on the door startles me. I quickly walk over and peek through the hole.

Three locks later, I am ready to jump on Memphis when I notice him looking at me strangely and realize I am a complete mess.

"Rough day, sweet cheeks?" he asks as he hands me one single white rose.

"It was, but it just got better. Come in." I step back. "Are you hungry?"

"Hungrier than Gandhi on day twenty-one."

I laugh. "That's hungry."

I turn to walk to the refrigerator, and his arm wraps around my waist and pulls me back.

"Tales." His voice is deep and rough.

"Oh … oh … um, shower."

"Perfect."

Once I turn around, his eyes are penetrating me. I seriously feel them everywhere. He wants me as much as I want him.

He leans down and kisses me, a growl escaping his throat, and I feel him against me. I suck on his tongue the way I want to suck on him, and then I pull back slowly as I hook my thumbs in his waistband and feel the steel of his piercing twitch against my touch.

"Oh, wow."

"I am going to fuck you so good, Tally."

I can't respond. The look of desire seems more intense than ever before.

"Once I'm in there again, I'm never coming out, you feel me?"

"Can't wait to." I scramble to unbutton his pants as he pulls my tank top over my head. I pull his tank top off, and he immediately yanks my shorts and underwear down.

"Pill?"

"Shot."

"Aw, fuck, Tales."

"Please." I have him in my hand, carefully stroking him up and down as he walks me backward to the bathroom.

"You miss me, Tales?"

"More than I can even—"

"Show me, Tales." He reaches around me and starts the shower. "Stroke me harder."

I squeeze him, and he rocks his hips into me.

"Fuck," He hisses. I tighten my grip even more and feel the steel running through him. "*Fuck*!"

I want him so badly I set my foot on the side of the bathtub and rub him against me. He hisses, and I moan when he pushes against me, sliding up and down the lips of my vagina.

"You're soaked, Tally. So fucking wet." He nudges me, and his piercing hits my clit.

"Oh, yes."

"Yeah, Tales."

"Yeah, oh, yes." I feel the metal of his dolphin piercing rub up and down me, and I push against it, trembling.

"Fuck." He does it again, and I come from the friction alone.

He then lines himself up and pushes inside of me. I feel his heat, the metal, the pressure of his size. He reaches underneath my leg that's still on the side of the tub and pushes slowly in.

"Easy," I cry.

"Fuck, Tales, does it hurt?"

"Just different."

"Sorry. Fuck, what was I thinking?" he says, starting to pull away.

"No! No, don't pull out. Different isn't bad, just different." I wrap my leg around him and push against him.

"Better?"

"Yes," I whimper.

"I'll rock you slow, Tales." His hips circle, and then he pushes in a little. Circle and more, again and again, as he cups my breasts and kisses my neck. "Wrap your other leg around me," he says, and I do.

With one hand, he holds me, squeezing my ass. I feel his finger rubbing from the back side of my opening and around my back entry.

I open my eyes, trying to decide if I will tell him no, and then get completely lost in the reflection of his ass with my legs wrapped around him as the warm water cascades down his back.

OMG! His piercing isn't the only thing that's different. Forever Steel and… I look closer, an emerald. I can't believe he did that. Wow, just wow. Absolutely beautiful.

The water changes course at each ripple of muscle and in the dimples above his very round, hard, muscular ass.

I begin to meet him, delicious thrust for delicious thrust, watching our entwined bodies in the mirror.

Beautiful, erotic, sensual, stimulating.

"I love you, Memphis," I moan into his neck, still watching us.

"I love you, Tallia," he growls.

"Right there?" I ask as I push into her, and she moans. "I'll take that as a yes."

"More," she begs.

I'm kneeling in front of her with her legs wrapped around me. I pull one leg up and rest it on my shoulder.

"No, no, no, no—"

"Okay, damn girl, the view from up here was fine, though."

"Too much pressure." She wraps her long, lean leg back around my waist as I hold her hip in my hands.

I lean down and suck hard on her left nipple, making her back arch. I keep sucking as I slowly lift her leg to put it back on my shoulder, and she opens her eyes.

"Really?" She laughs as she pulls it back down.

"Get out of your head, Tales. Just enjoy the feels, babe."

We've been at it for hours, trying different positions with the new and improved steel. Some, she clearly likes better than others.

"I'm enjoying. Are you?" She sits up and wraps her legs securely around me as she grabs my face. “Tell me we can stay like this forever.”

“Do that again.” I smirk.

“What?”

“Sit up while you’re impaled.”

She kisses me. “See?” She leans back then sits up again. “Don’t even need a gym. I have you.”

“You’ve got me, all right, by the dick, by the balls …” She rolls her eyes. “By the heart and by the soul.”

That gains me a sweet, little look and some lip action. That lip action gains her missionary position with a happy ending had by all.

I flop on my back, panting while holding her hand as she does the same.

I glance over at the clock. “Tales, it’s fucking three in the morning,” I groan as I sit up.

“Don’t leave.”

I look back down at her, totally naked with marks from my mouth still on her tits. “I have to be at an interview at seven in the—”

“Please,” she whispers, closing her eyes.

“You do know the reason I can’t stay is because waking up with you in Miami was amazing, and I know damn well I won’t be able to leave this bed with you draped over me.”

“I promise to kick you out at six.”

“In three hours, Tales?”

“If you drive back to your place, it’ll give you even less time to sleep,” she argues, batting her lashes at me.

I stand up then lean down to kiss her. “I can’t fuck this up, Tales.”

“Fine,” she says, her lips popping out right

before she rolls over.

Stake to the heart.

I walk around the bed and grab a quarter off the nightstand. “Flip for it?”

She opens her eyes and smiles. “Tails, you stay?”

“Sure.”

“Heads, I use my mouth as an alarm clock?”

“Shit, Tales.” I smile. “When did you get so naughty?” I say as I flip the coin.

“That time I stayed with a bunch of rock stars in Miami.” She smiles.

“I see.” I look down at the coin. “Ha, heads, I win.”

She giggles and scoots over. “Go to sleep.”

I lie down, and then I think about what just happened.

“Tales?”

“Yeah?”

“You just manipulated that coin toss to your benefit. Either way, I was gonna end up staying.”

She yawns and turns off the light. “It was mutually beneficial.”

I wake up to her hand on my cock and glance over. Five forty-five in the morning. I pretend to be asleep because I hate getting woken up, fucking hate it. Then her lips wrap around me, and suddenly I’m a morning person.

***

It’s two days before the show when I walk into Forever Four and realize I’m the only person here.

I look at my phone to check the time. I'm an hour early.

Fuck.

I grab my phone and call Tallia. She answers, and I know damn well she went back to bed.

"Tales, you up?"

"Yeah, of course."

"I call bullshit."

She giggles.

"Not funny, sweet cheeks. You did that shit on purpose, didn't you?"

"Did what?"

"Woke me up early."

"No, actually it wasn't on purpose."

"No? Then what was it?"

"A craving, I guess?"

"You guess?"

She yawns. "Uh-huh."

"You know what they say about payback, right?"

"Yep, that if someone loves you, there is no such thing as—"

"No, it's a bitch, Tales. That's what they say. Payback is a bitch."

"Be nice."

"We'll see."

"Okay, well, you have a good day. I love you."

"I love you, too."

I hang up the phone and toss it on the couch then flop down beside it. I can't sleep, though. My head is high on daily fuck sessions, a lot of overnights with Tales, and the high of two days from now when I'll be standing on the stage. Just three months ago, we were an opening act, and now we are going to be the main fucking attraction.

I stand up and pace the floor for what must be an hour before the guys walk in behind Xavier.

"All right." He claps his hands and rubs them together. "We have an announcement. Change in plans. Our opening act shit the bed, which caused a big fucking headache last night, but we pulled off one hell of a hat trick. You all remember Stevie Danielle? Kick ass rocker chick who didn't get shit for attention she deserved because of her old man's fucked-up career?"

"Yeah, her old man was a douchebag. Talented as fuck, but didn't know how to take no for an answer," River says, cracking open a Red Bull. "Four women came forward, claiming rape, and everyone rallied around him until she stepped up with missing security footage from their Beverly Hills house. Yeah, who the hell doesn't know the story? She got shunned by the industry as a whole."

"Well, she's gonna open for STD, and—"

"X-man, I don't think that's a good idea," I say, feeling my head start to spin.

"I disagree." Taelyn walks in, throwing a file on the table. "Your band's name pegs you as a bunch of irresponsible hot boys in tight pants who want to 'spread around your disease'." She air quotes the hell out of it. "She has a huge following in the women's liberation community, and if they will rally behind you, you'll sell more tickets so we can get the rest of this year booked up."

"I still don't like it," Finn says nervously.

"No? If we sell out ten more stadiums, you'll

each walk away with about seven hundred fifty thousand dollars in income. If we sell out twenty, everyone's gonna follow suit, and you double that."

"I think it's a terrific idea." River laughs. "Millionaires, can you imagine what—"

"Now it's an even worse idea," Finn grumbles. "You'll end up so fucked up—"

"He'll be fine," Billy says then gives Finn a nasty-ass glare.

"X, you should know something about Stevie Danielle."

He gives me a look like *spill it*.

"I fucked her," Finn confesses. "Seven years ago, I fucked the chick, and I wasn't even legal. I don't want that bitch around."

"She violated you?" Taelyn gasped.

"Fuck no. I violated the hell out of her and her ass, but—"

"All right!" Xavier yells, pointing a finger at Finn. "Watch your tone with my wife."

"Xavier Steel." Taelyn laughs loudly. "You are all about violating—"

"Irish, don't you even go there," he warns her

Finn stands up and walks to the door. "She's a fucking cunt."

River gasps and looks at Taelyn, and she starts laughing and throws her hands in the air. "Did I lose my honorary brass balls over night? Stop acting like I'm made of glass, guys."

"I'm gonna have to say I am on Finn's side here," I say louder this time because my opinion doesn't seem to matter right now.

"Why? Because she's a cunt?" Taelyn laughs.

"Irish, you shouldn't say shit like that." Xavier looks at her sternly.

She smirks.

"Okay, remember when I went to the woodshed in Tampa?" I say a little too loudly, and they all look at me. "I came back with "Bang Bang"?"

Finn walks back in, leans against the door jamb, and crosses his arms over his chest. "You fucked her, too?"

"I didn't just fuck her; I violated every orifice that woman had. I don't trust this one fucking bit. She's fucked two of us."

"Every orifice?" River asks inquisitively. Finn and I both nod. "Well, hell, I say keep her. I'd like to test those waters, too."

"Keep your dicks in your pants, and it'll be fine." He hits a few keys on the keyboard. "Her assistant, Sonya, is driving sales." He turns the monitor to face us. "Social media marketing at its finest. We do the show, and you four behave. We are respectful, and we walk away after it's all done with. I'm not one to ever cry boss, but today I am. Suck it up, and fuck it up, and then it's off to Texas." Xavier smirks.

I get in the Escalade, and Finn, River, and Billy jump in. Then I send Tales a message.

Gonna need some down time for a couple days to get prepped for the concert. You good with that?

As long as I get you after the show. <3

I stand in front of the mirror, wearing the tightest tank top known to man, all leopard print and sequins, paired with black silk, boy shorts and thigh-high, six-inch, black leather boots. My makeup is stage-ready times a million, and my hair is blown out, resembling an afro.

I look like a freaking stripper—no, a hooker. I turn and look at my butt. POW! should have a for sale sign on it. Right now, I wish I had on ballet pink. I look awful, and worse yet, I feel awful.

When I found out Stevie Danielle's band was opening for STD, I was nervous and excited. I couldn't wait to surprise Memphis, but then Stevie started acting like a diva and changing everything up that we had perfected, and when I say perfected, I mean it. I'm self-critical about everything.

My phone rings, and it's Memphis, so I answer immediately.

"Tales, are you coming tonight?"

"Of course I am. Wouldn't miss it for the world," I say, hoping he doesn't catch the hint of sadness in my voice.

"Good. Mads is gonna meet you at gate six

with your VIP pass."

"So I'll be a VIP?" I joke.

"Of course you will, Tales. Why the hell are you even asking a question like that?" He sounds angry.

"I was joking, Memphis. Geesh."

"Sorry, sweet cheeks. I am amped. Wish you were here."

"Where are you?" I ask, looking around and knowing he is done with sound checks.

"Getting in a car. Just finished sound checks. Now the opening act is going to do theirs, and then it's show time, Tales. Fuck, this is crazy."

"Is the opening act any good?"

"Some say so, I guess. I don't know. Why would you ask that? I mean, really, who gives a shit, right?"

"Right." Wow, he is nervous. "Well, you are going to kill it. I just know it."

"It's a given." I laugh, and he sighs. "Miss you."

"I've missed you, too."

Sonya pokes her head in the dressing room, and I press mute. "Stage, Tally."

"Right." I take the phone off mute. "Hey, what do rock stars get after a show? Flowers? A card?"

"Dome." His tone is serious.

"Wow."

"It's expected."

"Is that so?"

"Yeah, sweet cheeks, it's so. Hey, see you soon?"

"Of course. Break a leg, Memphis."

"Let's fucking hope not."

I shove the phone in my bag then quickly make my way on stage. Everyone is there, and Stevie looks pissed when she sees me.

"You do know who the star is, correct?"

I give her a smile. "Stevie Danielle."

She rolls her eyes. "One last minute change. This song just won't go away. I was very inspired one hot as hell night, and well, let's just say that inspiration has returned." She is all starry-eyed and looks downright smitten. Good for her. "You know what they say; you can't keep a hard man … or is it a good man down?" Everyone laughs, including me.

"Dancers"—*so now we are nameless?* I think to myself—"Same beat as "Go, Go". I think you can keep up."

I walk up the ramp to the center.

"Shit, Tallia, I need you in the cage." She points to the tall cage, left of center. "You can freestyle this one. Show off that wild animal inside of you. No one can pull that off like you can with all that … hair." She looks at me in disgust, but then she smiles. "And no one on this stage can move like you—well, except me."

"All right girls, let's do this!" She smiles as I climb in the cage.

My stomach is in knots. I don't ever go on stage unprepared. It's unacceptable.

Kellie taps the sticks, and the band starts a familiar beat. I've got this.

Black leather at the bar, he's looking at me.

Glazed blue eyes give me all I need.
I feel the weight of his desire.
I feel it everywhere.
I give him what he wants.
I dance for him.
He stands up slowly, the look of sin.
No slowing it down, this heat we feel
He takes my hand, and we seal the deal.

Bang, bang. My heart beats like drum.
Bang, bang. No choice but to succumb.
Bang, bang. Not sent from above.
Bang, bang. Fits like a glove
Bang, bang. He's driving it home.
Bang, bang. A rocker's syndrome
Bang, bang. He's a loaded gun.
Bang, bang. Two seconds to run.
Bang, bang. No room for love.
Bang, bang. Not sent from above.

I freeze. I feel sick. I want to scream. Then the speakers go dead.

"What the fuck is that?" booms over the microphone.

I look toward the sound booth to see a black man covered in tattoos storming toward the stage.

"Is there something wrong?" Stevie asks.

"You know damn well there's something wrong," he says as he hops the fence and jumps on stage. "That's not your fucking song, Stevie."

"Sure is, Nickie."

"That's STD's song. Memphis wrote that song. It's already fucking copyrighted and recorded. It releases tomorrow!"

"I had no idea."

"No? Really?"

"Well, I didn't expect him to release the song our time together inspired." She pauses and covers her face. "God, of course he would."

"He wrote the song, so of course he—"

"He may have written the words, but I didn't think he would ever record it without me. Our night inspired every lyric, every emotion, every—"

"Now why the fuck would he not record a song he fucking wrote?"

"He didn't mention it when we saw each other again in Florida the day before he left to come here, and he hasn't mentioned it in the two days we have spent together."

I can't listen to any more. God, how could I have trusted him? His behavior has been off, and I should have known. I should have seen it coming.

I climb down from the cage and quickly make it off stage, hoping I haven't been seen.

"Tales?" I look up to see Madison. "What the hell?" She laughs. "Does Memphis know you're—?"

"No, and please don't tell him."

"You're going to surprise him? That's a fabulous idea. Then what? Will you come to work for STD? I mean, Memphis has talked about maybe getting you involved with contests for opening acts. Says it's taxing, and he …" She keeps talking.

My head is spinning, and my ears are ringing. *Taxing?* Yeah, I bet.

"Tales?"

"Yeah?" I ask.

"Why are you crying?"

"Oh." I wipe away a tear that has escaped. "Just overwhelmed."

"Don't be. I heard him tell River, '*Yeah, I fucking love her. Now shut the fuck up*,' so that must be love, right?"

All I can do is smile and force a nod.

"I miss you. I really hope this means you'll join STD's tour. They are selling out stadiums, Tales. I never knew what went into putting on a show. It blows my mind how this team works. It's exhausting yet thrilling."

I hug her. "See you soon?"

"Yeah, really soon. Oh, man, I can't wait to see the shock on his face."

Sonya walks up to me. "Let's go. Stage, Tally. What the hell is your problem?"

I follow her out and do my best to get through the sound check, and then I wonder why I even have to be at a sound check. This is messed up, so incredibly messed up.

I look up to see the man who was giving Stevie hell with his phone to his ear.

"We've got a fucking problem. This bitch is fucking crazy, Xavier, like padded cell shit." He walks away, and I can't hear him anymore.

I look left and see Sonya and Stevie whispering.

Then Stevie laughs and claps her hands. "That tape will go viral if they fuck with me. That song is going to put me back in the spotlight." I see her pull something out of her bra and hand it to Sonya. "This is the only copy. Guard it with your life. Now get that little bitch on stage so she can look like the nothing she is."

Sonya nods and drops what I assume is a flash drive of the two of them having sex into her bag. I then see the man, Nickie, rushing an equally as large, even more tattooed man in through the rear entrance—Xavier.

Sonya looks up, and my eyes are locked on her. Her almost amber eyes narrow as we literally stare each other down.

I want that flash drive. I want to see with my own eyes that Memphis Black is what the world thinks him to be—a walking STD waiting to explode.

"Xavier, she's fucking dangerous," Nickie says as they walk by.

"Xavier Steel?" I ask.

He stops and looks at me as if he doesn't recognize me. "If I know you from a past life—"

I see Sonya start to walk away, and I grab his hand. "Come with me."

"Girl, I'm a married man, have a kid and shit. No can do."

"My name is Tallia Priest. We met in Miami," I say as I try my best to drag him, hoping Sonya doesn't get away with my evidence and whatever else is on the damn drive.

"Tales?" He laughs. "Sorry, but—"

"Would you just shut up and come with me!"

"Nickie, get Memphis. His little lady seems to have drunk the crazy Kool-Aid."

"Screw you," I growl. "Don't get him," I snap

at Nickie as Sonya walks toward the door. "Bitch, you better stop right there," I call out to her.

"Oh, damn, a girl fight." Xavier laughs.

I let go of his hand and run at her as she grabs the door handle. I grab a fistful of her hair and pull her back, then grab her bag as she turns to hit me. I have her bag, and Nickie now has her. Adrenaline kicks in, and I start to run toward the gravel parking lot in six-inch, thigh-high, leather boots.

I look back to see everyone is running at me. Xavier Steel is looking at me like I'm crazy. Then I run into the brick wall that is Finn Beckett.

"Tales, you stealing purses now?" Finn looks at me like I'm a lunatic and then laughs. "Or selling your body?"

"Fuck you," I say, stepping back, and the damn heel breaks on the boot.

I am just about ready to fall on my ass when I'm swooped up into the arms of a very angry looking Memphis Black.

"I hate you!" I spit at him.

"Is that so?" he snaps at me.

"Put me down, you asshole." I start to kick and scream.

"My purse!" Sonya comes at me.

"Bring it on, bitch!" I scream, kick, flail, and the purse slips out of my hand.

I look up at Finn who has grabbed it, telling me, "You better hope there is something in this."

Billy has Sonya now, and River is laughing while Nickie opens the door to the stretch Hummer.

"Get them inside!"

"Put me down, or I'll scream!"

"You *are* fucking screaming, you loon!" Memphis pushes me into the vehicle and to the far bench before he and everyone else follows. "Now explain what the fuck is going on, Tales, before I bend you over my knee and beat the literal shit out of POW!"

"You'll never touch my ass again, you, you—"

"*Enough*!" I look up to see Xavier glaring at me. "Now what the hell—"

"She has a sex tape!" I point at Sonya, "of you and your little rocker whore, Memphis."

I can't take it. I hit Memphis in the chest. It feels good, so I do it again.

"Now the whole world can see what you are! How the hell did I believe a word you said to me?! I hate—"

He grabs my hands and holds them so I can't hit him anymore. "Shut the fuck up, Tales! Just shut the—" He stops when Finn dumps her purse on the floor.

Sonya quickly snatches up something on a chain, a necklace of some sort, and Finn grabs the flash drive.

"You wanna tell me what the fuck is on this?" he asks Sonya.

"None of your business. Now give me back my belongings and let me out, or I call the cops," she says in an oddly calm voice.

Finn doesn't respond; he just looks at her. "What's your name?"

"Sonya. Sonya none-of-your-damn-business," she says as she picks up her wallet, a pocket-sized photo album, and her phone.

"Okay, let's just calm the hell down and sort this all out," Xavier Steel says in an authoritative, take charge, but don't mess with me voice. "Sonya, what's on that drive?" She looks out the window. "Sonya …"

"It's not mine, haven't seen it, don't know, and really don't give a damn."

Nickie opens his laptop and pops it in. "*Fuck me, Memphis. Oh, yeah, baby, fuck me just like that.*" It's Stevie's voice.

"*I'm gonna fuck you my way. You just lie back*," He groans. "*And enjoy the show*."

I've had enough. I pull my hands away from Memphis and cover my face while my tears run freely.

"You sure that's me?" Memphis says.

"If it looks like a duck, sounds like a duck, then fuck, it's a duck," River says, sitting back. "But we already knew this. Well, not all of us."

"She knew! She saw me the next morning, all marked up." I feel him grab my wrist. "Tales, you fucking knew."

I pull my arm away then slap the tears off my face. "Let me out."

"Tales, seriously?"

"You should have told me. You should have—
"

"You should have told me! Here I think you are practicing for a dance tour, and you're working for *her*! Yet, you won't even consider traveling with me!"

"Let me out. You have your tape. I overheard

the conversation; it was the only copy. Now let me out. And, Memphis, don't ever talk to me again."

"You're fucking insane! Don't talk to you again? You fucking lied to me. I didn't lie to you."

"I know you fucked her after I left Florida, and for the past two days, you've been with her and too busy to see me!"

"Doing press shit, Tales, not banging her. And, fuck no, I didn't fuck her after you left without so much as a goodbye. I was fucking healing, Tales!"

"Yeah, well, it's your story." I get on my feet and bend as I make my way through everyone to the door. "Good luck tonight, and you're welcome for stopping that from going viral." I need to get away from him. Far away, so I do.

I get out and see Madison.

"Tales, what's going on?"

I unzip my boots and hand them to her. "Can you give these to Stevie? Tell her I quit."

"Tales, wait." Madison grabs my hand.

"Madison, I need some time, okay?"

"Sure, but—"

"Please. I just need—"

"To listen to me for a fucking minute," Memphis says from behind me.

When she doesn't respond, I take her hand. "I didn't fuck her again." She looks away. "Come on! You know damn well—"

"I don't know!" She sobs, her hand trembling. "I don't know anything." I pick her up, and she grabs my neck and cries against my chest. "I am so mad at you."

"Well, then you do know something," I say, and then her scent hits me.

"*Hey*!" I look up to see Stevie. "I need you onstage."

"She's done," I spit out. Why the fuck did she take a job with this bitch and not me?!

"She's under contract!"

"It's been broken. I'm breaking it!" I tell the bitch as Tales pulls away. "Tales, you don't—"

"That's right," Stevie bites out. "She knows she needs this. What else does she have? A couple classes—"

"You can fucking leave. You're done, too." I flip shit.

"Says who!" Stevie spits at me.

"Memphis, let go of my hand," Tally whispers. "I signed a contract." She pulls her hand away.

"That's right; let's get this show on the road," Stevie taunts.

"No, fuck that."

"It's not your decision, Memphis." Tales shakes her head.

"I didn't have sex with her after that one night." I grab her shoulder and shake her. "You hear me."

"I hear you," she says as she walks away, broken, and all I can do is watch her.

"Fuck!" I scream as I fist my hair. "Tell her the fucking truth, Stevie. Tales, you know me better than that. You. Know. Me.!"

"Not going after her?" I look behind me to see Stevie's drummer, Kellie, throw down a cigarette and stomp it out.

"It's none of your damn business."

"Right." She shakes her head and walks away. Then she turns back. "Grow a set."

I am shocked at her audacity, but I don't respond.

My phone rings, and I fish it out of my pocket. "Sup?"

"All handled man," Finn says.

"No, it is not," I hear in the background.

"Who's that?" I ask.

"Sonya. She's a pain in the ass, but she'll conform." He forces a laugh, and I know he's being tried right now. Finn doesn't do confrontation well.

"You good?" I ask.

"You?" He laughs uncomfortably.

"We have a show tonight. Get your ass here."

"On my way," he says then, "Bitch, are you

trying to bite me!"

"Where's Billy?"

"Billy! Come take this little shit off my hands!" he yells.

"You good?" I ask as I walk toward the back door of Bader.

"Stop fucking asking me shit like that!" With that, he hangs up.

When I walk through the door, Madison is standing in front of me.

"Just leave her alone!"

"I didn't do shit, Mads." My voice breaks. "I didn't do shit!"

"Well, right now she's out there, and you're staying here. You need to get ready, and so does she."

***

I stand backstage where Mads tells me to. I don't normally listen to the little queen, but Tales is up there, shaking her ass, and I know she doesn't want to, but she's no quitter. Sonya, the girl who, had the flash drive will vouch for me if need be, but I don't want to owe her any favors. Besides, Tally better not doubt me.

I love watching her move, but not like this, and not for that bitch. That bitch who is going to walk off stage and be bombarded with Forever Four's lawyers and have major fucking issues if she doesn't back the fuck down.

Finn took off with River, and that's not cool at all. He's a fucking mess and doesn't touch even a prescribed drug. When he asked River to take a walk with him, I felt sick, but I'm so fucked up right now I can't do shit except stand and stare where she can't see me because Mads is cock-blocking like a motherfucker.

When Stevie Danielles' band ends, I look out at the crowd. They fucking love them and it makes me sick. I wish they were throwing tomatoes or booing that bitch.

"Memphis, go; she'll see you." Mads pushes me. "Go!"

I walk down the hall and find the room meant for us to chill, relax, and fucking celebrate all we've accomplished, and I haven't even stepped foot inside it until now.

I open the door, seeing Finn and River sitting there, all fucking pie-eyed.

"You're kidding me, right?"

River sighs. "Just took the edge off."

"Where is it?" I ask.

Billy walks out of the bathroom, chillz in hand.

"No shit?"

Billy grins. "Just to take the edge off."

"Aw, fuck, man, give me that." I snatch up chillz and hit the bathroom. I spark him up, take two pulls, and that's enough. It feels good, too.

When I walk out, the three of them are looking at me.

"It's either the beginning or the end. We started this together; we end it together. Let's fucking go rock them our way."

"We do it for us," Finn says as we stand in a circle.

"In the words of the great Eddie Vedder, 'It's a great time to be me.' " I throw my fist in.

"Jimmy Page once said, 'I may not believe in myself, but I believe in what we're doing.' " Finn puts his fist in.

"Kurt Cobain, "Nobody dies a virgin; life fucks us all.' " River fists in.

"The amazing Billy Holiday once said, 'The difficult, I will do right now. The impossible will take a while.' "

"We have done the impossible. Fuck, Billy learned guitar, River has laid off the heavy shit, and Finn … not sure what to say? Best bass around, and apparently he decided today was the day to put an end to the 'Just Say No,' campaign, which I need the story behind, fuck-stick."

He nods and grumbles.

"And you've got a steel dick." River laughs his fool head off.

"Shit bird." I laugh, too, because it's funny, and I'm fucking soarin'. "All right, STD, let's hit 'em hard"—we bump fists—"light 'em up"—we do our own little version of an explosion with our hands—"and let's go fucking rock 'em our way!"

We walk out into the hallway where the entire Steel crew is, including Momma Joe, and we're all fucked up.

Shit.

Xavier narrows his eyes at us. "You fucking kidding me right now?"

"Ready to rock, man." I chuckle and grin.

I look at the guys. Finn's lip is curled, and his eyes are fixed on the chick Sonya while she scowls at him. I hear him growl, and then he fucking snaps his teeth and barks at her. I shit you not. He fucking barked!

I start rolling.

"She get her fucking shots yet?" Finn asks X-man.

"You, too?" he gasps then throws his hands up in the air and walks away, calling out, "What a fucking day!"

I see Mads and Tally round the corner. Tally is looking at the ground, and Mads is basically pulling her toward me. She has her head hung down as well she should. She should know better.

"Kiss and make up," Mads demands then walks away.

"Tales."

"Memphis."

"What, I'm not asshole anymore?"

"Sometimes."

"But right now?" I tip her chin up with my finger.

"No." She looks up, and I get Emerald City. Fucking beautiful. "Are you high?" And angry.

"Been a fucked up day, Tales. I needed to take the edge off."

"Great. Well, good luck, break a leg, keep your dick in your pants, and—"

I grab her and pick her up, bringing her eye to eye, and she whimpers.

"You sure about that last part?"

She smiles like I knew she would.

"I mean, how am I gonna get dome when I'm done if they stay on?"

She fists my hair and pushes her forehead against mine. "I hate her."

"Don't blame you, Tales. I'm not a fan, either." I inhale. "You smell good. How do you taste, Tales? Give me them lips."

She does, and she gives them to me hard.

I pull back when I hear the crowd start chanting, "*STD! STD! STD*!"

"I watched you dance, Tales, the whole time. Inside, I was praying you fucking believed me 'cause, if you didn't, I would be gone." I set her down and step back. "Don't you ever doubt me again. That shit hurt." Her lip quivers, and she nods. "I love you, Tales. That doesn't just mean something; it means everything."

"I love you so much." She chokes back a sob.

"I know you do." I give her a quick kiss on the cheek then turn to walk away. I don't want to go onstage with bitch pants on.

I step up to the rest of the band, and the four of us look at each other.

"Nickie D, X-man, and Taelyn are standing to the left like the proud parents who just gave birth to the most well-hung kid in the nursery, just like my parents must have thought." I laugh.

"Shit, we have something in common, then." River gives me a fist bump.

The crowd gets louder as I look at my boys. "Who's first?"

"Let's do it together." Billy nods, fucking with his strings.

I look back and see Mom, Mads, and Tales hanging to the right, all smiling. Tales is the brightest. Mom? Didn't even know she was coming.

She mouths, '*I love you.*'

I yell, "You better."

She laughs as she wipes a tear away. I'm pretty sure it's a happy one.

"Let's rock!"

We run out on stage, and I make a mental note to work on that entry. We look like a bunch of teenage, eager boys who are gonna blow their load way before it's time.

"Hello, New Jersey!" I hold the mic out for the crowd's roar, and they give me more than I am looking for. My head is buzzing, and so is my soul.

"I'm Memphis Black, lead singer for Steel Total Destruction!"

I let them scream. Fuck, I egg them on.

"The buzz I catch off of that is bigger than the one we caught backstage!" I laugh.

They fucking go crazy, and I am all energy.

"It's like a spiritual erection, a transcendent orgy to my soul, a divine intervention with every cell in my body. You're getting me hard." I grab my dick then look off stage at Tales and wink. She covers her mouth, laughing.

"You ready for some STD? You ready to get rocked so hard you can't walk straight for a week?"

They scream. They shout. They lust for our music … and for us.

"I like the way you sound!"

"Get ready, ladies. Get ready for it, men!" I bounce up and down on my feet because I am that fucking pumped. "Give it to them, Finn!"

The fucking condom cannons jizz all over the crowd. They scramble around, screaming and grabbing the fucking condoms like little crack whores—our little crack whores.

River spanks the drums, the crack and pop of the snare proceeding. Finn finger bangs his G and L tribute. Billy is on his new Fender; and I begin to sing our first hit song, "Going Down."

The crowd screams. The girls in the front row dance, trying to gain our attention. They have it. For the next two and a half hours, they will get more than they paid for.

The song ends, and I look around at the guys and laugh. All of us are perma-grinning. I'm not sure if it's the high or the *high*. Maybe both.

"You wanna little story?"

The crowd screams.

"Not even two years ago, we sat in this kick-ass studio, looking around and thinking the owner was just a punk ass kid who wanted to play the role of big time music producer with family money." I look at the guys, who laugh and nod. "I still think he's a punk sometimes, but he's got mad respect from me."

I lift my shirt and turn around. "Forever Steel, bro."

I look over where Taelyn is beaming, and X is trying his best to act unaffected, but I see it. I see the love.

"Well, he and the real reason we stuck around—his hot ass wife" —I glance back at X-man, who flips me off—"sat us down, and he told me why this was important to him. He said, 'I want to find the damn kid who was picked on because he wasn't cool enough to hang, the one who, instead of banging the cheer captain, went home and finger-fucked his guitar or banged his drums like he wanted to bang the football captain's girl. I want the kid who went to bed every goddamn night with headphones on, listening to his favorite songs to escape the reality of an abusive or absent father. I want the girl who wasn't good enough to hang with the "it" crowd and dove into the piano, letting her fingers tickle the ivory while she created perfection because she *was* fucking good enough. I want the guy dressed in all black to have his voice and the notes he belts out be his ultimate orgasm. I want the people who were told they couldn't be shit to live and breathe something other than a twisted up blunt. I want their high to be the notes, the melodies, the beats, the songs that live inside them. I want them to be who they are and be seen, not what the stuffy ass production company suit told them to be. I want to be the one to help them find who they are without walking on to a stage where some British fuck tells them they're not marketable'." I pause, and the crowd roars. "He found us. He stuck by us, and we hope to make him proud."

I look up and shake my head. "Now enough of the head trip. Get ready for the night of your life. Are you ready to rock?"

They scream.

Pandemonium.

"I said, are you ready to rock?"

Chaos.

"*Are you fucking ready to get rocked*!"

Mayhem.

Two hours of rock and roll, two hours of nonstop fucking jamming, two of the best hours of my life!

"Look beside you, ladies. Is he what you want? Eyes back here, babe. If he's not, do yourselves a favor and find the one you were meant to be with."

I look off stage and find Emerald City.

"Here's a song for all you lovers out there. "Surface to Soul"."

Awaken beast, you took my all.
Taboo desires, burn out of control.
Intoxicated youth, a troubled teen.
Still both inside, eternal flames.
Surface to soul.

But I'm chasing the light,
Chasing my goal,
Chasing the girl who owns my soul.
Chasing the night,
Chasing the score,
Chasing the need to rock this floor.
I'm missing you. Oo-oo-oo
I'm missing you. Oo-oo-oo

Chasing my dream.
You chase the same.
We're chasing away the fucking game.
Chasing the right.
Chasing the wrong.
Chasing the words to write your song.

I'm missing you. Oo-oo-oo.
I'm missing you. Oo-oo-oo.

Down on my knees, I beg you now.
I can't let go, Tales. I don't know how.
A tender heart, a taken toll.
What was surface took my soul.
Surface to soul.

But I'm chasing the light.
Chasing my goal.
Chasing the girl who owns my soul.
Chasing the night,
Chasing the score,
Chasing the need to rock this floor.
I'm missing you. Oo-oo-oo.
I'm missing you. Oo-oo-oo.

Chasing my dream.
You chase the same.
We're chasing away the fucking game.
Chasing the right,
Chasing the wrong,
Chasing the words to write your song.
I'm missing you. Oo-oo-oo.

But I'm chasing the light,
Chasing my goal,
Chasing the girl who owns my soul.
Chasing the night,
Chasing the score,
Chasing the need to rock this floor.
I'm missing you. Oo-oo-oo

I'm missing you. Oo-oo-oo

Chasing my dream.
You chase the same.
We're chasing away the fucking game.
Chasing the right,
Chasing the wrong,
Chasing the words to write your song.
I'm missing you. Oo-oo-oo.

Back stage, I shower and then stand in an empty dressing room. I told the guys I would catch up with them later. I know they all picked out their treat for the night, and I have mine picked out, too.

The door opens, and Tally slides in.

"Tales …" I begin.

"Shh," she says with her finger to her mouth as she walks toward me.

She grips the towel and pulls me toward her before kissing my chest then continuing on a downward path. She pulls the towel down, going to her knees, and grabs my dick with both hands, pumping while her tongue swipes across my head once, twice, three times. Then she tugs on the ring, and I groan.

"You need to stop teasing my cock, babe, and … fuck. Yeah, just like that. Fuck," I hiss as I feel my head hit the back of her throat as she pumps my dick in her hands. She doesn't stop, either. It's relentless, almost punishing.

She then reaches up, takes my hand, places it on the back of her head, puts her hand over it, and pushes.

"Fuck, Tales. Oh, fuck."

Her hand leaves mine to it, and the selfish fuck in me takes what she is giving. I fist her hair and pump into her, taking what she is giving, fucking her mouth. I get lost in it—the pleasure the indulgence, the hedonism—until I feel her tense, and I look down.

"Holy fuck, Tales." I pull her up.

"No, don't. I want you so badly."

"Then you'll have me, sweet cheeks." I push those little, silky shorts to the side and feel the heat and how drenched she is through the material. I bend enough to line myself up and nearly come from the sound she makes. "You need my cock that badly, Tales?"

"Please," she begs.

I push in just a little, grabbing her ass.

"Wrap 'em round."

She immediately wraps her legs around my waist. Then I lean back against the wall and pump slowly in and out, giving her a little at a time. Her pussy contracts, and I know she's already gone.

I turn us around so her back hits the wall, and then I push in without restraint again and again and again as she cries out my name over and over and over.

Later, we walk out of Bader, hand in hand. She is so happy, and I don't know how after the hell Stevie put her through today. And God only knows how long it's been going on, crazy-ass bitch.

"Can't go back, Tales." I open the door for her. "I won't let you."

She nods, and I hide the excitement from her

agreeing.

"You'll tour with the band, work for Forever Four."

She sighs as she looks at me. I get another nod.

"And you and I are moving in together." I swear my fingers are crossed behind my back.

She looks down as I shut the door. She will. I know she will. She loves me, and I love her.

Forever Steel.

Tales insists I speak to my father and I argue I have nothing to say.

"You have plenty to say," She smiles up at me with those big sad green eyes, that cat, the one from…Shrek-Puss in Boots. He had younger Tales all 'aw,' all the time. Adorable. "Please, just tell him you forgive him."

"I don't fucking forgive him."

"Then tell him that Memphis, just tell him something."

When she gets off the tour bus leaving me alone, I do.

I get his voicemail, and I tell him, "You fucked up a good thing. You cheated on not only Mom, but Mads and I, too. You also fucked up bad as a man, Dad. You were banging a man who died, leaving his wife and daughter with nothing, and you what? Looked the other way?

"If someone had asked me who taught me how wrong that was a year ago, I would have proudly said, 'My old man,' but hell, we both know that shit's not the truth. Mom taught me that.

"I'm not asking for shit from you, but Tale's mom, she doesn't need to know a damn thing but if you ever feel the need to buy me a fucking car again, do me a favor, give Mrs. Priest the cash. She deserves that, she and my mother are good women. You DAD," I emphasis Dad, "Deserve shit."

"I will tell you I love you man, but liking you is a whole different story."

***

"This is crazy," Tally says, looking around the beach house.

"Really not crazy, Tales. The Miami house was crazy. This is just—"

"Insane?" She laughs and then squeals as she dances around the stark white kitchen with black marble counters and stainless steel appliances.

"God, you're beautiful." I'm getting hard.

"I should be so pissed at you." She tries to look angry, but then grins as she runs up and jumps on me, wrapping her legs around me and kissing my face over and over again. "We were just looking."

"And you had a notebook of drawings that showed how it would be perfect. I just took that as a sign."

"I love you."

Painfully hard.

"See? I told you you'd love moving in with me, pain in the ass." I laugh as she continues kissing me.

"We've been together nonstop since Bader, and it's October," she says, running her fingers through my hair.

"We have three weeks until the craziness starts again."

"But then a break at Christmas." She smiles, her legs tightening around me as she raises her hands in the air. "Thank you, God, for this crazy life."

I look at her, watch her. She hasn't mentioned God since our fathers' secret was uncovered. It feels good to see her like this again. My Tales is coming back, and it makes me deliriously happy.

"Garage apartment?" she says after she does her little praise Jesus thing.

"Falcon said a week."

"He's the," she pauses and smiles, "tall contractor who's—"

"Gonna get fired if you light up like that about him again."

"He's nice. He's making my mom a home, and his kid is adorable."

"Fired."

She laughs.

She laughs a lot, and I not only live for her laughs, but I love them.

I set her on the island and spread her legs wide before hiking up that long, flowing skirt. "First meal at the new place." I don't wait for her to say yes; I just dive in.

She cries out, "Memphis."

That's better than any applause.

Check out an excerpt from The Original Sin

By

Angelica Chase, Daryl Banner, Chelsea Camaron, MJ Fields, MX King, and Ripp Baker

HE IS *sin.*

HE IS EVERYTHING WRONG IN MY LIFE. ON THE FLIP SIDE OF THE COIN, HE HOLDS POWER OVER EVERYTHING I THOUGHT I DID RIGHT IN MY LIFE.

SIN IS A TRICKY THING LIKE THAT.

HE HAS HIS SECRETS, AND I HAVE MINE. WHAT BEGAN AS A YOUNG GIRL'S DREAM WAS TURNED INTO A TWISTED GAME OF CRIME AND PUNISHMENT. HE COMMITS THE CRIME; I DOLE OUT THE PUNISHMENT I SEE FIT.

ONLY, LIKE EVERYTHING ELSE IN PORN STAR SIMON SIN'S WORLD, HE ALWAYS KEEPS THE UPPER HAND. HIS SUMMER OF SIN REVEAL BECOMES MY SUMMER OF SIN RETOLD. WHAT HAPPENS WHEN EVERYONE'S SECRETS ARE SHARED?

Chapter One

SIMON SIN

Sadi

ASK ANY HOLLYWOOD STARLET WANNA be if they know Simon Sin, and the answer from a girl who's been here for more than a year, doing anything to make a buck —and I mean anything—will be a resounding, 'Hell, yes!'

He isn't Hugh Heffner or Larry Flint; he's fucking Simon Sin, six-foot-three-inches of lean muscle and sexuality. His jet-black hair is parted to the side and slicked back, his piercing brown eyes deep set, his full lips lush, and his smirk is nothing but a sinful reminder of his intent.

Sin is ageless. No one knows for sure, but the guess is that he is in his late thirties to early forties. He has slight lines around his eyes and even a laugh line or two, but one can never know how old someone is based on that alone.

The man is charisma on legs, his character a product of his awareness of his own good looks and the legendary sexual skills that back it up.

What the public does know about Sin is that he is the king of porn, and he owns a mansion in the Hollywood Hills that is said to have twenty-five bedrooms, an indoor and outdoor pool, sauna, seven hot tubs, a gym, theatre, two kitchens, three dining rooms, and a playroom that would rival any sex club in the world. The world also knows Sin has ten inches of thick perfection between his strong, muscular thighs.

His size is no myth, no urban legend. It is real and has appeared in over three hundred porno films around the world. The most recent skin-filled movie is with me, Sadi Dee, as his "preferred partner," and only because I fought hard to make it that way.

Years ago, with a fake ID in hand, I landed a job as a cocktail waitress with the sole purpose of gaining Sin's attention and, even more ambitious, his affection. I was a sixteen-year-old runaway from the Chicago, Illinois foster care system.

I ran from a home with a handsy alcoholic foster father and a woman who worked two part-time jobs to afford her husband—her Sir, as I heard her call out from within their bedroom—the ability to try to make a go of his mail-order porn business.

I had heard him talk of Simon Sin, a man he knew growing up and despised. That is where my obsession with Sin began. Maybe it was my need to dream of bettering my situation or a dire need to side with the man who was my foster father's worst enemy because of how much I hated him. Whatever the reason, I clung to every word, ever detail regarding Simon Sin. I became fascinated by him and that, in turn, fueled me to seek him out as soon as I had the opportunity.

I trained myself in sexual etiquette by fucking half of my high school's eligible and ineligible bachelors when I was just a freshman. When that feat seemed to be too easy, I graduated to the seduction of men twice my age by the time I ran away.

My foster father had unknowingly navigated my future. Leaving the filth and discomfort behind me, I departed with an agenda in mind. I was looking to become the queen of an empire, and nothing would stand in my way.

The first night I saw Sin, he walked into the club, dressed in his signature black slacks, Italian leather loafers, and button down dress shirt—all custom tailored to fit him perfectly and enhance his broad build and trim waist. On his wrist was a steel Rolex, and around his neck was a silver chain with a cross hanging from it that rested just above his perfectly chiseled pecs.

For months, I watched Sin walk in like that and sit in the corner booth alone as he watched the girls on stage. For months, I watched as he handed a card to one of them, then walked out of the club without a sideways glance toward me. For months, I listened to the stories about the girls who had received the card and never returned to the club, only to turn up months later on her knees online, sucking off Sin and looking happy doing so.

I tried for two years to figure out what it was that made them so special, and when I did, I took the five grand I had saved from cocktail waitressing at Cheetahs and the money I had gotten from stripping at a shit hole club down the road, then upgraded my look.

If the size of my tips was any indication, I had a pretty impressive body. My long, silky, raven hair always seemed to do the trick with the fanfare at the club, but my slightly larger than normal pouty lips got me the most attention. My facial features had always been slightly exotic, giving me an edge. It was the only thing I had to thank my presence-lacking parents for, so I decided to upgrade the only department I was lacking in. I bought myself double Ds for my eighteenth birthday and disappeared for six weeks to heal.

When I returned to Cheetahs, I was given the go ahead to dance for the manager. He almost didn't believe I was Sadi, but I was promoted immediately. I had to admit, my investment paid off. My entire silhouette had been transformed, making my petite frame look even more delicate and shapely, and I had taught myself how to move just so, in order to enhance all my assets, both given and purchased. I was now a dancer.

Two weeks later, Sin walked in with clear intent. He was looking for new talent. I was nervous as hell, yet still managed to dance my ass off, moving and grinding my body to showcase my every angle. Unfortunately, I was a curtain call behind Amber. When I noticed her being given a card from Sin halfway through my dance, I almost lost hope.

Almost.

"Amber," I yelled, running outside Cheetahs with a pill bottle in hand, "don't forget your pills. Wouldn't want you to have another outbreak. I know how much the last one cost you."

She looked behind her, stunned, while Sin leaned out the door of his black town car, looking equally as stunned.

"You said you were healthy," he sneered at her in that sexy rasp I had heard on over two hundred pornos of him.

"I am," she gasped.

I looked down and shook my head.

"Sadi?" he asked, stepping out and ripping the card from her hand. "That's your name, right?"

"Yes, sir," I said in a very well prepared, made for Sin, equally as sexy rasp back to him.

"You clean?"

"Yes, sir. I—"

"You little whore!" Amber lunged toward me but was caught by the elbow by Sin himself.

"Sadi, do you know what I expect?" he asked, snapping his fingers and pointing to the car.

"Not one hundred percent, but I am sure you can teach me." I saw his eyes light up and that sexy smirk appear. "I mean, I'm not as"—I looked at Amber, who was being escorted by Sin's driver back into the building—"seasoned as her—"

"Slut!" Amber yells.

I don't respond. I simply look down.

"Is that true, Sadi? Are you a little whore?" His voice was thick, and by the pitch of his pants, I knew my assumed innocence turned him on.

He reached up and, with the pad of his thumb, stroked my lower lip, keeping his eyes lingering on it, before turning the burning amber up to me.

"Well"—I twirled my silky locks around in my finger—"if you want me to be, I sure can try."

..*

Six months later, my lover and mentor sneaks out of his lair while I am half dead from the pounding he has given me. Unlike the past six months, however, he doesn't return.

I have been feeling his loss of interest in his new "pet" grow as time has passed. Helpless is not a good place to be for one's mind or body. Panic never overtakes me, though, only longing for Sin and aggravation at his lack of attention. He says what he is doing to me is "training," but I called bullshit the first time he kissed me, and I tasted pussy on his mouth—not my pussy, either, because he stopped going down on me two months prior.

A man like Sin is hard to keep sated, and though I never expected to be his only lover, I feel the betrayal of his actions as I lie here, tied to the bedposts, helpless and alone. I finally fall asleep and wake up to his sexual demand only when he remembers he has left me. Even when he releases me, I am not deterred.

"Bend over now," he demands.

Today, I am in no mood for punishment.

"No," I tell him, still a battered mess from our last session as I step toward the door.

We all have limits, and I have reached mine. I have gotten nowhere fast as just another one of

Sin's conquests, and at this point, I know he isn't taking me seriously enough to be his partner, let alone the queen of his empire.

"Excuse fucking me?" he yells, his eyes flaring in anger.

As I glare at him, he looks shocked. "You are no master, no Sir, no … man, Simon Sin! You left me for ten hours!"

"Training, precious," he says in a tone meant for seduction, but at present, he only pisses me off.

"Then you came back with someone else's pussy on your tongue!"

"You don't get to question me," he snaps. "You are mine to do with as I please, and you are not the only one." He laughs haughtily. "I never promised you that. Never."

"I have been for six months."

"You were my preferred partner, but now—" Simon begins, but I hold up my hand, walking through the door of his play palace with my clothes in hand.

"I'm done with you, Sin. I am still young, still beautiful, and I can still make something of myself."

He remains silent as I pack what little I have and leave him.

He doesn't follow me, but I am fed up at this point, so I don't care.

I have enough cash for a bus ticket back to Chicago and for at least four months of rent in a shared place with the couple of friends I have kept in touch with. With that goal in mind, I head east, alone, afraid, and ashamed of the fact that I thought a girl like me could fuck the sin out of a man like Sin.

A year later, broke, scared, and alone, I walk into Cheetahs and don't recognize anyone working the stage from before. Regardless, the owner remembers me and gives my job back to me.

In little to no time, I reestablish my relationship with a few regulars. I manipulate them with my body and seductive words and have them eating out of the palm of my hand.

I've still got it, and I vow to use this power to better my situation, no longer willing to settle for more than a queen's share.

Sex is a powerful weapon, and I have mastered my technique.

Sin shows up a few weeks after I return, looking like hell. As he is walking toward the door, he stops, turns around, and looks at me before he holds up his card.

I shake my head, and then I see him talking to one of the bouncers as my song ends. I walk off stage with my head held high, proud that I have resisted Sin. Who knew I had it in me? Too bad, it is a year too late. He goes to stop me as I exit the stage, but I walk past him indifferently, heading back to the dressing room.

Sitting in front of the vanity, I look in the mirror at a girl who, a year ago, thought she knew everything. It feels like a lifetime ago. In fact, it is.

"Sadi." Sin's rasp startles me.

I look up as he walks up to me, his gaze holding my eyes in the mirror. I let my eyes linger on him briefly, just to drink in his beauty. Despite his rougher than usual exterior, he is still insanely gorgeous.

I see a glimmer of hope in his eyes as he takes in my perusal of him, causing me to lower my gaze in protest of the stupid girl who still has lingering feelings for him.

"Save it, Sin. I have done a lot of growing in the past year. I—"

"You've grown even more beautiful, Sadi"," he says, as he pulls a chair up behind me and sits. "So fucking beautiful." He turns me around in my swivel chair so I am facing him. "Look at Daddy and tell me you don't crave my touch, miss my cock, my—"

"I don't want to be a piece of ass that fucks you on camera and gets tied up then forgotten," I state, giving it to him honestly.

"I could never forget you, Sadi." He takes my hand and kisses it, sending chills down my spine. "Look at me now and tell me you haven't missed me."

"Don't—" I try to stop our conversation before he can lead me down the trail of temptation.

"I'm not the same man, either."

"So I've heard. AIDS?"

"A rumor that has ruined my career." He sighs, his face showing subtle signs of the last hard year of his life. It seems neither of us has fared well, although I know his luck has everything to do with me.

Looking at him now, a part of me wants to believe he truly has missed me in his own way.

"So, you're clean?" I question him as mischief and some other emotion dance in his eyes.

"Yes, but not many people believe me. I might even have to sell the mansion."

"Oh," I say, looking into his eyes, "I think I have an idea."

I have him exactly where I want him in this moment. For the first time since I met this man, I feel powerful because I know he needs me.

Not wanting to give in so easily, I say, "No, forget it. I won't get sucked into Sin again."

"I won't ask you to suck on the sin stick, beautiful, but I sure as hell will go down on my knees and beg for a taste of heaven."

With that, Sin sinks to his knees, asking forgiveness as he pushes my robe aside, tosses my legs over his shoulder and begins ravaging my pussy like a man possessed. And, like an addict with a drug, I can't hold back.

"Sin," I cry out, "Oh, God, Sin."

"I need someone to believe me, someone to believe in me, Sadi," he coaxes as he expertly tongues my clit in just the right spot. I begin to buckle under the pressure as he laves at me, taking all of my orgasm into his mouth. "What good is hell without owning a little piece of heaven?" he finishes, plunging his tongue back into me as my heart rips slightly from his admission.

I already know I have failed on my own, and he seems sincere, but with Sin, you never can tell.

Maybe this time, just … maybe...

~THANK YOU~

To the owner of this book, thank you so very much. You are the reason I love what I do. Without your love and encouragement I would just be writing naughty stories with happy endings…for myself.

To Bobbie, a million thanks for being president of the STD fan club.

To my #foreversteel reader group, I LOVE YOU! You are my escape, support, and sisters from another mister...

To C&D chicks Kris and Ali, thank you so much for your hard work and ass kicking turn around.

To Kellie Montgomery WE FINALLY MET!!! Love you even more now. Thank you for your hard work and support.

To Shauna Kruse, Michael Fagone, and Jacqueline the cover picture you all worked on making perfect is just that, perfect. Thank you so much.

To Mel, thank you for kicking ass for me always.

To Kari, you are a magician and a mind reader as well as an amazing author.

To Ally, we've got this. You and me… always. Love you more <3

About the Author

MJ FIELDS

USA Today bestselling author MJ FIELDS's love of writing was in full swing by age eight.

Together with her cousins, she wrote a newsletter and sold it for ten cents to family members. She self-published her first New Adult romance in January 2013. Today she has completed six self-published series, The Love series, The Wrapped series, The Burning Souls series, The Men of Steel series, Ties of Steel series, and The Norfolk series.

MJ is a hybrid author and publishes an Indie book almost every month, and is signed with a traditional publisher, Loveswept, Penguin Random House, for her co- written series The Caldwell Brothers. Hendrix is available now, Morrison will be released on December 22nd, 2015.

There is always something in the works, and she has three, yes, three, new series coming out this summer, and fall.

MJ was a former small business owner, who closed shop so she could write full time.

MJ lives in central New York, surrounded by family and friends. Her house is full of pets, friends, and noise ninety percent of the time, and she would have it no other way.

She is represented by Marissa Corvisiero.

MORE FROM MJ FIELDS

MEN OF STEEL SERIES
FOREVER STEEL
JASE
JASE & CARLY
CYRUS
ZANDOR
XAVIER
Forever Family
And
Family

TIES OF STEEL SERIES
ABE
DOMINIC
SABTATO

The LRHA Legacy Series
A collection of series that follow the Links, Ross, Abraham, and Hines families through several generations.
Each series can be a standalone but is so much deeper read in order.

The Love Series
Blue Love
New Love
Sad Love
True Love

The Wrapped series
Wrapped in Silk
Wrapped in Armor
Wrapped Always and Forever

Burning Souls Series
Stained
Merged
Forged

And the latest releases
Love You Anyways
And Love Notes

Ava links story will be coming out in summer 2015

The Norfolk Series
Irons
Irons 2
Irons 3

CALDWELL BROTHERS SERIES
(Co-written with Chelsea Camaron)
HENDRIX

MORRISON
(Coming winter 2015)

JAGER
(Coming 2016)

Connect with MJ Fields

Email – mjfieldsbooks@gmail.com
Website – www.mjfieldsbooks.com
Facebook – http://tinyurl.com/mjfieldsfb
Tsu-https://www.tsu.co/mjfields
For more on the Ties of Steel series, sign up for the newsletter on MJ's Facebook page or at www.mjfieldsbooks.com
Would you like to receive text messages from MJ Fields?
Text MJFields to 96362
Standard texting fees apply
Follow MJ on Spotify and listen to songs that inspired this and many of her other books!

To Ally,
We will someday discuss….
I love you more.